Last of
the
Giants

D1526191

Other books by Christine Marshall

Charlie and the Giants series:

A Series of Retellings

Becoming Cinder

White as Snow

Forever Sleeping

Charlie's story

Rise of the Giants
Battle of the Giants
Last of the Giants

Last of the Giants

Book Six in
Charlie and the Giants

Christine Marshall

To my Mom & Dad

Thank you for always telling
me that I could do anything
I put my mind to.

The world is a different
place without you in it.
I miss you both every day.

Chapter 1

The City of Giants had fallen.

The buildings had been reduced to rubble. Chunks of brick and mortar the size of Charlie's house littered the roadways. The wooden frames of the buildings still stood, charred, and withered. Smoke billowed from the tops of the towering structures. Ashes thickened the air.

Charlie lifted her plain linen tunic over her nose and mouth so she could breathe. The ashes that fell like snow settled on her dark eyelashes and shoulders and turned her light-brown braid gray.

The view inside the shops and homes showed the hasty retreat of the city inhabitants: wooden furniture strewn about, unnecessary belongings piled on floors, interior doors with broken hinges. Pictures and tapestries hung crooked on the walls. Cabinet doors stood open, the shelves behind them picked clean of necessities. Yards and gardens next to homes had been trampled. A thin layer of ash coated almost everything.

Charlie's own home probably looked the same- minus the ash. If it even still stood. She had left so much behind. The giants had, too.

A trail of enormous belongings lined the path that the giants had taken to escape. A faded cloth doll twice Charlie's size lay crumpled and forgotten on the side of the road. A dozen huge books littered the ground; their pages as long as Charlie was tall flapped in the breeze. Buckets, utensils, tools, and items of clothing guided Charlie through the city, each item larger than life. Mingled with the abandoned belongings she saw broken arrows, a massive sword, several cracked shields, and even a badly dented armor chest-plate. Each item meant for people ten times Charlie's size.

Charlie's heart ached. Her throat tightened. Her eyes stung, from the smoke and from sorrow.

Who could Jessamine have convinced to do this to the City of Giants? And how many had there been to cause the nearly indestructible giants to flee for their lives? Why was Jessamine so intent on destroying everything good in the world? It wasn't fair.

Charlie's blood boiled. Her jaw clenched. Why couldn't Jessamine just leave everyone alone? Whatever she thought she was going to gain from all of this could not possibly be worth the sacrifices. But it was obvious that Jessamine didn't care about anyone except for herself.

Charlie forced herself to calm down. But it was hard. She wanted to take out her frustration on something. But she had no target. Not yet.

"The balance must be restored."

2

The voice whispered at the back of her mind. Again.

Lately when she became frustrated, sad, or discouraged, the voice reminded her that she needed to stop Jessamine. She had no idea how.

Willem had told her that the voice wasn't him. He and Charles and many other giants had agreed, though, that in order to be rid of Jessamine they must restore the balance. Many more giants had voted to stay out of the conflict completely.

Pepper zipped to Charlie's side and interrupted Charlie's thoughts. "I've looked all over." The tiny pixie hovered in front of Charlie, her hair a dull orange, no glow present, and her skin nearly translucent.

"Did you find any survivors?" Charlie could tell by the look on Pepper's face what the answer would be.

Pepper shook her head, her large orange eyes wide and sad.

"What about Willem? Are there *any* signs of his family?" Charlie's heart hurt for the giant she had just met a few weeks ago, who had sacrificed everything to help her.

"No." Pepper's tiny voice was barely above a whisper. "Nothing. He's becoming more distraught the longer we stay here."

"We should meet up and gather what we need." Charlie's thoughts lingered on Willem. He had left behind a wife and child to help Charlie. He must be devastated. "And Willem should get away from this place. Can you tell everyone to meet at the armory?"

The pixie nodded and zipped away.

Charlie worked her way toward the armory at the center of the city. She stubbed her foot on an old cast iron frying pan big enough for her to lie down in. Her gray tunic caught and tore at the hem on the sharp corner of broken stonework. She would mend it later. She avoided smoldering fires and skirted around the heaviest of the destruction. Her leather ankle boots protected her feet from the chunks of buildings that covered the ground. She barely recognized the parts of the city that should be familiar. Only the tall stone building at the center of town marked her destination. And that, too, had been half-toppled. With her sooty hands she wiped away the tears that leaked from her eyes.

Chapter 2

Charlie arrived at the armory before the others. The group had split apart to look for signs of survivors or evidence of what had occurred here. She must have been closest to the city center. She dropped her canvas pack onto the ash coated ground. She leaned her back against the wall and closed her eyes to wait. She did her best to keep her mind off the destruction around her.

A clatter came from inside the darkened armory. She startled. Her entire body tensed. She held her breath and listened.

Muffled voices echoed from within, followed by another loud clang. One of the voices shushed the other.

Who was in there? Was it a giant? No, a giant would have a much louder, deeper voice. Was it one of Jessamine's mercenaries? Charlie's palms started to sweat.

She edged toward the door. She should probably wait for the others. She paused and looked around. No sign of her friends yet.

The two voices whisper-argued with one another again.

She didn't want to risk whoever it was escaping before they could be found out. She shouldered her pack and paused to gaze at the door.

The door was massive, three times thicker than her own width, but loosely hinged. She pushed it open just far enough to slip inside unnoticed. She stayed still and peered around the room. A little light came through the narrow windows that ringed the top of the space. Dust sparkled in the rays. It didn't brighten the room, but it did keep it from being too dark to see.

She crept around the edge of the room, beneath tables, and around enormous vases, crates, and chests. Her footsteps made no noise. She kept her breathing steady and quiet. A large table that held artifacts and weapons stood between herself and the voices. She walked upright beneath it but stayed in the shadows close to the wall.

The next crash sounded closer this time. She pulled out her dagger from the ankle holster beneath her loose pants.

She peeked around a leg of the massive table. Where had the sound come from? She could just make out the whispered argument now.

"It's not like there's anyone left who needs it."

"But it's not ours."

The voices sounded familiar.

"Oh, come on. It would come in so handy. You know I'm right!"

"No. We aren't taking it. Put it back."

A scuffle broke out. One of the voices grunted. A thud followed.

"Hey! That hurt!" The first voice cried out in pain.

She knew that voice.

"Max! Eliot!" She put away her dagger and rushed toward them.

The pair of tiny men, brownies to be exact, startled. Max, the taller of the two brothers, dropped whatever it was that he wanted to steal. It hit the tile floor with a loud crash. Charlie couldn't tell what it was in the darkness, but it sounded metal. And heavy.

"We weren't doing anything!" He kicked the object behind him and stuffed his hands into his trouser pockets. The item clanged against the floor as it rolled away. The sound bounced off the tall walls.

Eliot rolled his pale eyes at his older brother. Then he leveled his piercing glare at Charlie. Even in the dim light Charlie could feel his wariness of her.

"I'm so glad to see you." Charlie relaxed, her words a sigh. She hadn't realized how much she had been worried about these two. And about finding them. Charlie needed their help. "What happened here? Did you see anything?"

"No, we didn't see anything," Max rushed his reply. "Nope, nothing."

"I'm talking about the city." Charlie's voice had an edge to it.

"The city," Max answered. "Riiiiight." He drew out the word as if shifting his thoughts to the correct topic.

"Yes, we were here." Eliot spoke directly to her.

She kept a straight face. Eliot hardly ever spoke to her. Would he say more?

Eliot didn't expound, so she prodded. "What

8

happened?"

Eliot shared a dark look with Max. What had they seen?

Just when Max opened his mouth to answer, the door to the armory swung all the way open and banged against the wall. The noise made her jump.

A rectangle of sunlight, dimmed from the ashes, spread across the room. Max hissed and covered his eyes. Eliot squinted against the light. Charlie kept her eyes on the pair.

Radcliffe's hooves echoed off the stone tiles and nearly bare walls. He held his double-bladed battle axe in one massive human hand. His other hand hung in a loose fist at his side. The muscles across his bare human torso tightened. His horse tail swished behind him.

Max nudged Eliot. He picked up his pack and slung it across his body. He signaled to Eliot and started to sidle away.

"Wait," Charlie reached out to block them, "Please, we need your help."

When Radcliffe heard Charlie, he moved across the room to join her.

"Oh, it's you." Radcliffe sheathed his battle axe and looked down his sharp nose at the brownies.

The brothers stopped in their tracks. They turned slowly around to face the centaur.

Max gave Radcliffe a sheepish wave.

Eliot stared.

Radcliffe stared back.

Eliot's eyes flicked to the new canteen that hung around Radcliffe's neck. Then he made eye contact with Radcliffe again.

Radcliffe gave the slightest nod.

Charlie looked back and forth between the miniscule

man, whose pointed hat barely reached her knees, and the centaur twice as tall as herself.

"What in the…?" Charlie started to ask.

Before she could finish, though, the others entered the room.

Alder assisted Charlie's injured father as he limped toward her. Princess Juliette followed close behind, carrying his things. Juliette's enormous brindle mastiff, Roxi, sniffed the ground and paused to look around with her one good eye, then padded faster to catch up with Juliette.

Pepper zipped to Charlie's side and landed lightly on her shoulder.

"Willem's family?" Charlie asked Juliette.

The Princess shook her head, eyes red with tears. She brushed them away with the sleeve of her light tunic.

Charlie looked at the floor and squeezed her eyes shut. The guilt blossomed inside. If Willem hadn't left to help her, then he would be with his family now. Her chest tightened. She forced herself to take slow, deep breaths. She sighed and turned back to the brownies.

"Can you tell us what happened here?" She asked again. "Please?"

The two little men shared a pained look. Max nodded.

Chapter 3

"We came here to convince the leaders to go to your wall " Max did all the talking, as usual, while Eliot listened carefully. "It was a hard sell. We offered some, let's just say, interesting trades…"

Eliot elbowed Max in the ribs and shook his head. "I know," Max mumbled before he continued.

"Anyway, after we convinced the giants to go to your wall and prepare to fight, we," Max paused and cleared his throat, "… decided to find Juliette's people. We knew they would be able to help you."

What had given the brownies the idea to do that? Charlie wanted to know but didn't want to distract Max from this story.

"We found the forest people and sent them your way. We, err, saw some things here that we were… interested in, so we thought we would come back. It didn't take us long to return, and most of the able men had left to fight. We…

hung around, making... trades..."

"Oh, stop," Pepper interrupted. She rolled her eyes at Max. "We all know you were swiping things while you had the chance. Moving on..." Pepper gestured for Max to finish his story.

"Alright, alright!" Max held up his hands in surrender, with a crooked grin on his face. "We poked around for several days, when out of the blue, one of the watchmen sounded the alarm. The city was under attack! Everyone scrambled around. Anyone who could fight raided the armory for weapons, and the others gathered the youngest and some belongings and started to leave the back way. Most of those able to fight had already left. There just weren't enough..."

Max sighed, eyes far away like he could see all this take place in his mind.

"Who was it, Max? *Who* attacked the City of Giants?" Pepper prodded Max. She hovered in front of him, her bare feet almost touching the floor, but not quite.

Max shook his head, unable to continue. His jaw clenched. He pulled his pointed hat off his head, exposing his messy white-blonde hair and pointed ears. He twisted the hat in his hands and his eyes filled with tears. He worked his jaw to try to control his emotions.

Eliot looked at his brother. "It was the other giants." Eliot spoke quiet, but clear.

What? What other giants? Jessamine's army of giants had been engaging the army from the City of Giants at Charlie's home. Did Jessamine have more giants under her control?

Pepper was the only one to voice what they all had to be thinking. "What do you mean?" Her skin reddened.

Max swallowed. His voice had lost all of its usual humor. "It was Jessamine's giants. A second, smaller army of them. They must have expected the giants here would go to your aid behind the wall and leave the city defenseless. No one expected this city to be attacked." Max's eyes widened, like he wouldn't have believed it if he hadn't seen it for himself.

"The army came through and destroyed everything." Max's voice cracked. "Those few giants who were prepared to fight knew they were no match for this army, so they fled. Jessamine's army chased them out of the city. We followed, but we couldn't stand to watch the fighting." He cleared his throat. A tear dripped out of each of his bright blue eyes.

"Jessamine's army killed everyone they could find." His voice was almost a whisper now. "The giants from the city fought back as best they could. We left the battlefield and came back here before the battle finished." His shoulders slumped and his whole demeanor sank. "We kept expecting giants to return, but no one has come back."

Max dropped his arms to his side. His hat fell to the floor. This little man looked utterly hopeless.

How could this have happened? It would take a mighty force to destroy the City of Giants. How could some of the giants themselves be the ones to do it? Charlie's heart broke just a little bit more.

Everyone, except for Radcliffe, sank to the floor.

Juliette leaned her head of blonde curls against Roxi. Pepper landed on Charlie's lap, skin pale and hair dull. Charlie's dad rested a hand on her shoulder from behind and let out a deep sigh. Alder kneeled right beside him. Radcliffe stayed close.

13

They were the only living beings left in the vast city. Except for Willem, who must be mourning his family somewhere beyond the walls of the armory.

Charlie didn't know what to say. The others stayed quiet too.

Her thoughts turned to home. The battle between the two giant armies had been fierce when she had left. The giants from the City of Giants had been well armed, but so had Jessamine's army. Each army had been roughly the same size, evenly matched. Had Charles and his army defeated Jessamine's army of giants? If they had, they would have been back by now, right? Did that mean that there were no survivors? And where had Jessamine's second army of giants come from? Where had they gone?

Radcliffe's knuckles cracked. She glanced at him. His face was hard, and his fists clenched. "How do we find her?" His voice rumbled low in the vast space.

They took turns looking at one another. No one knew the answer.

Charlie sighed. She ran into stumbling blocks at every turn. How could she fix this?

She returned her attention to the brownies. "You two seem to be able to find things- or people- that don't want to be found." Her words were laced with near-despair. "Do you have any idea how we can locate Jessamine?"

Max and Eliot shared a look. Max raised his eyebrows at his brother, but Eliot ever so slightly shook his head. Max's look turned pleading. Eliot left his face unreadable.

Max shrugged his shoulders and mumbled, "No." He briefly made eye contact with Charlie, then looked away.

Did the brownies know how to find Jessamine? If they did, they would say something, right? But clearly Eliot didn't want Max to say anything, one way or the other. She was sure that after finding Juliette's people, they would be able to find Jessamine. Why wouldn't they help? What were they hiding?

She'd have to figure this out later. When Eliot decided something, Max didn't argue. It wasn't worth pressing the issue. Yet.

She changed the subject. "I guess we should gather the supplies we need while we're here."

"Then what?" Pepper asked.

"I don't know." Charlie shrugged and stood. Her mind raced to figure out their next steps. Every time she thought she made the right move, she encountered more loss and dead ends.

"The balance must be restored."

Charlie wanted to scream at the voice that she knew that already. What she didn't know was *how*. She bit her tongue. She hadn't told anyone about the voice. Especially since she had started to hear it even when she wasn't asleep. Maybe she was going insane.

"We should find Willem," Juliette's quiet voice cut through the silence.

"I'll go," Alder volunteered. He stood to his full height, head and shoulders taller than herself. He ran his fingers through his messy dark brown hair and squeezed Charlie's shoulder with one of his warm, dark hands when he walked past. "You'll figure it out, don't worry." He spoke low into her ear so only she could hear. His breath tickled her neck.

He could always tell when she was troubled. She gave him a weak smile.

"Thanks." She watched him walk away to find Willem. She wished she had his confidence and ability to stay calm and positive even in the worst situations.

Radcliffe cleared his throat. She startled and met his gaze. He must have heard Alder, even when the others had not. His piercing gray eyes studied her face. How much of her thoughts and feelings did he pick up on?

She blushed and turned away.

Charlie recognized many of the artifacts in the armory from when she had been there before. The giants had removed most of the giant-sized armor and weapons from the rows of racks and hooks that had been full before, but many of the other artifacts remained. Books still lined the shelves, and the pedestal with a human-sized flight of stairs attached still stood nearby. The books looked like they had been reorganized since the giants had moved back into the city. A ladder had been installed that slid in front of the shelves that nearly reached the towering ceiling.

Rows of artifacts, odd looking boxes and chests, and rolled up parchments filled the shelves on the other end of the room. The oversized map table remained in the center of the space. Charlie couldn't see from below, but she imagined a new map that showed the way to the wall, and pieces to represent the battle that the giants had left to fight.

She made her way across the room until she saw the enormous tapestry that hung on the far wall. She tried to see what her giant friend had seen before: images of the Battle Horn and Sariah. What would her mother think about everything that had happened since Charlie left home? Charlie's view from the floor prevented her from seeing the details on the tapestry. She looked away, pushed the tapestry aside, and stepped behind it to the nook that stored the human armor and weapons.

The low, rounded ceiling gave the room a cave-like feel. Rough wooden benches lined the wall on one side. Charlie's eyes roved over the bows and crossbows that hung above each bench. She made her way across the room and stopped in front of a crate filled with arrows. Along the opposite wall, spears and battle axes stood upright in tall cubbies. The rack above the cubbies held sword after sword, some long and light, others heavy and wide. Which one would she choose? She made her way to the rear of the room where the rows of human armor hung, the intricate details so much like the designs her father used on his devices.

Charlie fingered one of the arm pieces: the Key of Sariah that activated the now destroyed Battle Horn. Her throat tightened.

"It feels just like yesterday sometimes, doesn't it?" Pepper spoke in Charlie's ear.

Charlie nodded. Her hand dropped to her side. She sighed and plopped herself on one of the wooden benches to wait for the others. She closed her eyes. She didn't want to remember the last time she had been here.

Christine Marshall

Chapter 4

Charlie's dad wanted to arm himself, but Charlie insisted that his leg injury had not healed enough to support him in battle. He still had a bad limp, and he tired too easily. He negotiated with her for a crossbow made of lightweight material and easy to use. She agreed, but only if he allowed her to carry it for him. She strapped it to her pack with leather cord. Then she set up a place for her father to rest in one corner of the room.

The others perused their options for arms. Charlie currently carried her dagger, a sling and stones, and the small sword she had chosen last time. She had a sinking feeling she would need something better. She had experience with the bow and arrows and figured she would end up using the crossbow she now carried for her father.

The sword Charlie had was small and light. But would it be enough? She asked Radcliffe for his opinion, and he helped her choose a sword that was still light, but longer and sharper. Radcliffe promised to teach her how to use it.

She strapped the sword in its sheath to her waist. The added weight probably wouldn't be too much of a problem. Especially with Willem to carry her.

Alder still had not returned with the giant. She looked toward the outer entrance of the armory as if thinking about them might make them appear. It did not.

Charlie turned her attention to Juliette as she fingered the variety of weapons. Though uncomfortable with violence, Juliette handled herself well when the situation required it. She chose a shorter, lighter sword than the one Radcliffe had picked out for Charlie.

By the time the others finished arming themselves, Alder had returned. He, too, chose a small sword meant for self-defense and nothing more.

How was she supposed to keep them safe if they weren't prepared? What if they ended up having to fight? Charlie's heart grew heavier every time she thought of any more of her friends becoming injured, or worse, in the upcoming battle with Jessamine. She had to find a way to protect them all.

Willem stayed in the shadows of the outer room. He did not speak to anyone. He only sat hunched over with his head underneath his folded arms.

"I think we should stay the night." Charlie didn't think Willem was in any condition to travel. She asked Pepper to gather the others again.

They set up makeshift beds within the smaller room and leaned their packs and new weapons against the walls. Charlie settled near her dad. Radcliffe stood watch, as usual.

No one spoke much. They must have all been as weary and heart sore as Charlie.

Charlie munched on the dried food from her pack. Her mind wandered to all the possible outcomes to the oncoming confrontation with Jessamine, as well as the ever-present reminders of the fact that she needed to "restore the balance."

She drifted off to sleep long after the others had succumbed.

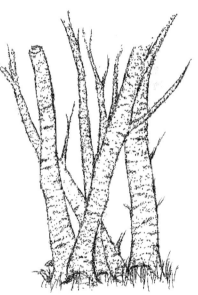

Charlie stood alone in the woods. Tall thin birch trees surrounded her. Dappled sunlight spotted the ground. The only sound came from her own heartbeat. She didn't have her pack or her weapons. She turned in a slow circle. What was she supposed to see? Or do?

"You must restore the balance."

The voice came from all around her, but also from inside of her.

"How? How do I restore the balance?" She hollered at the trees, the sky.

A movement in the shadows to her left caught her eye. She turned to face whoever, or whatever, was there.

Her heart raced. She tensed.

"You must stop Jessamine."

She took careful steps toward the voice. The trees that surrounded her all looked the same.

21

"Who keeps saying that? What do you want me to do?" She shouted ahead of her, certain that's where the voice had come from.

She continued forward.

She could see that the trees thinned up ahead. She hurried her steps. The forest opened onto a lush meadow. *The* meadow. Excitement and nervousness fought for a place in her chest. Would he be there?

She stopped in the center of the meadow and turned in a quick circle. Her eyes desperately searched for any sign of her friend.

"Where are you? I need you!" A sob caught in Charlie's throat. She fell to her knees. Tears leaked from her eyes. "I can't do this alone."

Would her words find her friend? Would he come to help her?

When Charlie awoke, her face was wet with tears. She wanted to stay curled under her scratchy wool blanket. She wanted to dream more, to receive advice from the giant. Or, better yet, have him tell her that she was done and could go home. That everything had returned to the way it was before.

She kept her eyes closed and imagined returning home with her father. He would be healed. They would slip back into their old routine of him tinkering in his shop, and she helping him, studying, and trying to stay busy. Her heart sank. That wasn't much of a life, was it? Not now that she had seen and done so much more. And made actual friends. The life she lived before had been lonely. As much as she wanted things to be normal again, she didn't want to be alone anymore.

A heavy sigh escaped her lungs. She rubbed her eyes and sat up. Some of the others had already begun preparing for the day.

With her heart heavy, she did the same.

Christine Marshall

Chapter 5

The group agreed that they should be on their way as soon as possible. None of them had a clear idea of where they should go. They walked in silence and headed for the main gate of the city. They were almost there when Charlie remembered something.

"Wait," Charlie called to her friends. "There are some hidden caves this way. We should check them out for survivors."

Willem's head whipped to look at Charlie. Did he not know about the caves? Charlie assumed all the giants knew. Had he forgotten in his grief?

The group followed Charlie and Pepper to the caves. Charlie's hands became clammy as they neared the entrance. Even though it was tall enough for a smaller than average giant to walk upright into, the thought of going under the mountain still made her feel claustrophobic. She swallowed and led everyone into the cave.

Their footsteps echoed in the vast underground cavern. Huge stalactites hung from the ceiling. The water that dripped into puddles on the ground pattered like rain. The moist, earthy air closed in around them. The humidity did not help Charlie's feeling of being closed in. The others stayed silent as they made their way deeper under the mountain. Charlie listened for movement or the voices of potential survivors.

It took forever to make any progress. Charlie had been carried through here by her giant friend last time. It had gone much quicker then. Their pace on the ground, however, was sluggish in comparison. But she didn't think it would be right to ask Willem for a ride.

As the light diminished, Pepper set her hair aflame and flew in front of the others to provide enough light to see. But still, the surrounding darkness pressed in on Charlie. When would they reach one of the tunnel openings?

A clatter bounced off the walls from the tunnels. Radcliffe motioned for everyone to stop and stay silent. He stepped into the blackness.

Charlie bit her lip. She expected him to return at any moment, but she waited and waited. Nothing. What had happened to him? She whispered to the others. Should they go ahead to find him?

Before anyone could answer, she heard a crash that reverberated off the walls. The ground shook. Dust and rock rained from above.

Charlie dropped to the ground. Her arms circled her head. One of the huge stalactites was sure to dislodge, fall down, and crush her.

A second later, she heard shouting. And Radcliffe's war cry.

She called for Pepper and rushed toward the sound of the fight. She stumbled through the darkness. Pepper's light showed the cave split into two different caverns. Which way should she go? She stopped. She strained her eyes and ears against the darkness.

The sounds of struggle came from the left. Charlie motioned to Pepper. The pixie lit the way. The pair rushed through the tunnel.

Charlie stopped short when the tunnel opened into an enormous cavern. Pepper's light only shone a short distance around them. The rest of the cavern was black.

Scrapes, grunts, and clashes echoed around the cavern. It was impossible to tell where the sounds came from. Pepper searched the cavern with her light. She discovered Radcliffe and his foe in no time.

Charlie could only make out the shadows on the far wall of the cave, cast from Pepper's bright light. Radcliffe's shadow danced larger than life. His opponent loomed above him, at least three times his size.

Radcliffe defended himself from dozens of legs and pinchers. Spines protruded from the long, worm-like body of the monster he battled. Radcliffe dodged the strikes from the massive creature. Just as Charlie was about to rush forward, sword in hand, Juliette and the others joined her in the cavern. Everyone but Willem.

"Stay back!" roared Radcliffe. He must have heard the group arrive.

The ground rumbled. The walls shook. Dirt and small rocks rained from above. Charlie braced herself against the cave. Her eyes strained to find the danger in the darkness.

A giant barged into the cavern and charged full speed toward the fight. Charlie recognized Willem as he barreled

27

into the huge creature. Their shadows merged as they tumbled to the ground. Charlie couldn't tell what was happening, but she wasn't about to get any closer. Radcliffe and Willem shouted in rage and pain. Strange, high screeches came from the creature.

The fight became more intense. Charlie had no idea who would win.

The ground rumbled again. *This is it*, Charlie thought. They're going to lose this battle. The cave would collapse. They were all going to die.

A light shone into the cavern. It came from another tunnel to Charlie's right. Two more giants appeared. They wore full armor and carried huge double-bladed axes. They raced toward the fight. In mere minutes the giants and Radcliffe finished off the creature. It screeched and wailed as the life left its body.

The two new giants made their way toward Charlie and her group. One carried a torch. Willem followed close behind. Radcliffe pulled up the rear.

"We should move away, quickly now," said one of the giants, whom Charlie now recognized as female.

"This way," said the other giantess. She led the group back down the tunnel that they had emerged from.

Charlie and the others followed. No one spoke.

Before long, they arrived at another large cavern. Quiet talking echoed in the vast space. They walked through the center of a makeshift camp. Enormous women and young giants sat in small groups around several campfires. The smoke drifted toward the roof of the cavern and escaped through a small shaft near the top.

These must be the survivors from the City of Giants. Willem searched each of the dozen makeshift tents and campsites. His movements became more frantic as he moved around the circle.

Huge eyes met Willem's at every turn. But they weren't the eyes he wanted to see. Charlie stood still as realization hit Willem that his family had not found refuge in the cavern. They may not have survived at all.

His legs buckled. He fell into a heap on the hard ground. His shoulders shook with sobs.

Charlie's heart fractured. How much more loss would they have to endure?

Radcliffe stepped toward the two giants who had saved him. "What was that creature? And are there more of them?"

"There are others," replied the giantess holding the torch, "but they are averse to light. They have mostly stayed away from us."

"Yeah, well, I'm not planning on sticking around long enough to see if that's true," muttered Max. Eliot elbowed his brother and gave him a stern look.

"Are there any other survivors?" Juliette's words glowed with hope.

Charlie had been thinking the same thing. Maybe Willem's family had found someplace else to shelter.

"I'm afraid not," said the giantess. Her voice cracked and pain etched lines in her face.

"What now?" Alder's voice was as broken as Charlie's heart.

Charlie thought for a moment. The giants were in hiding. Jessamine's army controlled her own home. But where was Jessamine? They had to find her. To put a stop to all of this.

"We continue. We can't give up." Charlie needed to convince herself that this was true. She had to have hope. She held back the sob that tried to escape.

"Willem has decided to stay, just in case his family comes back," Pepper announced to the group.

"I do not blame him. I hope all will be well for him," Juliette sent a longing look at Willem.

He was still in distress. But there was nothing they could do for him. At least, not until they stopped Jessamine.

Charlie had to admit to herself that she was disappointed, though. Without Willem, their travels would take much longer. And it never hurt to have a giant on your side in a battle. But she could understand his need to stay. There were less than three dozen giants left. She hoped more had found other hiding places. But that didn't seem very likely.

They decided not to backtrack, but to exit the cave on the other side of the mountain. One of the giants in hiding explained which way to go, and they maneuvered through the tunnels as quickly as they could.

Charlie was relieved to see the light of day when they made it out of the mountain. She would be happy for the rest of her life if she never had to go under that mountain, or any mountain, ever again.

Now they just had to figure out where to find Jessamine.

Christine Marshall

Chapter 6

Max and Eliot whispered to one another. Max pointed, and Eliot nodded. Charlie again had the feeling they were hiding something.

"Pepper," she whispered to her winged friend, "could you go see what they are talking about? They seem to like you, so maybe they'll be more open about what they know."

Pepper's body turned pink. She flitted to the brownies and stood near them with her hands behind her back, and a sweet smile on her face. She inched toward Eliot. She leaned close and put her hand to his ear. She whispered something to him.

Eliot nodded to Pepper. Max looked back and forth between the two, clearly feeling left out of the exchange. Something he was probably not used to.

Pepper spoke to the two of them for a few minutes. She pointed at Charlie. Max and Eliot nodded but looked reluctant. Then Pepper flew back to Charlie.

"They think they know which way we should go," she said.

Charlie motioned for Radcliffe and the others to move closer so they could all hear. The brownies kept themselves separated. They edged away from the group, like they wanted to sneak off again.

Pepper rolled her eyes at Max. She told everyone what the brownies had told her: they weren't exactly sure where Jessamine was, but they thought they should head north.

"How do they know which way to go?" Radcliffe quizzed Pepper.

Pepper shrugged. "I dunno. But where else are we going to go? North is as good a direction as any."

Radcliffe grumbled under his breath.

Pepper's skin turned rusty. "Do you have a better idea?" She folded her arms and glared at Radcliffe.

The centaur huffed but did not answer.

Charlie looked at the others. They all looked at her like they expected her to tell them what to do. She was supposed to lead them.

"We'll go north." She tried to sound confident.

"Is everything alright, Charlie?" Juliette touched Charlie's shoulder.

"Yeah, I'm fine. I just want to get this over with." She sighed. "Let's go."

"Charlie," Alder interrupted. He grasped her hand and tugged on it. "You are not in this alone. Do not be discouraged."

"I know." But did she know? She felt strongly that she was the one who needed to stop Jessamine and protect her friends. But could she do it alone?

"He's right." Her father draped his arm across her shoulders and gave her a squeeze. "You know all of us would do anything for you. And we trust you."

Charlie nodded. Her eyes stung.

"There is strength in numbers, Charlie." Radcliffe gave her a significant look. Did he suspect she would leave them behind if she had to?

"We are with you, too," Eliot spoke.

Charlie hadn't noticed the brownies join the group. She was surprised that Eliot had spoken in front of everyone, but it looked like he wasn't going to say any more.

Max chimed in. "We'll do *whatever* we need to in order to help." He gave his brother a stern look when he said this. What were they up to?

She was glad that she would have her friends with her. But she had to keep them safe. No matter what.

She took a deep breath and held it for a moment. She listed each of her worries quickly in her mind. Then she let it all out, sending her doubts out with her exhale. She imagined them floating away. She would do her best to be the leader she needed to be.

Charlie led the way north, away from the caves and mountains. The prairie stretched east of them, and the mountains to the west curved northward far in the distance.

Where were they headed? And how long would it take to get there?

The rolling hills stretched all the way to the mountains. The deep valleys between the hills only received full sunlight during the middle of the day. Shadows stretched long as evening drew close.

Groves of papery birch, bushy cottonwood, and shimmery quaking aspens scattered the grassy ground.

35

Between the clusters of trees, sagebrush and juniper kept a low profile. Fields of wildflowers that included buttercups, star-shaped aster flowers, and soft blossoming clover filled in the empty spaces.

They edged around a very large field of needlegrass. Alder warned them that the blades would pierce their skin and be very difficult to remove.

Roxi alerted the group, through Juliette, of a porcupine that hid nearby, camouflaged in a clump of sagebrush.

Ground squirrels chased each other through the groves of trees. Their chatter sounded like scolding to Charlie. Were they scolding each other, or Charlie and her friends?

A "V" of migrating geese honked in the sky. Was it nearing fall already? The weeks had gone fast. But the days of walking over the past several months had been long. The brief respite riding Willem's shoulder from her home to the City of Giants hadn't lasted long enough. The remainder of her journey would be on foot.

By sunset Charlie was ready to stop. She was sure her father was worn out. Everyone else looked like they could keep going. She hesitated but stuck with her gut feeling. They would find a place to rest for the night.

A nearby grove of aspen trees turned out to be the perfect spot. A creek flowed nearby, plenty of firewood littered the area, and thick clover carpeted the ground.

"What will Willem do now?" Alder wondered out loud.

They sat in a circle around the fire, munching on the food that Radcliffe and Juliette had prepared. Alder shared

a log with Charlie, and Juliette sat cross legged on the soft ground. The smaller members of their party were huddled under a summer plum bush. Pepper slurped on plums; purple juice dripped down her tiny arms. Max and Eliot poured over the parchment in Eliot's lap.

Charlie looked at Radcliffe, who sat on her other side, near where her father rested. His jaw clenched and he stared into the bright flames.

What had he done when his family had been killed? He had hunted for revenge. But Willem didn't seem like he would do that. She was more worried that Willem would sink into despair. She hadn't known him very long, but she hoped he would find peace.

"I cannot imagine what Willem must be feeling." Juliette's voice was soft and low.

Alder nodded. "He must be heartbroken. How will he go on?"

Radcliffe stood abruptly and left the group.

Charlie watched him go. She knew he didn't want to talk to anyone, so she let him be.

"Did we say something wrong?" Alder looked wide-eyed and worried.

"This is all bringing back a lot of painful memories for Radcliffe." Charlie explained to Alder that Radcliffe's family had been killed by the giants who worked for Jessamine.

An embarrassed shadow fell over Alder's face.

Charlie hurried to reassure him. "You didn't know, Alder. It's fine. He's not angry with you. He'll be back, don't worry." She squeezed his knee.

He took her hand and squeezed back. He gave her a warm smile. She blushed and slipped her hand away to continue her meal.

Radcliffe returned when the fire had dimmed, and Charlie had already stretched out on the ground. The aspen leaves shook in the breeze. It sounded like running water. The gentle noise lulled Charlie to sleep faster than she expected.

Birch trees surrounded Charlie again.

"You must restore the balance," echoed through the woods.

A movement to her left caught her eye.

She followed the movement until she reached the meadow.

She looked all around, but no one was there.

"I need help!" She shouted. "I can't do this alone!"

"You're not alone," a sly voice said from behind.

She whipped around.

Jessamine stood before her. Behind Jessamine, the birch forest had been replaced by dried grass, spiky mountains, and stormy skies.

Charlie found herself on the battlefield instead of in the woods. She held a sword in one hand and wore armor on her body. She lowered her stance.

Jessamine had a hunger in her dark eyes. She bared her teeth and snarled.

She lunged for Charlie.

Charlie sat up. The cool night air against her moist neck and back gave her a chill. She shivered, curled into a ball, and lay on her side to wait for morning.

39

Charlie let Radcliffe lead the way the next day. They still tromped up and down the endless sea of hills and valleys. The brownies had not suggested a different direction yet, so they still traveled north. For how long? She had no idea. But she didn't need to lead right now. Radcliffe enjoyed the constant sense of alertness that leading the group provided. She stayed in the back with Alder and her father.

Alder was so gentle with her dad. He let her dad lean on him for support. He walked as slow as her dad needed. He offered her dad food and water often. He took breaks for her dad to rest. The going was slow. Really slow.

The others outpaced them in no time. Charlie couldn't even see Pepper and the brownies very well from the gap between them. And Juliette and Roxi were even further ahead. Radcliffe was a speck in the distance.

But the mood with Alder was so calm and peaceful. And his kindness chased away Charlie's worries and lifted her mood.

Alder also carried the conversation well. She never would have guessed that he suffered internally from his lack of connection with the plant life, save for the fleeting look of sorrow in his eyes every once in a while. He spent so much time caring for her dad, that he didn't have time to worry about himself.

She should take a leaf off that vine.

She laughed at herself with a snort. Then covered her nose and mouth with her hands. She hated when she did that! And Alder was right there! Her face must be as red as Pepper's angry skin.

Alder chuckled at her embarrassment.

"Stop!" Charlie laughed some more. She pushed lightly

on his shoulder.

"It was cute, don't worry," Alder said. His grin stretched across his entire face.

It made Charlie weak in the knees. She blushed some more. But she, too, could not stop smiling.

"I need to fill my canteen, I'll be right back." Charlie had to escape this moment! She started to step away.

"No way! I want to hear that snort again!" Alder tugged Charlie's canteen from her hands.

Charlie looked at him with mock surprise.

"Actually, I'll go fill the canteens. You can stay with your father." Alder bounded away with all three water canteens toward the nearby stream.

She watched him go, still grinning.

"I like him," her dad said in her ear.

She jumped, composed herself, and looped her arm through his. She avoided looking at his face. She had never had any friendships, let alone relationships, with boys before. She didn't need to start anything now. Not when things ahead looked so grim.

Her thoughts must have been easy to read.

"It's natural to connect with people, Charlie. You need this. Do not push him away." Her dad sounded so calm. And wise.

She met his eyes. They were filled with love.

"Oh, Dad!" She squeezed her eyes shut and willed herself not to cry. She had been doing that way too much lately. "I don't know what to do. I'm supposed to stop Jessamine. But I don't want you and my friends to get hurt. I don't want anyone else to die. I won't let it happen. But how do I stop it from happening? I'll never forgive myself if I mess up."

He reached his arm across himself and covered her hand with his. He didn't offer any wisdom. But he looked thoughtful.

She waited.

"I have continued to not dream, Charlie. I don't know if I can help. But I am here for you always."

She leaned on him, before she remembered that he needed to lean on her. This was all so backwards! "Thanks, Dad."

"Have you talked to Radcliffe about this? He may be the one you need to speak with. He has experience where I do not."

Charlie nodded. "I'll try to talk to him."

Why hadn't she talked to Radcliffe already? Was she embarrassed to admit to him that she didn't know what she was doing? But her dad was right. Radcliffe might be able to offer some kind of advice on what to do next.

Alder returned with the water. He looked concerned at Charlie's unhappiness.

"Is something wrong?" He looked carefully into her eyes.

She met his gaze. Her heart beat a little faster. "I'm good." She gave him a weak smile.

He poked her arm. "Good." He grinned back at her.

Then he took up his usual place on her dad's other side. He talked about his garden that he grew back home, the variety of plants he cared for, and the hybrids he created. His whole face lit up when he talked about these things.

She had to help him get his abilities back.

It wasn't until another night of disturbing dreams of Jessamine and her army attacking and destroying Charlie and each of her friends one by one, and the voice repeating the same words to her, and another half day of walking and worrying, that Charlie decided to talk to Radcliffe.

Would he dismiss her dreams and think she was crazy for hearing voices? Or that she might be possessed or something? But he listened carefully to what the voice had said to her and what she had seen in her dreams.

"What am I supposed to do? Hearing '*You must restore the balance,*' and '*You must stop Jessamine,*' over and over again isn't helping." She mimicked the deep voice that she kept hearing. *"How* do I do those things?" She knew frustration edged her words, but she was at the end of her rope.

"You need to dream. Or we're all dead." His words came out flat.

That's it? That's all he had to say? That was about as helpful as "*You must stop Jessamine.*"

"Gee, thanks," she grumbled at him.

He looked sideways at her, down his sharp nose. That look always made her feel judged. Maybe she shouldn't have come to him for help.

She could feel her agitation grow. It gave her a queasy feeling, and made her lightheaded, like she hadn't eaten enough.

"Are you alright?" Radcliffe stopped and turned to face her.

She didn't feel alright. She shook her head.

Her vision blurred. Her knees buckled.

Everything went black.

Chapter 7

Birch trees. Check.

Spotty sunlight. Check.

Movement to her left. Check.

Here we go again.

She stomped toward the meadow.

"Well?" she hollered at the sky once she arrived. "Aren't you going to tell me to stop Jessamine and restore the balance?"

She spun in a circle. Her hands clenched into fists. She was so sick of this!

She heard a deep, slow chuckle behind her.

She turned on her heels.

It was the giant. He was here. Finally.

She rushed toward him and hugged his leg tight. At least, as much of his leg as she could get her arms around.

"I've been expecting you for so long!" She spoke with a tight throat.

"I've missed you too, Little Dreamer."

Her heart slowed. She relaxed for the first time in a long time. Now she would get the answers she needed.

She gazed up at her friend who sat with his legs stretched out in front of him. He leaned on a massive boulder. He smiled down at her.

"How am I supposed to restore the balance and stop Jessamine? I don't understand what needs to be done. And I don't know how to keep everyone I care about safe anymore. Please, you have to help me." Her fingers twisted in front of her. The anxiety inched closer to the surface.

"You must Dream, Charlie. Your dreams will guide you."

She already knew that. "But nothing I dream about is helping. And that voice. I don't understand!"

Her heart beat faster.

"We've talked about this before, Charlie. Fear keeps you from dreaming."

"I don't feel afraid. I just feel like I don't know where to go or what to do. I need the dreams to lead me. Not just tell me what the outcome has to be. How do I do that?"

"You must see things from a different perspective. You must focus on what you *need*, not what you are worried about. You must take this journey one step, one day at a time. You must allow the dreams to consume your wants, including the well-being of those around you. You must *become* a Dreamer."

Charlie couldn't take her eyes off him when he finished. She took a moment to allow his words to burn into her memory.

"I believe in you, Charlie. We all do."

Her surroundings began to fade.

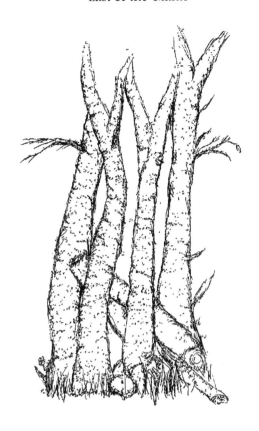

"Charlie? Charlie!" Radcliffe called from somewhere nearby, but his voice sounded funny. Kind of echoey.

She opened her eyes to find herself lying on the ground, her head and shoulders in Radcliffe's arms.

"What happened?" Her head felt fuzzy. She had a hard time focusing her eyes.

Radcliffe heaved a deep sigh. He looked at the clouds for a moment, before returning his sharp gaze at her. "You passed out." His jaw clenched so tight that the words had to slip out between his teeth.

She focused on him. Was he angry? He looked really pale.

"Are you sick or something, Radcliffe? You don't look very well."

His mouth turned into a sideways grin. Color returned to his face. He squeezed her shoulder and lowered her to the ground.

The vision of the giant and the words he had spoken to her rushed into her mind.

"I didn't pass out. I had a dream… or something. I saw the giant. He spoke to me. He told me I need to become a Dreamer."

She pushed herself into a sitting position. Radcliffe had his horse legs tucked beneath his body beside her. "The thing is, Radcliffe, I thought I *was* a Dreamer. But he said I have to see things from a different perspective. I have to let the dreams consume my wants. Including your safety."

She locked eyes with Radcliffe.

How could she not want her friends to be safe? And how could she let go of that?

He nodded. Like he could read her thoughts.

"It will take time and work, Charlie. But you can become a Dreamer. I would like to assist, if you will allow it." Radcliffe stood on his feet again, then reached a hand to Charlie.

She grasped his wrist and he pulled her into a standing position.

She brushed the dust off her backside.

"Thanks, Radcliffe. I think I'm going to need all the help I can get. But I don't want to worry my father or any of the others, either. This has to stay between you and I."

"Agreed." Radcliffe rested a heavy hand on her

shoulder. His grey eyes peered into hers. "You are not alone."

Charlie had thought that Radcliffe would train her on how to use her weapons and how to fight. But she really needed him to train her on how to use her dreams.

He told her he would begin when they stopped for the night. The day was almost halfway over. She couldn't wait to get started.

Charlie slowed her pace so the others could catch up to her. Juliette and Roxi were the first to join her. She asked Juliette about their surroundings, the plants and animals that lived there. And the changes that Juliette may have noticed taking place.

The world was still out of balance. Charlie knew that much. But she didn't know enough about everything to be able to tell what exactly was not normal.

Juliette pointed out that there should be patches of goldenrod, marigolds, and beauty berries covering the steep, rocky slopes of the hillsides. Instead, creeping vines covered large areas of the ground. She said that the vines were not native to the area and would choke out other natural species.

Charlie noticed vines crawling up aspen and cottonwood trunks, too. And the patches of clover that should be blossoming were dotted with spiny phlox flowers instead.

The phlox would deter pollinating insects from the clover. The clover would not blossom.

There should also have been over two hundred different bird species and variations along their travels. But Juliette said she had only encountered a handful.

"The ones I have seen did not look healthy," she told Charlie. "I can only assume the others have all left the area. But to where, I do not know. The only other explanation

would be that they have all died out. And that is not something I can willingly accept."

Charlie could see the despair on her friend's face and hear it in her voice. She gave Juliette a sideways hug.

It wasn't long before Pepper and the brownies caught up, too.

Pepper flitted around Charlie, recounting the race Max and Eliot had run.

"You should have seen it! Eliot drank some special drink, and then they raced. He ran so much faster than Max! I mean, he almost looked like he was flying! I could have sworn his skin looked different, too, but it was probably just my imagination."

Eliot and Max shared a mischievous look.

"What did you drink?" Juliette looked back and forth between the brownies.

"Oh, just some juice that we made from… er… some… speed weed?" It sounded like a question more than an answer.

Charlie rolled her eyes. They were up to their old antics again.

"Just be careful. And don't involve Pepper in your little experiments, remember?"

Pepper grinned. "Can you imagine how fast I could fly if I drank some?" Her eyes had a spark to them.

Charlie nodded. "Yes, I can. And I'm not sure that would be a good thing."

Max looked thoughtful. Like he had a clever idea. "Don't worry," he told Charlie, almost as an afterthought. "We wouldn't do anything to harm Pepper."

Pepper pouted a little. "Just a sip?"

Max shook his head.

Charlie nodded. "Good."

Alder and Charlie's dad didn't catch up to the group until near dusk. Her dad's progress seemed to be getting worse, not better, even with Alder's healing teas and careful attention. Juliette attempted to aid as well, but none of her techniques helped. He still limped. He looked tired all the time. He didn't sleep well. The long hours of walking each day didn't help. How much longer would he be able to travel before it was too much?

After their evening meal, Charlie made sure her father was as comfortable as possible and sat with him until he fell asleep.

She watched Radcliffe speak with Max and Eliot away from the others. She always had the impression that he didn't like the brownies very much. But he seemed to respect them.

When the others had settled in, Charlie followed Radcliffe a little away from camp. It was time for him to help her learn how to become a Dreamer. Hopefully it would work.

"The first thing you need to do is learn to focus." Radcliffe began his instruction. "We will begin small and work our way up. Find a comfortable place on the ground."

Charlie sat with her knees bent and ankles crossed in front of her, like butterfly wings.

Radcliffe tucked his legs beneath him. It looked awkward. But he seemed comfortable. What would it be like to have a horse body and four legs?

"Notice your body." He interrupted her thoughts.

She blushed and brought her mind back to the moment. This was all about learning to focus. She shouldn't be thinking about other random things.

"Close your eyes and relax. Feel your breath as it goes in and back out again." Radcliffe demonstrated.

She watched him breathe for a minute. Should she take deep breaths? He was. She closed her eyes and breathed in really deep, then let it all out. She did that a few times. How long would they do this for? Her mind started to wander again, this time to her father not healing right, and wondering if Willem found his family yet.

"When your mind begins to wander, come back to the breathing." Radcliffe's voice was calm and quiet.

How did he know her mind had wandered?

"Continue to focus on your breath for a few more

minutes." He continued his own breathing.

She breathed in… and out. In… and out. In… and out. The fire crackled. The wind rustled the leaves. In… and out. Her body relaxed. Her mind sharpened.

"You must restore the balance."

The voice startled her. She inhaled a sharp breath and opened her eyes.

Radcliffe continued to breathe steady, like he hadn't even noticed.

She closed her eyes and tried to focus on her breathing again. She breathed, but couldn't relax and focus anymore.

A few minutes later, Radcliffe spoke softly again. "Open your eyes, slowly look up. Take in your surroundings. Notice the sounds around you, your body, your thoughts and emotions."

He stayed quiet for another minute or two.

"How do you feel?" he asked her when he was finished.

She squirmed a little under his gaze. "Good, I guess. It worked for a little bit. But then I got distracted…" She didn't meet his eyes.

"That is well, Charlie. This is new. You must not be hard on yourself or judge your thoughts or feelings during the process. When you sit down to do this, you are telling yourself that you believe in change. That you believe you can become a Dreamer. That you believe you can make it real."

Charlie nodded.

Radcliffe stood. "We will do this again tomorrow evening. Try to focus on your breathing as you fall asleep tonight. We will discuss any dreams you may have in the morning."

Charlie followed Radcliffe back to camp in silence.

Would this meditation really help her be a successful Dreamer?

She stretched out on her blanket, near her father, but not too close. She did what Radcliffe had told her. She tried to just focus on her breathing with her eyes closed. Her mind wandered to her home, to the City of Giants, to her worries about her father, and what would happen to her friends. Each time she tried to bring her thoughts back to her breath. In... and out. In... and out.

Max stood on a boulder near the edge of their camp. The others surrounded him, Charlie in the center. The little man pointed; his arm extended in front of him.

"We need to go that way."

Eliot nodded beside the boulder.

Charlie shouldered her pack and led the way in the direction that Max had indicated.

The others followed.

Spiky mountains and a shadow in the distance called to Charlie. Jessamine was there. She was sure of it.

"You must restore the balance."

Chapter 8

In the morning, Charlie watched the two brownies sneak away and hide behind a bush. The others were distracted by their morning meal preparations and packing away their few belongings.

Max and Eliot whispered to one another out of earshot.

How did Max and Eliot know which way to go? Were they just leading them on a wild goose chase? Were they really heading toward Jessamine at all?

After a while, Charlie gave up watching the little men and returned to her own preparations for a light breakfast.

By the time Charlie had finished eating and had packed her bag, Max and Eliot emerged from the bushes.

Max announced that they knew which direction to go next.

Charlie and the others looked up from their various activities.

Max motioned for everyone to gather around him as he climbed on a small boulder to look across the valley.

"We need to go that way." Max pointed northwest.

This was the exact scene she had seen in her dream. The others surrounded the rock, Charlie in the center. Eliot nodded to one side.

The others all looked bewildered at the serious expression on Max's face, but Charlie understood. He was pointing toward the enchanted forest.

In her dream, Charlie had done what Max suggested. But she had no idea that they would be headed straight for the enchanted forest! It was a bad idea.

"Why can't we go toward the lake?" Charlie asked him, all eyes on her now.

"It would take us in the wrong direction," Max answered.

"Sure, but wouldn't it be safe to take a less direct route?" Charlie had no desire to enter the forest again.

"Why don't you want to go that way, Charlie?" her father asked.

Charlie shifted, then answered. "Because of the forest."

Alder nodded. "I understand her hesitation. That is an enchanted forest…"

Juliette and Charlie's father looked surprised, while Radcliffe just rolled his eyes.

"I've been through enchanted places before," Radcliffe said. "It's nothing I can't handle."

"Actually," interrupted Alder, "this one is quite dangerous."

"Yeah, I know, I've been through it before," Charlie said.

Pepper nodded, looking wide eyed and apprehensive.

"If you've been through, then we should be fine," Radcliffe folded his arms.

"I had help. Even the giant I was with almost died in that place. A wood nymph saved us. We wouldn't have survived if he hadn't helped."

Charlie didn't want to argue, but this was an important decision to make. She couldn't bring herself to put their entire group in danger when it could easily be avoided.

"Fine, so we get him to help us again," countered Radcliffe.

"That is not easily done," Alder said. "Charlie, you were quite fortunate to have received a wood nymph's help. They don't become involved in the affairs of humans often, if ever."

His voice was grave, but Charlie had already known that she had been lucky the first time. That's why she didn't want to press her luck again.

"Can you help us, then?" Charlie's father asked Alder. "I understand you have certain... abilities?"

Alder shook his head, his shoulders sank. "I'm afraid I cannot. As you know, my connection with the natural world has been severed. It's not possible at the moment." He shrugged, a look of despair hiding behind his controlled expression.

"So, let's just go another way," Pepper announced. She looked down at the brownies from her position hovering near Charlie.

The two little men shared a look. "That would not be wise," Eliot maintained eye contact with his brother as he spoke.

"Why not?" Charlie asked.

"Do you trust us, or not?" Max asked. He sounded annoyed. And frustrated.

"Of course, we do," Juliette said without hesitation.

Radcliffe raised one eyebrow. The rest of his face remained stern.

Pepper blushed and nodded. Alder and Charlie's father both looked thoughtful.

Charlie wanted to trust them. They had only helped so far, even going above and beyond by finding Juliette's people so that Charlie's villagers would have a safe place to stay once they evacuated their homes. The brownies had always shown up right when they were needed.

But, they also seemed so secretive, whispering to one another and sneaking away without a word to the others. Even on this journey they had not been forthcoming with how they knew where to go, always saying it was just a hunch or they had heard about things happening in certain directions. There was definitely more going on than Charlie, or the others, knew anything about.

Whenever Pepper tried to find out more, though, they always brushed her off or diverted her questions.

Charlie knew that pressing the issue now, in front of the group, wouldn't do any good. They were sure to keep their secret, whatever it was.

The image from her dream filled her mind. She had gone the direction they had suggested. She supposed she should do the same now.

Charlie led the way. Radcliffe walked beside her. Pepper fluttered around Charlie, instead of traveling with the brownies. She flitted between Charlie and various patches of blossoming plants and groves of trees. The others stretched out at different paces behind them.

"Should we really go through the enchanted forest?" Charlie couldn't shake the feeling that it was a bad idea.

"What do you believe?" Radcliffe answered her question with another question.

"I think it's a terrible idea," Pepper answered Radcliffe before Charlie could. "It was rough last time. But, if Max and Eliot say we should go this way, then we should. Maybe we won't even go through the forest. Maybe we'll end up going around it, or in a different direction or something?"

Radcliffe nodded. "Charlie? What do you think?"

Charlie told Radcliffe about her dream of Max pointing the way and Charlie following his directions.

"Then you did the right thing."

"But it was such a small thing. So simple. Was it really that important that we go this direction? Unless Jessamine is *in* the enchanted forest, then why do we even need to go this way?"

"You focused before you slept, correct?" Radcliffe asked.

She nodded.

"Then you need to trust this dream. If it was some big revelation, or a major sacrifice, would you have hesitated to follow?"

She hadn't thought of that before. When her dreams told her something big, or scary, or important, she listened. "No, I would have done it."

"Right. Then why not do the small, simple things as well? It can't hurt."

"This could!" Pepper chimed. "Those vines, and flowers, and bees in the forest are intense!"

But Charlie knew what Radcliffe meant. If she wasn't willing to do the things that were relatively easy, then how could she be expected to do something that might require effort and sacrifice?

This may be a step toward the answers she needed. Even though she was still worried about traveling through the forest, she had to trust that this was what she was supposed to do.

"Speaking of Max and Eliot... Pepper, do you know how they figure out where we should go?" Charlie's thoughts turned to the brownies.

Pepper shook her head, her mouth full of some berry she had plucked from a nearby scraggly bush. She swallowed, then answered Charlie. "They always change the subject or offer me something sweet to eat. You know how I love sweets!"

Charlie chuckled. "Um, yeah. I know."

"I finally quit asking. Although, it was nice getting a treat every time I asked!" She giggled. "Now when they want to talk about stuff, they just politely ask me to go find them a certain plant or fruit or something. I know they are just trying to get rid of me so they can talk, but I don't mind." She shrugged.

"By the way," Pepper changed the subject now. "Have you noticed that the morning glories don't really glow that much anymore? And they taste bitter. They used to be so sweet!"

Was Pepper employing the same tactic as the brownies?

Changing the subject by distracting Charlie with something sweet? The thought made Charlie smile. Maybe so. But she wouldn't resist. She would keep trying to dream and follow the dreams. If that meant following Max and Eliot too, then so be it.

Pepper kept Charlie and Radcliffe entertained all morning long. She showed off her fighting techniques-mostly just burning her way through various shrubs and thickets. Charlie asked her to stop when she had to catch up and put out the beginning of a brush fire.

Pepper apologized and switched over to retelling several of Max and Eliot's tall tales. She talked about pirates on the high seas, an underwater adventure that involved a kraken, and some eerie story about ghostly figures that followed them through a mountain one time.

Charlie still didn't know if the stories were true. They sounded pretty far-fetched. But Pepper believed them. With each new tale they told, the pixie liked them more. Eliot more than Max, based on Pepper's giggles and blushing around the younger brother.

Late in the afternoon, Charlie could make out the shape of the enchanted forest in the distance. They had traveled in a straight line all day. And they would arrive dead center at the edge of the forest.

Charlie shuddered. Maybe not *dead* center. Right in the middle. She had to assume that they would, indeed, be entering the forest.

A river gully wound its way across the landscape to their left. Radcliffe announced that they should detour slightly so they could fill their canteens. It wouldn't take them off course, and it would only add a little bit of time until they reached their destination.

61

Willow trees laden with brown, dead leaves bordered the gully. These trees had died from thirst, not gone dormant due to seasonal changes. It should have been lush and green

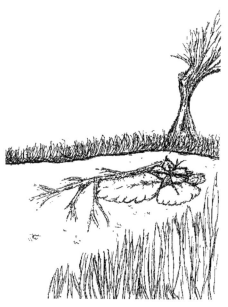

down into the gulch, but all the plants were brown and brittle, instead. At the bottom a thick layer of goopy mud coated the ground where a wide creek should have freely flowed.

A family of river otters lined the opposite bank. They dug in the mud as if they thought there may be water underneath. When they caught the movement of Charlie and her friends, they cowered and chattered to one another. Then they scurried and hid inside a hollow log on top of the mud.

"The poor dears," Juliette said. "Perhaps we should give them some of our water." She took a step toward the downhill slope, but Radcliffe stopped her with his arm.

"Wait," he demanded. "Listen."

Charlie couldn't hear anything.

Roxi whined from behind, where Charlie's fathers leaned on the great dog for support.

They all stayed quiet.

In an instant, the ground trembled. A split-second later

Charlie heard a roar that echoed down the gully.

"What is that?" she started to ask. But before anyone could answer, she saw for herself.

A massive wall of water raced through the gully. The front resembled galloping horses, their manes and bodies lost in the crashing waves behind them. Was it a trick of the eye, or her imagination? She could only guess.

"Oh!" Juliette cried beside her. "The otters!"

Charlie could tell she wanted to rescue the little guys, but Radcliffe continued to hold his arm out to block her.

And it was a good thing, too. Because the water raced in front of them and on down the gully so fast, that there was no way Juliette could have done anything to help the otters.

"They can swim, right?" Pepper asked.

Alder nodded.

But Juliette sounded sad when she answered. "Unless they become trapped in that log." She stared down the gully as if hoping she would see the little animals pop out of the water and swim to shore.

"I'm sure they will be safe," Alder added. He looked at Charlie with a worried expression though.

"Let's get moving." She encouraged the others to follow.

"What about filling the canteens?" Pepper asked.

"I think we should save that for another time. We have enough for today."

Charlie held Juliette's arm and led her away. The Princess was in a daze, as if she felt betrayed by the water for stopping her from helping the otters.

Alder walked with Charlie's dad, as usual. The group stayed together the rest of the afternoon. The pace was slow, but the companionship necessary.

63

Chapter 9

They neared the edge of the enchanted forest just before nightfall. Everyone stopped to stare at the ominous tree line. No one spoke. The darkness penetrated the gaps between the trees just like Charlie remembered.

How would they survive this time? Her dad was injured, the brownies were so tiny. It seemed impossible. Would Gerfott help? Was he even still here? What if his abilities had been lost, too? She sighed heavily.

"We should camp for the night," Radcliffe spoke low in Charlie's ear. "We will deal with the forest in the light of day."

Charlie agreed and they set up camp, as usual.

Again, after everyone had eaten and settled, Charlie followed Radcliffe away from the others.

He instructed Charlie to focus on her breathing, like last night. She nodded, made herself comfortable, and closed her eyes.

He guided her through the process in a soft, low voice.

"Breathe in. Breathe out. Focus. Feel your breath fill your lungs. Bring your thoughts back to your breath."

His voice soothed her. She relaxed. Her mind wandered less than it had the night before.

It didn't feel like it had been long when Radcliffe said, "Good. Now open your eyes slowly and notice the sounds, your thoughts, and your feelings."

She focused for a few more minutes.

"How do you feel?"

"Calm. At peace." It felt really good. It had been a while since she had felt that way. Like, a long while.

"While you are still relaxed, I want you to lie down on your blanket and continue to focus. Imagine every limb from head to toe relaxing completely. You should fall asleep rather quickly."

Charlie did as she was told, and Radcliffe was right. She fell asleep almost right away.

The sun brightened the sky. The forest loomed dark in front of her. She stood with the others, facing the forest.

"What are we waiting for?" grunted Radcliffe. With his battle axe in one huge hand and his sword in the other, he marched into the forest.

The others all looked at one another with wide, frightened eyes. One by one they followed Radcliffe into the dark thicket. Charlie watched each of her friends disappear from view.

"I should have been first," she scolded herself. Even her father had stepped into the darkness.

Charlie ran into the trees, the last to enter the forest. She would be the last one to encounter whatever lay ahead. Her heart hurt that she had let them all down once again.

In the morning, Charlie did not tell Radcliffe about her dream. Even though it had not yet happened, she was ashamed of the fact that she had allowed all the others to enter the forest in front of her. She knew she should be the one to lead. It's what her dreams had told her. It's what the giant had told her. She had to be willing to let go of her fears and insecurities and lead.

When the time came for them to enter the forest, she asked for everyone's attention. "This forest is dangerous. Do not touch anything. Keep a quick pace. Help one another. I don't know how long it will take to make it through."

She wasn't even sure they *should* go through the forest, but Max and Eliot had not changed their course. She had to trust them.

Pepper looked at her with wide eyes. Max and Eliot nodded.

"What are we waiting for?" Radcliffe grunted. He removed his battle axe from the holster on his back and gripped it tight in his left hand. He stepped toward the edge of the forest.

"Wait," Charlie found herself calling to him. "I'll go first."

He looked at her like she was crazy.

"Please. I need to do this."

He nodded and stepped aside.

She would not be the last one to face the danger. She would not let her friends be harmed. She felt a surge of courage blossom in her chest. She could do this.

She led at a fast pace, cutting branches out of her way. She couldn't go too fast because of the injured and short legs in their group. But she also wanted to hurry.

She jumped at every sound of a twig snapping or a tree branch rustling. But she realized quickly that it was herself and her companions making the sounds. The forest itself was still and silent. It was dark beneath the canopy, but not as dark as Charlie remembered. She could tell the sun was to her right as they traveled in a northerly direction. She shouldn't be able to tell which direction they traveled at all.

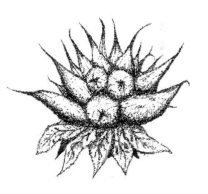

Unlike the other places she had traveled recently, the forest didn't look any different than any other forest. The various trees grew tall and straight, their branches fanned out to create the canopy. A variety of ground covers carpeted the forest floor. Moss hung from branches. Shrubs, laden with colorful berries, grew close to tree trunks. Wildflowers blossomed here and there.

She waited for something bad to happen. With every step she expected to be stung, bitten, or tangled. After they had been inside the forest for well over an hour the anticipation became almost unbearable. But no vines sprouted from the ground to entangle Charlie's feet. No pollen invaded her lungs to put her to sleep. No flowers tried to eat her hand.

Why hadn't the forest attacked them yet? Was Gerfott

protecting them? She didn't see him anywhere. He would have shown himself if he was helping them. She became more tense the longer they walked. Whatever the forest planned to do to them, she wished it would just happen so they could fight it and be on their way.

Eliot and Max signaled for the group to stop. She heeded their request.

"We need to bear north, and we are starting to head east," Max announced.

Charlie hadn't noticed, but they were right. She had led them in slightly the wrong direction. She had been distracted by the lack of resistance.

Radcliffe rolled his eyes. "Some enchanted forest," he mumbled. "I don't see what all the fuss was about before. This forest doesn't seem enchanted at all."

This thought poked at Charlie. He was right. The forest didn't seem enchanted at all. It seemed like any other ordinary forest.

"Maybe it's not," she said to herself.

"What was that, Charlie?" Her father stood beside her. He leaned close to hear her response.

"Maybe it's not enchanted," Charlie said louder.

"But you said this was the enchanted forest that you had traveled through before," Radcliffe pointed out.

"It is, but maybe it's not actually enchanted anymore." An idea began to take shape in her mind.

Radcliffe looked skeptical; the brownies a little too knowing.

"Think about it," she went on. "Juliette can no longer communicate with animals. Alder has lost his connection to the plants. The prairie and the mountains rejected our presence. It's hard to find things to eat. Water has even evaded us. Why wouldn't an enchanted forest no longer be enchanted. Everything is out of sorts."

Alder and Juliette shared a look. "I think she may be right," Alder said. Juliette nodded.

Roxi made a grumbling sound. Charlie assumed she agreed.

"Good, then the forest will be easy to pass through," Radcliffe stated. He sheathed his weapon.

"It may be good for us, but it is not a good thing for the world. The more power Jessamine gains, the more things will change." Juliette's voice sounded pained.

The balance must be restored.

That's what the voice had been telling Charlie. That's what the giant had said. And Jessamine was at the heart of all of it. She had to be stopped. And somehow, Charlie had to be the one to do it. Her brow furrowed.

The brownies glanced at one another. "We need to go that way," Max said, pointing in the direction he had indicated when they stopped.

"You said that already," Radcliffe said through gritted teeth. Then to the group, "If that witch is going to make things worse, then we should move. Take her out sooner rather than later."

"What he said," Max gestured at Radcliffe. "Let's go."

Part of Charlie wanted to talk more about the problem, but she knew that Radcliffe and the brownies were right. If Jessamine was changing so much of their world, they needed to solve the problem. Not stand around talking about it.

She led the others through the forest. Max occasionally altered their direction, and Charlie again wondered how they could know so precisely where they should go. But for now, she needed to place her trust in them.

Charlie didn't recognize anything in the forest. They were able to travel in a straight line, only varying their course to maneuver around the trees and shrubs. Nothing tried to stop their progress. No animals could be seen or heard. Pepper even commented on the lack of killer bees, for which Charlie was grateful.

They kept a steady pace. With Alder on one side and Juliette on the other, Charlie's dad maintained a faster speed than normal. They made excellent progress. They didn't stop again. After another two hours, they emerged from the tree line.

They took a quick break to rest, eat, and drink. Charlie checked on her dad. He rested on the ground, on his side, with his eyes closed. She looked on him for several long minutes. How much more of this could he handle? He never complained, but she knew he struggled with fatigue and pain. What if this proved to be too much for him?

Part of her wondered if this was really worth it. He should have stayed with Juliette's people. And where were they even going? Max and Eliot had not revealed a destination. How long would they wander out here before they found Jessamine and stopped her? And what would that look like, exactly?

She allowed her dad to rest a good while longer before she woke him and told him they needed to continue. Max and Eliot indicated that they should travel north still. Charlie picked up her pack and led the way.

For the next week she practiced her focused breathing each night. Radcliffe transitioned her into self-guided focus. She breathed and relaxed before she fell asleep. She slept harder and dreamed often. Her dreams showed her incremental details of her journey. She would see a landmark, or one of her companions do or say something. The following day, those things would happen, and she knew she was on the right path.

She also saw herself battle Jessamine over and over again. In all the versions, some or all of her friends did not survive. In many versions she did not survive. How did she expect to stop Jessamine when they were so outnumbered? Was she just leading them all to their deaths?

On the one hand, learning to focus and dream meant she would lead them where they needed to go. But on the other hand, was that even a good idea? She felt so torn.

The giant had told her that she had to let the dreams consume her wants. She had to be willing to let go. That was a lot harder than it sounded. The giant had also told her that only a Dreamer would be able to stop Jessamine. There must be a reason that she had been chosen. She had to believe that she had what it would take.

The more she focused, dreamt, and followed through on the day-to-day instructional dreams, the less stressed out and frustrated she became. When she allowed her worries for her father and friends to build, the focus and dreaming became more difficult. But she listened to Radcliffe's advice. And she remembered the giant's admonition to *become* a Dreamer.

Chapter 10

Charlie asked Radcliffe to train the group on fighting and defensive techniques each evening. Her dad wanted to participate, but Charlie insisted he rest. The hair around his temples had turned white, and his face appeared more aged. His posture had a slight bend to it, and he looked so tired all the time. She needed him to rest.

Pepper, on the other hand, insisted that she did NOT need Radcliffe to teach her anything. She attempted to show off her impressive fighting skills by shooting her miniscule bow she had crafted. Her arrows never traveled far. She ended up just bursting into flames and burning her target in a woosh of fire every time. Her dragon armor remained unharmed from her hot flames. She demonstrated her mid-air sword work, but Charlie doubted her toothpick of a sword could cause any real damage. Her bite, though, could incapacitate an opponent if she was angry enough. In the end, she didn't really need Radcliffe's help. But only because she lost her temper so often that she spent most of her training time aflame, which was far more dangerous than any weapon she could wield.

When Radcliffe wanted to teach the brownies to fight, they, too, announced that it would not be necessary. They assured the group that they had their own methods of defending themselves, as well as defeating an enemy. Charlie expected Radcliffe to be annoyed by this information. But instead, Eliot gave Radcliffe a significant look, and Radcliffe nodded. If Radcliffe believed them, then she wouldn't worry about it. Well, she would try not to worry, anyway.

Alder, Juliette, and Charlie had enough basic battle training to not need too many pointers, but the trio agreed that they should practice and train to improve muscle memory and prepare for the battle that loomed before them. Radcliffe observed and offered instruction as needed.

Charlie looked forward to their evening practice sessions. She liked parrying with Alder the most. She could tell he held back a little, but she didn't mind. She liked watching him move so sure on his feet and hold his sword like it weighed nothing. She didn't mind his eyes on her, either. They laughed and teased one another when they practiced. It helped Charlie forget her worries for just a little while.

During the days they walked through emerald green valleys between hilltops shadowed by groves of trees. The flowing water that had formed the valleys was missing. Dry river and creek beds led the way instead. One area that had once been flooded by a massive beaver dam had dried up. It left the area exposed. The grasses that had been matted down by flooding had begun to straighten. The massive beaver dam had been abandoned. Flies buzzed circles around rotting fish carcasses. Charlie held her finger under her nose to block out the smell.

One dusky evening a herd of pronghorn deer bounded across their path, but quite a distance away. The way they hopped on all four legs looked unnatural. Juliette assured her that it was perfectly normal. Pepper imitated their method of travel. Max egged her on. She landed on the ground, then burst straight up into the sky and flew a wide arc before she landed again. Charlie reminded her that the deer did not have wings. But Pepper paid her no mind. As long as Max and Eliot reacted to her antics, she would continue.

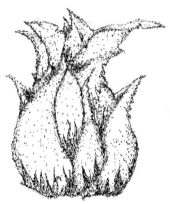

On the sixth night, Alder plopped down beside Charlie when they finished training. Both were out of breath. Alder asked her about her memories of the past, and what her hopes for her future were. He talked of his own upbringing, and even shared how he learned to use his abilities. Her heart ached for his missing connection with the plants, but he had hope that his abilities would be restored in the end.

"I believe in you, Charlie," he promised. He held out his hand for hers.

Her heart fluttered under his gaze. She rested her hand in his larger, dark hand. He laced his fingers between hers. She would not fail him.

When the time came for her to focus and dream, she found it easier to clear her mind and concentrate when she thought of him. She was glad Alder was with them, not only for her father's sake, but also for her own.

Jessamine called for her army to attack.

Alder stood shoulder to shoulder with Charlie.

She would not let him die in this fight.

She rushed toward Jessamine and swung her sword at the woman.

A look of surprise appeared on Jessamine's face, and she fell to the ground, lifeless.

Charlie panted.

She looked back at Alder. He had a look of horror on his face.

But she had saved his life. That had been the right thing to do, right?

Her head ached and everything went black.

She awoke to find herself shivering near the now cold campfire. She stayed awake for a long time, gazing at the stars and pondering what this new dream had meant.

The giant had said she must let go of her wants and be willing to make sacrifices. Did that mean letting Alder go?

She didn't want to do that! But wasn't that the whole point of letting go?

Her head continued to pound until morning.

Max and Eliot spent time alone each day, then returned to the group and announced the direction they should travel. Charlie's dreams continued to show her that she should follow their directions. She now led the group in a north-westerly direction.

After finishing their meal one night, the group made small talk about the condition of their supplies, the quality of the food, and the details of the flora around them. The brownies had snuck away again. Radcliffe excused himself from the makeshift camp.

A short while later, a roar sounded from behind a small rise not far away. Charlie leapt to her feet. What had caused Radcliffe to react this way? It was hard to tell sometimes if he was being attacked or was just really angry about something. It must be an attack. What could be making him that angry?

Charlie assumed a defensive position, tensed, and waited for the attacker to crash into their camp. The others formed a loose circle, backs toward one another, as Radcliffe had taught them. Roxi growled from deep within her chest. It was hard to see her father holding a weapon. He looked scared, and Charlie was sorry that he had to be going through this. She knew he was far out of his comfort zone. She shook these thoughts away. Now was not the time to worry about her father. She had to be ready to fight.

Her breath sped up and her heart raced while she waited for whatever it was to appear.

A moment later, Radcliffe burst over the hilltop. He held Max and Eliot, one in each hand, by the necks of their shirts.

He threw them down in the midst of the group, a look of pure rage on his face.

Charlie and her friends lowered their weapons a little. Where was the attacker?

"What is it, Radcliffe?" Charlie asked, still holding her sword out, just in case.

"Them!" he yelled and pointed at the brownies.

"What? What happened? Are we under attack?" Charlie begged for information.

"No. They have been lying to us!" Radcliffe answered. The veins in his neck popped up under his skin and his face turned as red as a autumn apple.

"So... no attack?" Charlie asked again, wary to lower her weapon until she was sure.

"NO!" yelled Radcliffe.

"Alright, alright. Sorry! Just checking." Charlie sheathed her sword, relieved, but frightened still at the same time.

"Don't put that away. You may need it yet," Radcliffe growled. His narrow eyes did not leave the brownies, who cowered together at his feet.

Pepper zipped down and approached her friends.

"Eliot? Max? What's going on?" she asked timidly.

"They LIED to us!" Radcliffe roared.

Pepper jumped and her hair lit up.

Roxi let out three sharp barks of warning.

Max and Eliot curled themselves into even smaller balls.

"Let us all take a deep breath and calm down," Juliette tried to neutralize the situation.

"I will NOT calm down!" Radcliffe bellowed.

"Radcliffe, hold on. What have they been lying to us about?" Charlie's heart slowed. They were not under attack.

What could have angered Radcliffe to this degree?

The brownies didn't look defiant or dangerous. They were clearly terrified of the centaur that loomed over them. They wouldn't even pull their heads out from under their arms to look at anyone. Not even Pepper.

Charlie was conflicted. Could she and the others have been tricked by these innocent looking men? She had learned the hard way that appearances can be deceiving. But she had also been trying to learn to trust. So, which should she do now?

"Radcliffe, can you please explain what has caused you to become so angry?" Juliette addressed the centaur, still attempting to calm him.

Charlie watched Radcliffe take a deep breath. He gritted his teeth and spoke. "I wanted to see why they were always sneaking off. I thought I knew," he glared at the brownies.

Charlie had seen him talk to them privately on several occasions. And she had seen him point at the small canteen that he carried. She assumed that he knew what they were up to. But she must have been wrong.

"So, I followed them. When I found them, they were looking at a half-finished map! They were drawing on it, discussing which way we should go next. They are leading us to nowhere!"

The volume of his voice increased.

"They are making up a map that leads to nowhere! They either don't know where that *witch* is located, or they are in her employ and intentionally leading us away from her.

They have been lying!" His muscles bulged and his eyes popped. He looked angrier than ever.

Charlie couldn't make sense of what Radcliffe had said. They were drawing a map? Why would they draw a fake map if they never showed it to anyone?

"Radcliffe, I don't get it. What are you talking about?"

"Ask THEM!" His face contorted with rage.

"Radcliffe, please do not yell. We have done nothing to deserve your wrath," Juliette implored the centaur.

It's a good thing that Juliette was there to mediate. Charlie never knew how to handle Radcliffe when he was so angry. It tended to frustrate her, which made her lash out back at him.

Alder and Charlie's father stayed silent on either side of Charlie, but she could feel them both tense with each of Radcliffe's outbursts.

"Max. Eliot. What is this about?" Juliette asked the brownies. She kneeled down and placed one hand on Max's back.

Max flinched at her touch. He scooted away from the Princess.

"It's not true," he pleaded. "We don't work for Jessamine." His voice was muffled beneath his arms.

"We trust you…" Juliette replied.

Was that true? Did Charlie truly trust them?

"Do you know where Jessamine is?" Juliette prodded for more information.

Max lifted his head just enough to see the Princess, eyes wide and a little wet. He made eye contact with Juliette, then looked away. His jaw was set, and Charlie knew he wasn't going to answer the question.

"Tell them," Eliot said in a small voice. He came out

from under his arms.

"No," Max said, a little panicked. "NO. We can't!"

"You've wanted to this whole time. Just get it over with." Eliot avoided looking at anyone.

"I kind of wanted to," Max agreed. "It would make things easier. But it would also put you in danger. You've been right all along. We can't say anything. It's not worth it." Max pleaded with Eliot.

"Tell us what?" Pepper wanted to know.

Charlie could tell by her pink hue that the pixie was hurt that she hadn't been let in on their secret, whatever it was, before now.

At this point, the brothers couldn't have a conversation like this in front of everyone and still keep their secret. And survive, anyway, by the look on Radcliffe's face.

"We trusted you!" Radcliffe seemed unable to hold in his anger any longer. His hooves stomped hard on the ground, and it was plain to see that he was barely holding himself back from destroying the two little men with his bare hands.

"Just tell them!" Eliot cried, louder this time.

Charlie had never seen him so passionate about anything before. He was always withdrawn, barely lighting up when Pepper came around at most.

"No! I... I can't, Eliot! I can't put you in any more danger. Not after what happened the last time someone found out. Not again." Max's voice cracked.

He was truly trying to protect his younger brother. All of his joking was a way to cover up his fear.

"We do trust you." The words left Charlie's mouth before she had decided to say them. She found them to be true, however, and continued.

83

"We know you aren't working for Jessamine. And we would never let anything happen to either of you. Max, I would *never* let anything happen to your brother. I will protect you. Both of you. I promise."

Max looked up at Charlie, real tears in his eyes now, his arms wrapped around himself like he was trying to hold himself together.

"I promise," Charlie said again, kneeling to better look Max in the eyes.

Pepper, and the others, watched as Max looked at them one by one, trying to read their reactions to see if they felt the same as Charlie. The only one who still looked skeptical was Radcliffe, who had folded his arms and turned his face away, nose in the air.

"Even from him," Charlie whispered for Max and Eliot's ears only.

"I heard that," Radcliffe said dryly, not moving a muscle.

Charlie had momentarily forgotten about Radcliffe's incredible hearing, but the fact that he hadn't moved had to be a good sign. She hoped.

"Please, Max, tell us what you cannot say," Juliette implored the brownie.

Max looked back and forth between Charlie and Juliette, swiped the tears from his eyes, and looked at Eliot for his permission. Eliot nodded once, then looked at his hands folded in his lap.

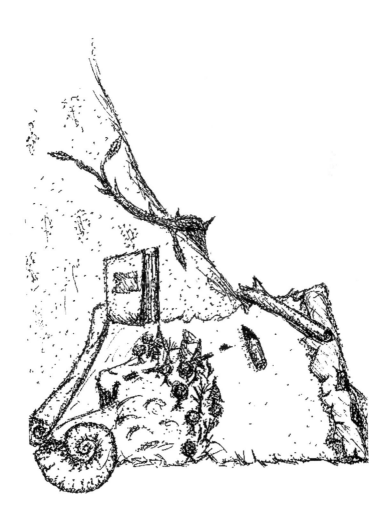

Christine Marshall

Chapter 11

"**Eliot** is a Mapmaker," Max announced.

Charlie looked at Max, not sure what it was he was trying to tell them. Eliot made maps? Why would that be such a big secret? She looked around at the others to see if any of them understood what Max meant by that.

Juliette looked as confused as Charlie felt, as did each of the others. Until her eyes came to rest on her father. He had a look of surprise, but the kind of surprise that meant he thought he would never meet a "Mapmaker," and that it was an honor to be doing so now. Charlie watched her father's eyes grow wide and his lips form a circle. He took a slight step forward, as if he wanted to get a better look at Eliot.

"Dad?" Charlie asked. Her single word expressed the confusion and curiosity that she knew the rest of them also felt.

"I never thought..." her dad whispered to himself, not taking his eyes off the little man. "After all this time..."

Charlie turned back to Max even as her father still

mumbled to himself in awe at Max and Eliot.

"Alright, Max. So… what's a 'Mapmaker?'" Charlie gently prodded.

Max stumbled over his words as he tried to explain. "He makes maps… secret places… dangerous." His words tumbled out as if he wasn't sure how to tell them the secret that he had kept hidden for so long.

"A Mapmaker has a gift." Charlie's father stepped closer and knelt beside Eliot. He couldn't take his eyes off Eliot's face. "He has the ability to find hidden things or places."

Charlie settled onto the grass beside Roxi, ready to hear Eliot's tale. Alder and Juliette did the same. Pepper sat as close to Eliot as he seemed comfortable with.

Radcliffe, however, continued to stand to the side, one eyebrow raised as though he doubted the truth of the revelation.

"It is not something that he can control," continued Charlie's father. "He is physically compelled to draw the map when the vision comes to his mind. He does not choose what the map is for or when he will draw one. It is just something he must do."

Charlie watched Eliot. Why would he care if others knew about this? She would think it would be something that he would have wanted to tell them, to explain his behavior.

"Then how is he drawing a map to Jessamine if he can't control when he makes one and what the map is for?" Radcliffe spoke through gritted teeth.

"He's doing something he's never been able to do before," Max spoke quietly. He kept his eyes on the ground. "He's choosing what the map is for this time. Only…" he looked at his brother with a worried expression. "… he has only received small portions of the map as we go. And it's taking a toll…"

"Hush," Eliot interrupted. "They do not need to know all."

Max nodded. He looked away, eyes tense and mouth turned down.

"I have always wanted to meet a Mapmaker," Charlie's father added. "It is truly a pleasure."

"Thank you," Eliot looked slightly uncomfortable.

"So," Radcliffe interrupted. "We are expected to believe that this tiny person has some magical ability to make a map that will lead us to Jessamine safely?" He stomped his front hooves.

"Yes," Juliette replied firmly. "Just as you believe in the ability to read your fate in the stars or take advice from a siren. I do believe Eliot is making a sacrifice to lead us where we must go. I do not understand how you can see and know everything that you do and not take his word for it."

Charlie hadn't heard Juliette speak so forcefully before.

Radcliffe huffed and rolled his eyes. He muttered something to himself and shifted his feet in the grass.

"She's right, Radcliffe," Charlie added. "Just because you've never heard of or seen a Mapmaker doesn't mean that he's lying to us."

Charlie turned back to the brownies, "Thank you for sharing your secret with us. We will guard it carefully."

Max nodded. Tears still wet his eyes. "Please, you must. If anyone finds out…"

"I can only imagine what this information in the wrong hands would accomplish," Alder nodded.

Charlie saw Eliot shudder as some fearful memory

passed his mind. What had happened to him before that would cause Max to behave this way? She didn't think it was her place to ask.

"What do you do with the maps once you make them?" Pepper wanted to know. She flitted above the brownies with excitement.

Charlie gave Pepper a look that said she shouldn't be asking questions like that.

The pixie just shrugged and waited for her friends to answer.

"We hide them," Max answered.

"What? Why??" Pepper exclaimed. "You could be rich and famous if you sold them!"

"It's not worth it," Max answered. "It's best just to hide them and let someone else chance upon them someday. Trust me, we know."

"But that's crazy! You should..." Pepper started.

"Pepper, that's enough," Charlie whispered to her friend.

Pepper grew sheepish and apologized. Max and Eliot smiled in return. It looked like a weight had been lifted from Eliot. Now that they all knew about his secret, he wouldn't have to run off and hide every time he added to the map. Maybe he would come out of his shell now that he didn't have to hide a big part of himself anymore.

"Well, if everyone is finished telling tales, then we should get some rest," Radcliffe grunted from behind.

"It's not a tale, it's the truth," Eliot spoke to the centaur firmly.

Radcliffe stopped, a stunned look on his face. Charlie held her breath as she waited for his reaction.

Radcliffe bowed his head at the brownies.

After everything Radcliffe, Max, and Eliot had been through together, it shouldn't be that hard for Radcliffe to have faith in them. Maybe now Radcliffe's trust would be complete.

Charlie raised her eyebrows at Radcliffe. He gave her a look as if to say that he had been mistaken about the loyalties of the brownies. Charlie nodded. He rolled his eyes at her, and she chuckled to herself.

That night Charlie had a new dream.

She saw Radcliffe battling a host of human soldiers. He was outnumbered by over a hundred armored men. He suffered blow after blow to his bare body. He would not survive.

Then his body transformed. His human torso and horse body changed before Charlie's eyes. His skin turned a mottled gray color. He yelled out in pain.

He was turning to stone!

Charlie searched frantically with her eyes for the source of the spell. She saw only Radcliffe and the men. Could one of the soldiers have done this?

She watched in horror as Radcliffe's skin became stiff. He was dying! She had to help!

"Radcliffe!" She called out to him.

He turned his head to face her.

"The balance must be restored."

Chapter 12

They encountered the first sink hole as they avoided a wood overgrown with thick, thorny vines dotted with beautiful flowers. Flowers that had thorns on the underside of their petals.

The sink hole had collapsed right beneath a grove of tulip trees. Everything in the grove had fallen below the surface. A scattering of the large, tulip shaped leaves and leftover yellow and orange tulip-like blossoms around the perimeter of the sinkhole was all that remained. The hole in the ground was so deep that the sun didn't reach the bottom.

Charlie didn't like it. Pepper flew right over it to see what it was like but couldn't convince Charlie to get very close to the edge.

"What if it collapses some more?" She didn't want to take any chances.

"I'm with you," Charlie's dad stood beside her.

Alder nodded.

Juliette, Roxi, and even Radcliffe stayed away from the edge.

Max and Eliot, though, scooted as close to the edge as possible. Max held Eliot's arm with both hands. He leaned back and allowed Eliot to use himself as a counterweight to lean forward and peer over the edge. After a minute, Eliot leaned toward his brother, and the brownies moved away from the edge.

The whole thing almost gave Charlie heart palpitations. She held a hand flat against her chest to calm herself.

"It's too dark to see down there." Max looked disappointed. Then his face lit up. "Want to light up for us Pepper? I'll lower Eliot down on a rope…"

Pepper nodded with enthusiasm, but Charlie insisted they keep moving. The last thing she wanted to do was to rescue the brownies from the bottom of a hole in the ground that was who knows how deep.

Pepper and Max reluctantly agreed to put the idea behind them, but they looked equally discouraged.

They came across three more sink holes that day. Was this ground even safe to walk on? Would they be swallowed by the land?

Radcliffe didn't think there was any danger. And Juliette, ever the optimist, agreed. Charlie let her worries fade to the back of her mind and focused on her breathing.

It wasn't long before Charlie had something new to worry about: her father. His leg had finally healed, but he had a significant limp. He insisted he could keep up with the others, and didn't need any special treatment, but Charlie knew he was having a harder time than he would admit to.

She tried to ask him about her worries, but he brushed off her concerns and insisted he was fine. She began to watch him more closely.

She dreamt of her father aging in a flash before her eyes, and then disappearing in a cloud of dust.

The dream felt so real, that when Charlie awoke, she nearly lost the contents of her stomach.

Seeing her father die like that had been the stuff of nightmares. But the possibility of it being true would not leave her thoughts. What would she do without him? He was the only family she had ever known. She couldn't lose him.

When she had the chance to speak with him alone one day, she confronted him.

"Dad, what's happening? Your limp is worse, your hair is going gray, and you look.... Older. How is this possible?" Her worry poured into her words.

He reached up and touched his hair at his temple. Had he even known that his hair was changing color? His eyes looked tired.

He sighed deeply. "It's true, Charlie, my body is aging. I expected some gradual aging upon leaving the wall, but it seems as if it has happened sooner and faster than I thought it would."

His eyes were full of worry, which alarmed Charlie more than his older appearance.

"Is it going to slow down?" Charlie's voice rose even higher.

He reached his arms out and pulled Charlie to him. "I don't know, Charlie," he mumbled into her hair.

Charlie's eyes stung and a lump formed in her throat.

Her father pulled back but kept his hands on her shoulders.

"It began right away, I noticed that my leg healed, but not fully. Then my joints became stiffer each morning. I've had a harder time keeping up on our daily trek.

"My back aches and my feet hurt. I've never felt fatigue like this before. I have some of the Deep Spring water still from home," he gestured to a pouch slung across his shoulder. "But I'm not sure if it will do much good. After the injury to my leg didn't heal with treatment from the water, I'm supposing it will make no difference to the rest of me now."

Charlie didn't understand. When she had been away from home the Deep Spring water had saved her life. But it was true that they had treated his wound with the water directly and by mouth, and neither had healed his wound. Something was wrong with the power the water had. For some reason, it no longer worked for her father.

What if the others that had left their homes behind were having the same problem? She couldn't imagine the confusion and panic if the people began to age this rapidly. Her father had memory from when the wall was built and the aging and memory protections were put into place, but the others didn't. This was all new for them and it would be difficult to explain now.

"You have been changing, too, Charlie." Her father looked over her now, as if inspecting one of his inventions for something out of place. "The changes are small, and others may not notice, but I have been watching you grow for a very long time. There are things about you that have changed since we were driven from our home. Your face is more mature looking, and you are just a little bit taller. Have you noticed?"

Charlie hadn't given it much thought. She didn't have a mirror to peer into, and never took the time to look at her reflection in the water when she washed. But now that he mentioned it, her clothes did feel a little shorter at the wrists and ankles, and a little tighter across her chest and hips. She patted herself down, as if she would be able to see the changes with her hands. Would she begin aging as quickly as her father?

At the rate he was aging he would be a very old man in a matter of weeks. She would appear older than Alder, and even Juliette, in just a few months. She groaned inwardly. She had always wanted to grow up faster, but not this fast. This was more than she could handle.

They had to figure out what they could do for him before he aged too much. They sought out Juliette to see if she had any advice. Alder was with Juliette, and Charlie was glad that he was in on the conversation. She knew her father was a private person and did not want to make a big deal out of his problem, or alert all the others to his predicament, but the fact remained that neither he nor Charlie knew what to do.

"It has to be connected with the disruptions being caused

by Jessamine's accumulation of power," Alder looked sorry.

Juliette agreed. "We have lost our abilities, and now your father has lost the protections of the Deep Spring. It could have something to do with the destruction of the wall, or the loss of protection from the giants." Juliette was guessing now, too.

"That does make some sense. It wasn't until your guardian friend left the wall that my body stopped healing..." Charlie's father said.

"But why you?" Charlie asked.

Her father gave her a knowing look to remind her that he was not the only one. Her body was aging, too.

Now her mind raced. If all the others were losing their abilities as Jessamine gained power, then eventually, or maybe not so eventually, she would lose her dreams.

Her dad seemed to know what she was thinking. He placed a comforting arm around her shoulder.

Juliette suggested that they should try to find a safe place for Charlie's father to go. This way, he would be safe from injuring himself on their journey and protected from Jessamine's army once they arrived at their destination.

To Charlie, it felt like someone had just put a time limit on her plans. If she took too long to find and stop Jessamine, her father may die. And if she wasn't with him, then she might never see him again. She wanted him to stay with her so they could be together, and she could take care of him while he aged, but Alder pointed out that she was the only one, besides Eliot, who had her abilities still. They needed her dreams to guide them.

She knew Alder was right. But she resisted. Her father wrapped his arms around her and assured her that she needed to continue to trust her dreams and allow them to guide her.

"I know, it's just…" Charlie tried to hold back her tears. "I don't want to lose you," she whispered.

"I will take him somewhere safe." Alder rubbed her arm, his brown eyes sincere.

"Do you have anything in mind?" Juliette asked.

Alder shook his head. "I will think on it."

"What about where our people are hiding?" Charlie asked Juliette.

Juliette shook her head. "I am afraid that would be much too far to travel. I fear you may not finish the journey." Juliette said the last part to Charlie's dad.

Charlie sighed. She squeezed her eyes shut to hold back the tears.

Her dad rubbed her back. "Maybe you'll dream something that will help."

Charlie nodded and hugged him tight. She let go and wiped her eyes with the backs of her hands. She nodded her thanks to Alder. If she had to send her father somewhere without her, she would have chosen Alder or Juliette to be with him. It comforted her that Alder had volunteered. Her dad seemed to like Alder and appreciate his helpfulness.

That night Charlie tried to focus on her dad as she fell asleep. She needed to dream about where he could go to be safe.

Instead, she had the same dream about him aging into a withered old man right in front her. It happened so fast that she didn't have time to even tell him that she loved him before he turned to dust and blew away.

She awoke with tears running down her cheeks. Pepper

rushed to her side and stroked her face to calm her. She sang her quiet pixie song that soothed Charlie. But Charlie's heart felt like it had cracked in her chest. What would she do without her dad?

"*The balance must be restored,*" echoed in the back of her mind. She wanted to yell at someone, anyone, that she knew that. That she was trying. And could whoever said that to her just give her some clues? Or time?

Chapter 13

"**Let's** set it on fire!" Max whispered a little too loudly.

Charlie could easily hear him.

"Oh, Pep-per!" He dragged out her name in a sing-songy way.

Pepper returned from the goldenrod patch she had been munching on and fluttered to Max's side. She walked beside him, in front of Charlie.

Charlie continued to eavesdrop.

The dried leaves beneath her feet crunched with every step. Her nose filled with the sweet aroma of decaying greenery.

It was not fall yet. The leaves had not fallen because of the season. The entire grove of cottonwood trees had simply died. The grasses and underbrush were very much alive, but the leaves on every single tree had turned brown and brittle. Most still clung tight to the branches. But some had fallen to the ground and crumbled beneath the feet of the travelers.

From what Max said to Pepper, it sounded like he wanted to set the entire grove of trees on fire. And that he wanted Pepper's assistance.

"That's not the best idea," Charlie caught up to the tiny trio.

"Drat," she heard Max mutter. "Just a small fire?"

Charlie rolled her eyes. "Why do you want to set things on fire? What do you get out of it?"

Max's eyes clouded for an instant before he gave Charlie a sideways grin. "Why do you want to know?" He folded his arms and looked up at her for her answer.

"I'm just trying to keep everyone safe, that's all. And that's hard to do with all the stunts you two pull. Not to mention how you lure Pepper into your shenanigans as often as possible."

Max mumbled something under his breath.

"Sorry, I didn't catch that…" Charlie waited for Max to repeat himself.

"Nothing. We'll leave the fire for tonight. Don't worry about us." He scampered away with Eliot right on his heels.

Charlie nodded. "Fine. Pepper, a word?"

Pepper flitted to Charlie's shoulder and hovered there.

"Don't be too hard on them," the pixie begged. "I think they're just trying to have fun; you know?"

"Just… be careful. Don't get into too much trouble with them, alright?"

Charlie watched Pepper catch up to walk between the brownies.

No more than a few minutes after he promised to stop being reckless, Max pointed to the tallest dead tree, and Eliot scampered up the trunk. Pepper followed and hovered beside him as Eliot climbed nimbly to the very top of the tree.

Pepper shrieked.

Charlie sighed.

Eliot plummeted to the ground.

Max rushed to his brother's side.

Eliot popped up, completely unharmed from the fall that should have at least broken some of his bones.

Charlie had a hard time understanding Max and Eliot. They wanted to be trusted. They clearly worried about keeping Eliot's secret, and Eliot himself, safe. Why were they so reckless, then? It didn't make sense.

She had to put it out of her mind. For now.

That night, when the brothers thought no one was looking, Charlie saw Eliot take a swig out of a small canteen. Very similar to the canteen that Radcliffe had suddenly started to carry a few weeks ago. Then the brownie stepped into the blazing fire. He stood in the flames for several long minutes, and then emerged. His clothes smoked a little, but besides that, he didn't seem to be any worse for the wear.

Max high fived his brother, and the two settled beside the flames and scribbled notes in Eliot's notebook. Max took the charcoal stick from his brother a few times and drew or wrote something. Then Eliot shook his head and scribbled over his brother's notes and wrote or drew something different. They kept their heads close together and spoke in very quiet tones. Charlie couldn't hear anything they said.

Charlie watched as Pepper sidled up to the little men. She settled herself beside Eliot and leaned over his shoulder while he wrote. Max reached into his bag and handed a tiny pouch to Pepper. He looked serious as he gestured at it and shook his head. She nodded with a grin and clutched the pouch tight in her hands, a wicked gleam in her eyes.

Charlie glanced at Radcliffe. He had his eyes locked on the pair, too. Could he hear what they said? Did it concern him as much as it did her?

As if he could sense her looking at him, his eyes flicked to hers. She looked away quickly. She stood and moved around the fire to sit between Alder and her dad.

"Any luck with the dreams?" Alder asked.

Charlie shook her head. "I'm having plenty of other dreams about things that we end up seeing the next day. So at least I know we're on the right path. But I still haven't figured out where you two should go."

Charlie's dad put his arm around her and squeezed.

Alder rested his hand on her knee. "You'll get there. I

104

believe in you."

Charlie's heart beat a little faster at his touch. Butterflies danced in her stomach. She swallowed and nodded.

Charlie's dad squeezed her shoulder again and poked her side with his other hand.

"Me, too. You haven't failed me yet." The smile he gave her lit up his whole face.

They both believed wholeheartedly that she could do this.

Most of the time, she did too.

But sometimes she felt like there was someone else who would be much better suited.

Charlie saw many more sinkholes scattered along the landscape that stretched far toward the mountains. Some large enough to swallow her entire village, others smaller than the well outside her house. There didn't appear to be a pattern to their locations.

Charlie steered the group around them every time. Eliot indicated that they continue to travel north. Nothing Charlie dreamed suggested otherwise.

As she had told Alder, she had a dream each night of some specific landmark or one of her companions doing or saying something. Then the next day, usually near the beginning of the day, whatever she saw in her dream she would see or hear for real. She assumed, and Radcliffe agreed, that it meant they were on the right path. It helped Charlie feel better about following an unfinished map drawn by someone she hadn't known for very long.

"There should be a settlement a little to the west of here," Radcliffe announced to the group one afternoon.

Charlie looked at Eliot.

He consulted his map and shrugged. "I don't see anything."

"How far?" she asked Radcliffe.

"A couple of hours at the most. Just beyond that stretch of hills."

Charlie nodded. "Let's head that direction. Maybe someone will know something about Jessamine or her followers. At the very least we may be able to obtain fresh food."

Radcliffe nodded.

"Lead the way." She gestured for him to alter their course.

Just as Radcliffe had estimated, they crested the last hill before the settlement a little less than two hours later. The sun had just started to dip toward dusk. The shadows stretched long, but the sun still brightened the sky.

A small river ran down one of the opposite hills and into the village center. Or, at least, where Charlie guessed the village center used to be.

Clear signs of farming surrounded the enormous sinkhole. Crops of leafy green vegetables grew in tidy rows in fields. Sheep grazed in pastures lined by hand hewn log fences. A llama with thick fuzzy wool looked at them with a wary eye near the sheep. But there were no people. Anywhere. And every other manufactured structure that she would expect to see in a settlement of this size had vanished. The earth had swallowed everyone and everything.

Charlie stared. Her mouth hung open. What had these people done to deserve this?

"We have to check for survivors!" Juliette hurried down

the hill.

Charlie and the others followed close behind.

"Spread out but be careful!" Radcliffe called to the group.

Charlie and Pepper made their way around the enormous hole in the ground. Pepper flew above it and reported to Charlie that it was full of water. Nothing of the people remained besides their crops and flocks. The animals seemed unaware of the disaster that had taken place.

The river that at one time must have run through the center of the settlement, now flowed directly into the sinkhole.

It had filled up, but there must have been cracks at the bottom that let the water trickle into the earth. The river flowed into the hole, but no water flowed out.

On the other side of the hole, the dry riverbed meandered through the fields and meadows beyond the village.

Charlie swallowed. What if there were remains of the people or their things floating in the water? She leaned forward to get a closer look.

The surface of the water was still, only disturbed a little by the inward flow. Charlie still didn't want to get too close to the edge, in case more of the ground collapsed.

The group stayed quiet. The magnitude of the loss was more than Charlie could comprehend. She didn't even know what to think, let alone what to say.

"Maybe they escaped?" Pepper offered in a hopeful voice.

"They would have taken their animals, at least," Alder answered.

Pepper nodded. Her face looked gloomy.

Radcliffe offered to fill Charlie's canteen for her, and

Juliette's too. He didn't comment on the destruction. Instead, he acted as if the only thing that happened here was an opportunity for fresh drinking water.

Radcliffe bent over the water near the inward flow to get the freshest water possible. Pepper flitted around, hunting for flowers, but didn't have much luck. Max and Eliot plopped down and poured over Eliot's larger parchment once more. Alder helped Charlie's father settle on a small incline and made sure he had a chance to drink and rest. Juliette and Roxi sat nearby.

Charlie thought about joining them, but instead sat a little apart with her legs folded beneath her and her pack in her lap. She tried to distract herself from the depressing scene around them. She had her own field journal out and she sketched the sink hole and added notes about some of the invasive plants they had seen that day. She kept her mind occupied. She didn't want to think about all the lives that had lived here. And what their fate may have been.

Radcliffe shouted.

Roxi barked.

Charlie jumped. Her book fell to the ground with the pages splayed open. Her head whipped to look at the place where Radcliffe had been filling their canteens.

Radcliffe's hooves slapped the ground. Three long, sleek black tentacles had wrapped themselves around both of Radcliffe's hands that still gripped the canteens tight.

Radcliffe let out an ear-splitting roar. His feet beat the ground and left sloppy, muddy divots in the earth. He slipped on the mud. His feet slid toward the water.

He pulled with all his strength and managed to take a few steps backward. Two more tentacles shot out and grabbed his arms. Radcliffe grunted. His face turned red from the effort of resisting.

"What should we do?" Charlie screeched.

Pepper couldn't help much, she couldn't swim.

Juliette looked just as lost as Charlie.

Alder and her father looked alarmed but frozen in place.

"We got this," Max announced.

Charlie whipped around.

Max took a bundle out of his bag, handed it to Eliot, and then retrieved his wisp lamp and a small canteen. The one she had seen Eliot drink from before. The one she was pretty sure held dragon's blood.

Her stomach turned.

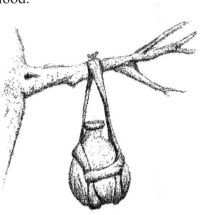

Eliot took a swig from Max's canteen, then Max drank. They bolted toward the water and jumped in. Max did a cannonball, splashing water all around him.

Pepper screamed. "What are they doing?"

Her hair aflame, she flew in quick circles above Radcliffe's struggle with the tentacled creature.

Radcliffe continued to fight. It was an even match, neither able to gain any ground.

Suddenly, an explosion came from below the surface. Radcliffe fell back. He landed in an awkward heap of horse legs, weapons, and Charlie's canteen.

Water shot high into the sky. It rained back down and soaked everyone. Black, slimy chunks of whatever the creature had been also rained down on them. Several landed in Charlie's hair and on her shoulders. She shrieked and brushed them off as fast as she could.

Max and Eliot emerged from the water and crawled back onto dry ground.

"Nice one, brother," Max said between breaths

They collapsed on the ground, panting. They carried neither the wisp lamp, nor the other bundle Max had pulled out of his bag.

They bumped fists as they worked to catch their breath. Wide smiles lit up both of their faces.

Chapter 14

Pepper landed between the brownies. "That was epic! What in the world did you guys do??" She was rosy with excitement.

After they had caught their breath, the brothers sat up. Eliot stood, brushed the debris off his clothes, and returned to his things. Max did the same. He shoved his canteen back into his bag. Then looked to Eliot for permission to share. Eliot nodded. Max grinned.

"Well, as you know, we harvested some of the dragon's blood from the graveyard." Max looked sideways at Charlie. She knew that he expected her to overreact. But she had given up trying to have any kind of influence over these two.

She rolled her eyes. Satisfied that Charlie was not going to reprimand him again, Max continued.

"We've been experimenting with it here and there along the way. Turns out, it's pretty explosive when heated. That came in handy, obviously. But it has other really interesting properties, too…"

Max stopped.

Everyone waited.

"Well, tell us!!" Pepper pleaded for Max to continue.

"Other properties… when consumed," Max started.

Pepper gagged. "You drank it??" She stuck out her tongue and made a disgusted face.

Juliette looked away and swallowed hard.

Max looked apologetic. He shrugged and continued to tell his story. "When consumed, it temporarily grants the toughness of dragon scales. You become basically invincible."

Radcliffe looked interested, but not surprised. He didn't say anything.

Alder nodded his head with a thoughtful look on his face. Did he know this about the blood from the dragon tree already?

"That's wild!" Pepper exclaimed.

Eliot nudged Max and pointed at his bag. Then he returned to his drawing.

Max pulled out his canteen and took a small sip.

"It doesn't matter how much you drink. But, watch." He dropped the canteen. He held out his arms. "Come closer."

The others surrounded him in a tight circle.

"Oh! My! Flaming! Hair!" Pepper cried.

And for good reason.

Max wasn't speaking figuratively when he said it gave the consumer the protection of dragon scales. Max's skin, from head to toe, at least what Charlie could see, had transformed into shimmery, pale gray dragon scales.

"Go ahead, hit me." Max gestured to Radcliffe.

Radcliffe looked reluctant. But Pepper was quick to oblige. She zipped down and punched Max on the arm.

"Ow!" she cried, shaking out her hand.

Well, how hard could a pixie hit, anyway? That didn't really prove much.

"Come on, Radcliffe, you know you want to." Max egged the centaur on.

The corner of Radcliffe's mouth twitched. He reached

for his sword and jabbed Max right in the chest.

Juliette gasped.

Charlie's hands flew to her mouth.

Charlie's dad chuckled.

Alder supported him with an arm across his back. He shared an alarmed look with Charlie.

Max stumbled off balance for a second but regained his footing. He pulled down his tunic to show where Radcliffe had stabbed him. The scales hadn't changed.

Radcliffe gave an interested, "Hm," and sheathed his sword.

"Like I said, indestructible. But it only lasts a couple of minutes, no matter how much or how little you drink."

As he spoke, the scales fell from his body and disintegrated before they hit the ground.

"Whoa! That was amazing!" Pepper flitted in circles around Max to see if the scales were really gone. Satisfied that it hadn't been some trick, she flew in front of him and landed on the ground.

"You totally saved Radcliffe back there." She pinched Max's cheek, then bent down and gave Eliot a tight hug. "You are so brave!" she sighed.

"Well, I don't know about..." Radcliffe started to say.

"Let them have this, Radcliffe." Alder stopped him. "Besides, you may not have lost against whatever that was, but you may not have won, either."

Charlie was still in shock. So, they had swiped the dragon's blood, experimented with it on themselves, and figured out that it could render someone invincible, even for just a few minutes?

"Why did you do it?" Charlie asked Max, interrupting the excited conversation happening around her.

All humor left his face, his eyes heavy with some past pain.

The others eyed one another with nervous expressions and collectively held their breath for Max's answer.

Max met Charlie's eyes. "So we could help. That's why we're together, right? To help one another?"

One by one Max met the eyes of each member of their party.

"We knew it had some magical properties. We have heard rumors. But we didn't know exactly what. We didn't want you guys to try it, in case it was dangerous, you know?"

He shrugged. "So, we tested it out. Now we know it's safe. And if any of you need it," he gave Radcliffe a pointed look, then returned his eyes to Charlie, "all you have to do is ask. I've got enough for emergencies." He patted his pack that held the canteen.

So, they weren't being reckless all this time? They were actually trying to help, without anyone getting hurt in the process. And Pepper was right, they had probably saved Radcliffe just now.

"I'm sorry for misjudging you," Charlie squatted to be closer to Max. "Thank you. For everything."

She held out her hand.

Max took it with his tiny one.

She squeezed.

Eliot kept his eyes on his parchment.

Max joined Pepper and Eliot on the ground. The three chattered away, Max back to his usual jovial self.

Charlie felt bad for having misunderstood their intentions. She would not think them reckless, useless, or undeserving anymore. They were part of the group. Part of

Charlie's new family.

Which only drove her need to find Jessamine and finish this even more.

Charlie's dad needed to rest. It became more apparent every day. He rode Roxi now, instead of walking. He slept whenever they stopped. He ate little. He looked bone tired all the time.

Charlie had to figure out where he was supposed to go. She focused solely on her father when she fell asleep each night.

Her dreams helped her know that they were still headed in the right direction.

The voice reminded her that she had to stop Jessamine and restore the balance.

But she dreamt nothing to help her know where Alder should take her father.

After several nights with no success, she fell asleep frustrated.

Her dream dropped her back in the birch forest.

This time, instead of a movement to her left, though, she saw Alder lead her father through the forest to her right.

Alder supported her dad with one of his own arms as they stumbled through the underbrush. Alder carried his own pack as well as Charlie's father's pack. They moved slowly away from Charlie.

She hurried to catch up. They couldn't see or hear her, but she followed just the same.

The scenery changed from a forest of only birch trees to

an alpine forest instead. Tall skinny pine trees laden with long pinecones surrounded her. Ferns and cone flowers grew on the forest floor.

Up ahead, a small group of forest people emerged from the trees to greet Alder. They assisted in carrying the packs and led Alder and her dad deeper into the forest.

Charlie stood and watched them fade away.

"Goodbye. I love you, Dad," she whispered to herself.

She woke up with tears on her cheeks.

She didn't know where they had gone, but at least she now had a clue.

In the morning she would check in with Alder to see if he could make sense of her vision.

In the meantime, she would try to get more sleep. And to not worry about whether she would ever see her dad again once he left her.

Alder told Charlie he knew of many alpine forests. And many groups of forest people.

Without more specific details, it would be difficult to understand what her dream meant or where he should take her father.

He encouraged her to not give up. He even gave her a tight hug when he saw the discouraged look on her face.

Juliette took Alder's spot with Charlie's dad, and Alder walked with her the rest of the day.

Eliot changed the course they took to a northeasterly

direction a few days later. And a day after that, they headed due east.

The mountain range that had been hazy in front of them throughout their journey now stretched into the distance to Charlie's left.

The elevation leveled out some, and Charlie could see the flat prairie far in the distance in the direction they traveled.

Great. The prairie. That had not gone well last time.

She wanted to question Eliot.

But in her dream the night before she had seen an indent in the ground. At the bottom, scattered among the shadows, she saw the enormous bones of animals with huge tusks.

Vines grew all over the space. Several of the bones had cracked from the squeezing of the vines over time. It looked like some kind of animal graveyard.

Not long after their afternoon meal, the group walked right past the graveyard that she had seen. This was the right way to go.

Before a week had passed, Charlie could see in the

distance the shape of the twin mountains that hid the Valley of the Giants. They walked straight toward the battlefield where her giant friend had died.

She would have never chosen to return to that place. Her chest ached. It hadn't been long enough.

Over the next several nights, she dreamed of the pine forest and her father and Alder meeting the forest people several more times.

She paid attention to every detail about her surroundings, and the forest people that emerged from the trees. But she saw nothing new that helped Alder understand where to go.

She promised she would continue to try.

Faster than she wanted, they arrived at the site of the battle between Jessamine's army and the awakened giants. A part of her had hoped that the brownies, or her dreams, would change their course and lead them another way.

Dark spots scattered the plain that stretched out in front of them, like freckles on the land. They varied greatly in size. When she drew closer, she saw that one of the larger freckles turned out to be the ruins of one of Jessamine's catapult launchers. And when they were even closer, she saw that the smaller freckles were the leftover armor and weapons from the fallen human soldiers.

There were so many. More than she had expected.

The giants had removed their fallen and taken them back to the City of Giants. But those in Jessamine's army who had survived the battle had fled. And no one had come back for their dead.

Charlie's heart ached. These men had fought for Jessamine, but they were still people. They might have had families waiting for them. She tried not blame herself. It had been a series of events that involved her, but she had not caused Jessamine to lust for power and immortality. The fault, as usual, belonged to Jessamine.

And now Charlie actively sought out her enemy, probably to face battle once again.

At least, that's what her dreams had shown her. A huge field. Jessamine's massive army of more fearsome creatures than a human army. And Charlie, basically defenseless, facing them.

Death always followed the standoff. No version of the dream had a happy ending. Not for Charlie and her friends.

How would she stop Jessamine? She really didn't want to fight again. The thought of harming or killing another enemy made her feel sick. There had to be another way. But so far, she had no idea what that would be.

Radcliffe joined Charlie as they picked their way through the battle graveyard and toward the ravine.

"How do you do it?" she asked him.

"Do what?"

"This." Charlie gestured at the endless number of fallen soldiers that surrounded them. "How do you do it, and stay sane?"

"The centaur way of life includes battle and death. We follow our fate." His demeanor stayed stoic. His posture stiff and proud. "If this is what was meant to be, then nothing you could have done would have changed anything. It would have happened, one way or another."

"But you look for ways to get revenge. You blame others for your losses. How does that work?" Charlie didn't understand. If "fate" could not be changed, then why try to stop bad things from happening?

"If I am to revenge my losses, then that is what fate dictates." Radcliffe seemed to barely notice the remnants of the battle that surrounded them. To him, it had to be this way. Fate had decided.

Charlie didn't believe it. She decided her own destiny. Her dreams guided her, but each choice she made was her own, as well as the consequences that followed. It would be easy to blame some "fate" for the way things turned out.

But wasn't that just it? If it was easy, then she wouldn't learn and grow from her experiences. If her destiny was chosen for her, then what was the point of trying to do better? To *be* better?

Radcliffe could say he believed in fate. That the loss of his family had been beyond his control. He could say that the revenge he sought had already been decided one way or the other. But she wouldn't believe that. Only *she* could decide her own future. Only *she* could decide to be a good person or not. The choices she made now would decide the person that she would become in this life.

"Do not fear, Charlie." Radcliffe interrupted her flow of thoughts. "You will come out of this unharmed." He sounded certain.

Her giant friend had said something like that to her before, too. He had had a dream about her. How did Radcliffe know that she would be safe?

"You sound like you *know*. How can you be so sure?"

He looked sideways at her.

She waited for his answer.

He avoided eye contact. "I just am."

Then he trotted away.

He looked like Max when the brownies kept secrets from the others. What did Radcliffe know? And why wouldn't he just tell her?

Chapter 15

The ravine stretched out in both directions along the base of the mountain range, as if the edge of the plain had been ripped away from the mountains. Darkness and shadows obscured the view of the bottom. To the left and right the blackness extended as far as Charlie could see.

Jessamine's army had attempted to construct a bridge. The less-than-half-finished bridge extended over the ravine to Charlie's left, where it ended abruptly part way across the chasm. Signs of decay were evident. They would not be able to use that bridge to cross.

Charlie looked to her right. A rock-pillar-bridge should be there, somewhere. But there was no sign of it.

"What is going on, why are we just standing here?" Radcliffe looked at the brownies for an answer.

Max and Eliot studied the map they held in front of them. They looked back and forth from the map to the ravine. Charlie couldn't see their faces, but she had the sense that something troubled them.

"Eliot?" Juliette stepped toward the little man. "Is everything all right?"

Eliot didn't answer. Charlie thought she saw his shoulders slump.

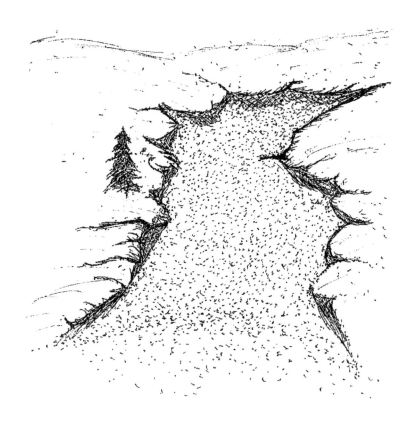

"Max?" Juliette inquired of the other brother.

"I don't know." His voice trailed off. "The map clearly led us to this point, but there is no way to cross the ravine." He continued to look back and forth between the paper and the scenery.

"There was a bridge here, before," Charlie piped in.

The brownies turned and looked up at Charlie, eyes wide and mouths turned down.

"What?" Charlie asked, not sure what they were thinking. "I was here for this battle. A rock pillar fell across the ravine when I activated the Battle Horn, and it made a bridge. I crossed it to get back to this side and try to save…" Charlie didn't finish her story. She had managed to not dwell on her personal history with this place, and she didn't want to talk about it in front of everyone.

Juliette squeezed Charlie's shoulders with one arm. Alder came to her other side and reached for her hand. Charlie appreciated their intentions, but their affection brought her emotions closer to the surface. She slipped away from them both and toward the brownies.

She pointed across the ravine. "You can see the base of it over there. It looks like it must have crumbled away at some point."

"This doesn't make sense," Eliot said flatly. "We are supposed to go this direction."

Max and Eliot shared a concerned look and folded up the map.

"So, what do we do now?" Radcliffe asked.

"I guess we'll have to go around," Max said.

"That will take too long," Radcliffe insisted.

"We do not appear to have much choice. Unless you plan on throwing us across the ravine." Charlie's father said with a smile to Radcliffe.

He looked thoughtful, as if considering the suggestion.

Charlie rolled her eyes at him. "Max and Eliot are right. We'll have to go around."

She turned to the little men. "Do you know where our destination is yet?"

Eliot shook his head. Max looked apologetic.

If Charlie knew where they were headed, then she could choose as direct a route as possible. But without a destination, it would feel like aimless wandering.

Charlie groaned.

"Maybe you'll have a dream..." her father suggested.

The others nodded.

Charlie decided she would lead them away from the leftover destruction to set up camp for the night.

They worked together to prepare their meal, avoided discussing the remains of the battle or the missing bridge, and turned in not long after the sun dipped below the horizon.

Charlie walked alone along the edge of the ravine. She needed time to think. If she didn't figure out where they were supposed to go, they would never find Jessamine.

Well, they would find her eventually, because Charlie still dreamed about it. But she had no idea how long it would take. And time wasn't exactly on her side.

Her eyes traced the ground as her mind wandered. Out of the corner of her eye she saw a strange movement.

She froze in place.

A green stem sprung from the ground. Its papery leaves unfolded as it stretched upwards. A second later, an orange, feathery blossom burst from the top.

The whole thing took only seconds. Charlie had never seen anything like it.

She took a step toward the blossom. She jumped when a second stem shot out of the ground and blossomed instantly, just beyond the first.

What were these flowers? How did they sprout and blossom so fast?

She took a step back and started to turn around in order to find the others. She could ask Alder if he knew what they were.

But when she stepped away from the flowers, they vanished into nothing.

She stopped short. How would she be able to ask Alder about them if they disappeared? She stepped toward the spot. Instantly two more blossoms burst from the ground. She hesitated. She took a tiny step closer. A third blossom sprang forth beyond the second.

Another step brought her another flower. Charlie stopped, then carefully stepped backwards. The furthest two blossoms faded away.

Were the flowers trying to lead her somewhere? Charlie shook her head. Impossible. They were flowers.

She stepped beside the first blossom. Two more flowers sprouted where the two had just died, and another beyond them.

She desperately wanted to find Alder and see what he thought. But would she miss her chance to see what the flowers wanted her to see?

Even though that line of thought seemed ridiculous, she shrugged her shoulders. She had seen stranger things, she supposed, so why not this?

She followed the ever-lengthening trail of bright orange flowers. It led her away from her friends.

It wasn't long before she found herself at the edge of the ravine. The trail of flowers stopped right at the edge. Charlie stepped forward, afraid to get too close in case the ground collapsed beneath her feet. But to her surprise, a makeshift trail switch-backed all the way down the side of the ravine to the bottom. When she leaned over to get a better look, orange flowers grew along the entire length of the trail. A huge patch colored the floor of the ravine orange.

She had to tell the others. Once she stepped away, though, the flowers would vanish. She bent down to pluck one of the blossoms. It withered before her hand even touched it.

She wanted to know what these blossoms were. But she couldn't take one with her, and if she walked away, they would disappear. How would she find her way back to the trail if they died every time she walked away?

She looked around. Could she mark the spot with something? The ground was just dirt. No rocks, plants, twigs. Nothing.

She stood frozen to that spot. What should she do?

"Charlie!" One of her friends called from the distance. "Charlie!"

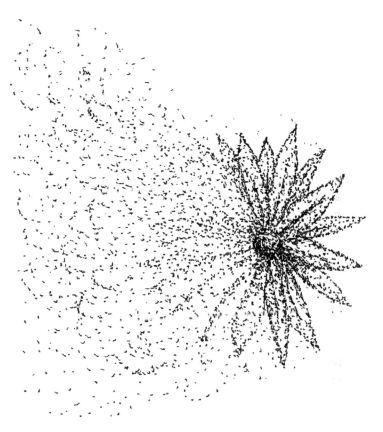

She cupped her hands around her mouth. "I'm over here!"

They must not have heard her, because the sounds of her friends calling for her faded. They looked for her in the wrong direction.

If she moved from this spot, she might not find it again. But if she stayed, her friends might not be able to find her.

What was she going to do?

It was too much to decide.

She couldn't move.
She wanted to scream.
"The balance must be restored."

She sat up. Darkness surrounded her except for the coals of the evening fire. And the flame of her tiny friend right in her face. The sound of her own scream echoed across the plain and bounced off the nearby mountains.

"Charlie! Charlie! Are you alright?" Pepper flew in a frenzy around Charlie.

Charlie took a deep breath. She allowed her eyes to adjust to the darkness. She willed her heart and mind to slow. "Yeah, I'm fine. Just had a weird dream..."

Pepper's light went out. She settled on Charlie's shoulder. "You were moving a lot in your sleep, and then you screamed. Are you sure everything is alright? Did you have a dream about Jessamine or something?"

"No, not Jessamine. Just... some flowers." Charlie couldn't shake the image of those orange flowers trailing down the side of the ravine. What did they mean?

"Flowers? What kind? Are they around here? Maybe they have sweet nectar in them." Pepper stood on Charlie's shoulder to get a better view.

Charlie chuckled. "No, not around here. I don't know if they have good nectar. I've never seen flowers like them before. Sorry, Pepper."

The pixie plopped onto Charlie's shoulder again. Her bottom lip stuck out in a pout. "Oh."

Charlie looked around to see if she had awoken anyone else, but everyone still slept. She had only disturbed Pepper. She told the pixie that she wanted to try to go back to sleep.

Charlie stretched out on her blanket again. She really did try to go back to sleep, but the dream wouldn't leave her mind. She tossed and turned until the sky paled.

She wanted to ask Alder about the flowers first thing but felt silly asking him about something she had only dreamt about. She didn't even know if the flowers existed.

She didn't want to tell anyone else, either. They all hoped she would dream about which way to go to find Jessamine. They looked at her expectantly. She didn't want anyone to get their hopes up about this strange flower dream until she knew for sure whether it meant something important or not.

After breakfast, the group made their way toward the mountains once more. Charlie supposed they would reach the foothills within the next day or two, and then they would move further away from the ravine. She fought with herself about whether she should ask for advice or tell anyone about her dream; one minute convincing herself to say something and the next deciding it was pointless. She didn't want them to waste time searching the edge of the ravine for a path that may not even exist.

She sighed as these thoughts weighed her down. Pepper had flown off to be near Max and Eliot in case the brownies received any inspiration about their course.

Radcliffe traveled far ahead of the others to scout for danger and hunt for their next meal.

Juliette and Roxi accompanied Charlie's father behind her. Her father rode on Roxi's back.

She sighed again.

"Is everything alright, Charlie?" Alder caught up to walk beside her. She felt the warmth of his presence at her side.

She only nodded, not sure how to voice all the thoughts that tumbled around inside her head right then.

He reached for her hand and gave it a reassuring squeeze. "You've changed, Charlie."

She looked up at him. What did he mean? Hopefully only good things.

"For the better," he added in a hurry. Then he chuckled at himself. "Sorry, I didn't mean for you to think anything other than for the better." He smiled wide at her.

His cheerful outlook usually helped lift her spirits, even just a little. But she just wasn't feeling it today. She smiled weakly back and then looked away.

"What's wrong, Charlie?" Alder's voice sounded concerned again.

Charlie just shrugged. Her throat squeezed tight, and her eyes started to prickle. She didn't think she would be able to say anything without tears leaking out.

After a long pause, Alder said, "You *have* changed for the better, you know." He gave her hand a squeeze.

Her heart leapt in her chest. She willed it to stay calm.

Alder hadn't noticed. He kept talking. "You are a confident leader now, and you hesitate less when you must make an important decision. You are careful about not putting those around you in danger. You always want to help everyone, even when there isn't anything you can do." He paused for a second to let his compliments sink in.

"Those are all great qualities to have. But you shouldn't place too much burden on yourself. Others must make their own choices, too. You can do your best to lead and protect, but sometimes you can't protect everyone all the time.

"I can see that your roots have grown stronger, you seem more anchored and surer of yourself than before. But you must allow yourself to blossom as well. When you are weighed down by your worries for others, you stifle your growth. Don't put so much pressure on yourself, or the best parts of you could wither away."

Charlie thought about his words. She knew he was right, but it was easier said than done. Everyone counted on her right now to fix the massive mess she had made of everything. How could she not worry? Everything fell apart around her, and she was the only one who could fix it. Wasn't she?

Alder continued to walk beside her. He didn't say anything else. She peeked at him. He looked so content and sure of himself. Even though his own abilities had been lost, maybe forever. Juliette seemed the same way. She could tell sometimes that they were sad about their disconnect from the world around them, but they never let it get them down for long.

Distracted by her own thoughts, she barely noticed Alder let go of her hand and step away for a second, then jog back to join her again.

"Here, for you. This will help brighten your day." A big grin lit up his face. He handed her a straight stem with papery pale green leaves and topped by a bright orange flower.

Christine Marshall

Chapter 16

She stopped dead in her tracks. Alder stumbled a couple of steps.

Charlie stared at the flower he had given her. It looked exactly like the flowers from her dream. Her mouth hung open.

"Charlie, what is it?" Alder's voice rang with alarm.

"This flower. Where did you get it?" She peered in every direction but didn't see any.

"It's called desert ghost. They grow in rocky, dry places, and they do quite well for themselves. See how the…"

"But where, *exactly*, did you find it?" She needed to see for herself if there were more.

She held the flower out in front of her as if it could lead her to more. She walked back the direction they had come and scanned the ground all around herself.

Alder hurried to catch up. "What's going on?"

"I need to know where you found this, Alder. Right

135

now."

Alder looked stunned. She had probably sounded harsh. She felt bad, but she needed to know.

He answered her question. "They grow sporadically in places like this. That was the only one. I thought its bright color would cheer you up... Why, do you want more?" Alder's brow furrowed.

She groaned. Why was everything always so hard for her? For once couldn't something be as easy as following a trail of flowers to the path that would lead them exactly where they needed to go?

"I'm sure we'll see more as we travel, Charlie." Alder rubbed her arm and watched her carefully.

She ignored his efforts to comfort her and searched the area, all the way to the edge of the ravine, for desert ghost flowers. Once at the edge, she walked back and forth along the cliff top. She just needed to see some sign of a trail down into the ravine. Or at least more flowers.

Alder followed her. He no longer asked questions or offered comfort. He probably just wanted to make sure she didn't fall over the cliff to her death or something.

She didn't see any sign of a trail, and no bright patches of orange led her anywhere. She continued to grip the stem of her flower and conceded to herself that she wasn't going to find a trail of them. They would just have to continue on.

"Tell me if you see any more, please." Charlie didn't take her eyes off the ground.

Alder nodded. She didn't notice the concerned look on his face as he followed a half-step behind her.

She didn't really care if he thought she was crazy. But she felt kind of bad about the way she had interrupted him when he had been so excited to tell her about the flowers.

And for the way she had ignored him while she consumed herself for nearly an hour searching the top of the ravine for more.

"Sorry about before," Charlie said to him. "Please, tell me about the flowers."

He gave her a look as if to ask if she was sure. She nodded and smiled at him. He spent the next little while talking to her about the orange flowers, and other kinds of plants that grow in such an arid environment with rocky soil. It helped distract her from worry, but at the same time allowed her to still be able to walk quickly and search the ground along the way.

When the sun began to sink toward the horizon, Charlie's heart sank along with it. Alder had told her everything about the native plants. They spent the rest of the afternoon on other topics. Charlie's spirits had been lifted. At any moment she would come across at least one more desert ghost to reassure her that her dream might mean something after all. But now the darkness would descend quick. Too soon they came upon Radcliffe setting up their camp for the night.

Alder left Charlie to help Radcliffe. Soon the brownies, Pepper, Juliette, Roxi, and Charlie's dad arrived at the campsite. They all pitched in to prepare the meal and make sure everyone had a safe, somewhat comfortable place to sleep. Charlie focused on her part and tried not to think about orange flowers. But the image of a trail of flowers never left the back of her mind.

Charlie awoke the next morning even more frustrated. She hadn't dreamt of the flowers again. She hadn't dreamt about anything at all. When she got up and everyone stared at her, she slipped away to have a private moment.

When she returned, she avoided eye contact. She only spoke quietly to her father. He continued to age rapidly. Alder knew of no place nearby to take him to rest. Charlie offered to travel with him, but he insisted she not wait for him. She resigned herself to a day alone. She hardly expected Alder to voluntarily join her again after her off-putting behavior from the day before.

She was right. They all started out together as a group, but before long Radcliffe led the way far ahead of the others. Roxi soon lagged; she kept a slow pace for the sake of Charlie's father. Alder and Juliette accompanied him together. Charlie naturally walked quicker than the brownies when she was in a hurry, so all too soon she found herself alone.

The longer she walked alone, the thicker the cloud of doubt and frustration grew over her, until she felt as if she moved through a thick fog. She chewed on some nuts that Juliette had gathered for them and thought about how to find more orange flowers. Her eyes never left the ground, especially closer to the edge of the ravine.

The nearer they got to the mountains, the more urgent Charlie's drive to find the flowers or the trail. She couldn't leave the ravine behind until she found the path.

The sun began to sink. She picked up her pace. She would do anything to find the path. The shadows grew longer. She would not stop until she found those flowers, even if it took her all night.

Pepper flew up beside Charlie and asked her what was wrong. Charlie explained to her that she had to find some orange flowers that grew in dry, rocky soil.

"The ones from your dream?" Pepper asked

Charlie hesitated. Did she have to explain the whole thing? There wasn't time. She nodded. She described them to Pepper, and the pixie zoomed away along the edge of the ravine to find the elusive flowers.

Charlie paced back and forth while she waited for Pepper to return. She bit her nails and kicked at the ground with her feet. She willed Pepper to hurry back with good news.

It took what felt like forever for Pepper to fly back. Her skin was pink with exertion when she returned.

"I found them, Charlie." Pepper panted as she worked to catch her breath. "They're not too far from here, actually. There's a lot of them!"

Relief washed over Charlie. "Show me."

Pepper flew slower this time, in order for Charlie to keep up.

Charlie bent over to examine the flowers. They were the ones from her dream. They spread out in a thin, wide patch, and almost made a trail to the edge of the ravine. Just like Charlie had hoped.

She walked alongside the scattered trail with care. She did not want to damage any of the amazing blossoms.

Her heart raced as she neared the edge of the ravine. She paused before she looked over the edge. Would there be a path down to the bottom? Was this the direction she and her friends were supposed to go? Or was she only leading them into more danger?

She took a deep breath and let it out slowly. No sense in worrying about the path if there wasn't even a path there.

She took a hesitant step toward the rim of the ravine, leaned carefully forward, and peered over the edge.

Christine Marshall

Chapter 17

"Are you sure about this?" Charlie's father looked overly worried. And exhausted.

"Yes. Absolutely. I dreamed about the flowers leading me to the trail, and Pepper found them. The exact flowers at a trailhead to the bottom of the ravine. We've been hoping for a way across, right?"

"But how would we make it up the other side? The cliff is equally as steep across the ravine," Alder wondered.

Charlie knew her friends didn't doubt her dream or her explanation of where they should go next. But they had to think it through before they ran headlong into a bad situation. Still, it stung a little that they weren't all as excited as her about the path. She took a deep breath and let the conversation continue.

"Perhaps she will have another dream," Radcliffe offered.

"Or maybe Eliot will be able to make progress on the map?" Pepper suggested.

"That is possible." Juliette hesitated. "But, Charlie, what about... your father? I do not believe he would be able to handle a steep trail such as this. Even with our help." Juliette looked at Charlie's father apologetically. He smiled weakly back but didn't seem offended.

Charlie had tried not to worry about the changes to his body, but each day her father grew older and weaker. She knew Juliette was right.

Charlie desperately wanted to find out what was at the bottom of the ravine. She was sure that was the way they were supposed to go. But she also did not wish to put her father in any more danger than necessary. She faced a crossroads. She must decide. Leave the trail behind and continue as a group? Or send her father away with Alder and maybe never see him again? Which was the right choice?

Charlie sighed. She met her dad's eyes, as if asking what he wished for her to say. He looked back lovingly for a moment, and then turned to address Alder.

"Maybe now would be a good time for you and I to seek refuge somewhere. Do you have any ideas as to where we might be able to find safety?"

Alder thought for a moment. "Based on Charlie's dream of the alpine forest and my people within, I have a couple of ideas of where we could go that would not be too far away. If we continue into the mountains, perhaps we would find... or be found by... the forest people there."

"Do you think they still have their abilities?" Charlie interrupted. "Would they be able to find you?"

Alder smiled and nodded. "Even if they have lost their abilities, they would still be very much aware of who might be travelling through the forest on the other side of these

142

mountains. I believe if we travel in the right direction, they will find us before we find them."

Charlie didn't want to let her father go. What if they didn't find the help they needed? They could wander in the mountains for too long, and then it might be too late for her dad. Her chest tightened. What should she do?

Alder put her fears to rest. He placed his hands on her shoulders and bent down to look into her eyes. "If we don't find my people, I will make sure your father is safe, I promise." He took her hand and squeezed.

Her hand tingled inside of his. She held on tight.

Roxi grumbled something to Juliette, who said, "Roxi, are you sure?" She placed a hand on the big dog's muzzle.

Roxi whined in reply.

"You know I must continue on…" Juliette spoke in a whisper to the dog.

Roxi let out a light bark. Juliette nodded with moist eyes.

"Roxi wishes to continue to aid your father." Juliette swallowed. "She insists."

Charlie stood with mouth agape as she looked between the dog and the Princess. "What? Are you sure?"

Juliette nodded. "She has grown attached to him and desires to be sure of his safety. The journey will be much easier if he continues to ride on Roxi's back. Even though it pains me to say so, I must agree. It is the right choice in this situation."

"You should accompany us, too, then," Alder offered.

Juliette shook her head. "I must find Jessamine. I feel as though, somehow, much of what she has become is because of me…"

A chorus of voices protested and reassured Juliette at one time. She held her hand up to indicate for them to stop so she could continue.

"Please. No matter what you say, a part of me knows that if I had tried harder when we were young, she would have grown into a much different woman. I must try to reason with her. Perhaps I may convince her of her wrongdoing, and she will choose to change. I must try..." she let out a small sob.

Roxi nuzzled her shoulder.

Juliette wrapped her arms around the dog's neck. Tears flowed down her face. "I will miss you so."

This separation would be difficult for Juliette. When Roxi left, Juliette would be completely cut off from her realm. She would feel more alone than ever, even with the presence of the other travelers. This was a massive sacrifice for Juliette. Charlie hoped she would be able to handle it on the remainder of their journey.

They decided not to waste any time, and parted ways at first light the next morning.

Juliette spoke to Roxi alone.

Radcliffe, Pepper, Max, and Eliot waited at the trailhead. Radcliffe's hoofs beat impatiently at the ground, which squished many of the ghost flowers underfoot. Charlie flinched at the sight. But they were just flowers, after all.

Charlie's father stood beside Alder, who supported him heavily. Charlie approached to say goodbye. Her throat began to close. What if her father continued to age too fast, and he died before she could stop Jessamine? She couldn't bear the idea of never seeing him again. She had lived five hundred years without a single worry about him. He healed quickly, aged too slow to notice, and was always there for her. His presence in her life had always been a given. How could she even think of going on if he wouldn't be there when she returned?

For a moment she considered not following the trail but joining her father instead. But that was not the right choice. She, too, felt a responsibility for finding Jessamine, although she expected her experience with the woman to be much less amicable than what Juliette hoped for.

Charlie threw her arms around her dad's neck. She willed the tears to stay put inside her eyes. She could feel her dad swallow hard as he fought back tears, too. They were too much alike in that way.

She wished that she had told him she loved him every single day now that she would not see him again for a long time.

She squeezed tight one more time, then stepped back.

"You're in good hands." Charlie's voice strained as she gestured toward Alder and Roxi.

"I know," he croaked back.

Charlie nodded.

Alder reached for Charlie and his arms swallowed her up in a tender embrace. "He will be alright," he whispered into her hair. He held her for several heartbeats before he released her. He cupped his hands around her face and looked deep into her eyes, then nodded his reassurance.

"Thank you," she whispered back. Her face warmed beneath his touch.

He bent his head and brushed her cheek with his lips.

The tears welled up in her eyes again. She swiped at them and stepped away.

Roxi and Juliette made their way over. Alder invited Charlie's dad with a gesture to climb onto Roxi's back.

"I love you." Charlie reached out to touch her dad's arm one last time.

"I love you too, My Little Charlie."

Maybe this wouldn't be a forever goodbye. She had to believe it, or she would go crazy with worry. She smiled at her dad, nodded to Alder and Roxi, and turned to join her friends at the trailhead.

The path, lined with more of the orange desert ghost flowers, led them back and forth down the steep wall of the ravine. Loose gravel covered the narrow path. Charlie hugged the wall of the ravine. Her heart raced as her feet slipped on the loose earth. She really didn't want to fall over the edge. Her legs shook and dust covered her from head to toe by the time she reached the bottom.

Just like in the dream, the end of the path led to a huge patch of the flowers.

Pepper flitted from one to the next but came back disappointed. "No sweet nectar." Her wings drooped. "It must be too dry."

"Maybe the nectar would be gross. You lucked out!" Max hollered at Pepper.

Charlie smiled, and Pepper flew back to be with Max and Eliot.

Charlie joined Juliette as the Princess descended behind the brownies into the patch of flowers. She looked as worn out as Charlie felt.

Radcliffe stumbled into the patch of flowers last. He stamped down many of them as he shook off the layer of dust that had settled into his coat of wiry hair on his horse body. He looked irritated.

Charlie gazed up to the top of the cliff they had just

descended. From the top, the ravine had seemed like a narrow crack in the ground, dividing the prairies from the rolling hills, and the Valley of Giants. But from her new perspective, she stood in a great canyon. The height of the walls stretched more than three times the height of Charles, Willem, and most of the other giants she had met. They were steep and rocky, forming sheer cliffs on either side. The path they had traveled down could not be seen from this perspective. If Charlie hadn't just made her way down, she wouldn't have even known it existed.

The afternoon sun tried to reach the bottom of the ravine, but they remained in shadow. Night would come early once the sun set below the walls of the ravine, giving them no light whatsoever. Toward the mountain range, the ravine ran in a mostly straight line before it disappeared between the high mountain peaks. How far on the other side of the range did it go? The other direction, back toward the Valley of Giants, the ravine curved a little. She couldn't see around the nearest bend.

The orange flowers filled a decent sized area, but beyond that, the dry, rocky ground had cracks all over it. Large stones that had fallen from the walls sat here and there. Patches of sage grew sporadically, along with clumps of tall, dry grass.

There was no sign of water. Charlie told herself that it would be fine. They would find their way up the other side of the ravine soon enough.

They had agreed that they should make their way toward the broken bridge, since that was where Max and Eliot's map had led them from above. Then they would be able to find another path up the opposite wall and make their way toward Jessamine. Whether through a dream of hers or the brownie's map, she would be able to figure it out.

Once again, Charlie found herself in the lead. And once again, she inwardly wondered if she should really be the one to lead them. Radcliffe seemed the obvious choice. He was big and formidable. Any enemy they may face would have a second thought before choosing to face him. But he seemed to be uncomfortable on the uneven ground. He was grouchy and Charlie thought it best to let him stay in the rear. Besides, she didn't think they would come across any enemies in the basin of this long canyon.

Max, Eliot, and Pepper followed close behind Charlie. They whispered to each other when they thought Charlie might be able to hear their conversation.

Juliette had chosen to travel behind the small ones. She remained sullen. Charlie knew Juliette missed Roxi and needed some time alone.

The absence of Roxi, Alder, and her father hung heavy over Charlie. Especially the looming feeling that she would never see her dad again. But she couldn't allow herself to let her thoughts stray in that direction, or she would lose focus and have a hard time completing her task.

She allowed her body to carry her along the ravine. They now traveled exactly the direction they had come, except at a much lower elevation. Frustration knit her brown together as her feet beat a path along the ravine floor.

The crack in the earth twisted and turned, almost like the path a river would take. Their water pouches had some water in them, but not enough to last long. Another day, maybe.

Charlie startled, her mind lost in thought, when Pepper landed on her shoulder. It had been some time since her tiny friend had traveled with her. She usually spent her time with Max and Eliot during the day and spent her evenings with Charlie.

"Do you hear that?" Pepper asked while Charlie pulled her thoughts back to the moment.

Charlie focused on her surroundings and strained her ears to process the sounds around her. The brownies and Juliette soon joined her. Each of them listened for the sound that Pepper had pointed out. Radcliffe was still some distance behind.

A strange, rhythmic noise echoed along the ravine ahead of them. Charlie could feel a grinding sensation in her feet and a steady, low hum in her chest. The ground vibrated. Charlie couldn't place the sounds.

She turned to the others with the question in her eyes. Did they know what it was? They each shook their heads or shrugged their shoulders.

Radcliffe joined them after a few minutes.

Charlie asked him. Her heart beat a little faster.

Was it some monstrous creature that would block their path? Would they have to fight? Would they be able to continue at all? They were nowhere near the location of the broken-down bridge yet; they wouldn't reach it for another day, at least.

What would they do if there was something between them and their destination? They were in a bad spot for fighting, and running away was not an option at this point, either. They needed to move forward.

Charlie dreaded what Radcliffe might say.

Chapter 18

"Miners." Radcliffe breezed past Charlie and continued forward.

"What do you mean?" Charlie hurried to catch up.

"Those are the sounds of miners. They must be mining the walls of the ravine for some sort of ore. I can hear their voices. There are a lot of men beyond this curve." Radcliffe remained calm as he spoke, like it was no big deal to come across a huge group of men digging at the sides of a cliff.

"So... what do we do? How do we know if they are a threat or not?" Pepper wondered out loud.

"I suggest we scout out the situation before we proceed. It would be better to be cautious than to walk headlong into a disaster." Radcliffe stopped so they could plan.

They bounced ideas back and forth. Radcliffe wanted to scout the situation but feared he would not be able to be stealth enough on the uneven ground. Charlie didn't know what to look for. Juliette took a step back when her name came up, obviously not interested in spying.

"Uh, guys?" Pepper flew close to Charlie. She tugged on her sleeve.

"Yes?" Radcliffe sounded annoyed at the interruption.

"Look," Pepper pointed ahead of them.

Max and Eliot hopped from rock to rock far ahead of the group. As they went along, one of them pushed the other off a rock. The brother who fell shot back up, raced ahead, and pushed the other off a rock. They threw things at each other and seemed to be more concerned with play than spying on a group of possibly dangerous men who stood in the way of their destination.

Radcliffe groaned and rolled his eyes. "What are those two doing, the little..." he finished his sentence under his breath.

He didn't mean the insults, though. Not really. Charlie saw him speak with the brownies in private from time to time. He trusted them.

"They said they would be able to find out pretty quick who the miners are and whether we should be worried." Pepper shrugged. "Then they just took off. Should I follow them?"

"No, that's fine." Charlie remembered the other times the little men had wandered off only to return with information or "borrowed" items. "They probably can find out what we need to know. They seem to have a way of not being noticed."

Juliette nodded. She found a decent sized boulder to rest on. Her shoulders still sagged from the absence of her traveling companion.

Charlie and Pepper joined her on her boulder, and they made small talk, while Radcliffe stood uncomfortably in place. He glared down the ravine for a sign of the brothers' return.

The brownies came back before too long. They each gnawed on sticks of cooked meat they had stolen right off a spit over a fire. Eliot offered Pepper a bite, but she politely refused. He shrugged and continued to chew on the charred meat.

"So, they work for Jessamine," Max said between bites, as if the information was as dull as dwarves mining for diamonds.

"What??" Charlie jumped from her spot.

"They work for Jessamine." Max shrugged. "I guess there's some good granite or something in the cliffs that she wants. They are digging it out in big chunks and putting it in these big cart things. I don't know how they expect to get it out of the ravine. But, hey, that's not our problem, right?" Max grinned up at the others.

When he didn't get a jovial reply from anyone, he turned to his brother and said, "What? What did I say?" He tossed his empty roasting stick onto the ground and picked at his teeth.

"I think we are all just a little surprised these men work for Jessamine," Pepper tried to explain.

"And that you were even able to figure that out so quickly!" Juliette offered.

Max and Eliot looked at each other and shrugged, clearly not about to share how they came across this information, or how they were able to wander through the camp and steal meat without being noticed.

"If these men are working for Jessamine, then it would be prudent for us to not be noticed by them," Radcliffe growled a little. "We must pass by them without being seen.

Can you tell me how the camp was laid out and where the men are digging?" Radcliffe prepared to plan for their safe avoidance of the miners.

Max and Eliot described the layout of the camp, drawing in the dirt with a stick to give Radcliffe a clearer visual of who was where within the camp. They recounted how many men they had seen, and Radcliffe estimated how many more may be beyond the camp, digging in the walls further down the ravine. He asked the brownies about weapons, and they told him that only a few of the men had been armed, and they were the ones sitting around camp eating and drinking and being all around lazy. Radcliffe nodded, as if he expected that to be the case.

Charlie wondered how Radcliffe seemed to know so much about a group of men mining, but she didn't think they really had time, nor needed, a prolonged explanation, so she put the thought out of her mind and continued to listen to the back-and-forth reporting and questioning by Radcliffe, Max, and Eliot.

After a lengthy conversation, Radcliffe announced that he knew where they would go around the camp, and that they would need to travel at night, preferably when the men were having a meal or being loud. The louder the better, he said, so they wouldn't have to worry about being quiet as they made their way past. Since it was only early afternoon, that meant they would spend the rest of the daylight hours waiting for the sky to grow dark.

Charlie wondered out loud if they might be able to "borrow" some water from the camp as they made their way through. She had checked with the others and all their canteens were running low.

She asked Max and Eliot whether this would be

possible, and they both nodded as Max said, "Sure, no problem. We'll take care of it. Is there anything else you might want?" He had a gleam in his eyes.

"No. No stealing anything else." Charlie spoke firmly to Max. "We'll take water because we desperately need it, and this delay is going to prevent us from refilling our pouches soon enough. But we don't need anything else. Anything. Got it?" She made him look her in the eyes and promise he wouldn't take anything.

She wasn't sure she believed him, but what else she could do about it at this point? With the plans made, the group waited out the afternoon.

Radcliffe tried to find a comfortable place to fold his legs underneath him to rest, but he got up and repositioned so often, that he ended up not resting much at all. He was probably more anxious than Charlie to get out of this ravine.

The rest of them found a spot to wait beneath a low overhang on the cliff. Charlie leaned her back against the stone. She soon began to doze against the warm rocks.

Darkness enveloped Charlie. The only light came from a faint glow in the distance. A slight breeze rustled her hair, and her lungs filled with dusty air. She coughed for a minute and waited for the dust to be pushed aside by the breeze. She strained her eyes to see her surroundings.

Her eyes could not penetrate the darkness. She shivered from the cool, moist air that brushed her bare arms. She sat on rough, but solid ground. No dirt and dry cracks covered the ground beneath her. She stood up and called out for her friends.

Her voice echoed back to her. She was alone. How had she gotten into a cave? Had someone carried her? Where were her friends?

She turned in a circle and faced the faint light in the distance. She stood in a dead end. The faint light came from the same direction as the breeze. Which meant it must be the way out.

She took a step forward and stumbled on the uneven ground. It was so dark it was impossible to see anything. Her hands grew clammy, and her chest tightened. She hated small, dark spaces. And she especially hated them when she was alone.

Her breath came faster. Her head began to spin. She was going to faint. As she fell in slow motion toward the ground, she heard the voice of her guardian.

"It's going to be fine, Little Dreamer. You are not alone…"

Charlie startled. She banged her head on the low overhang that had provided her shade.

"Ow!" Her eyes stung from the surprise.

She wasn't in the dark, silent cave by herself. She sat in the ravine. And a quick glance around proved that her friends still surrounded her.

Her head throbbed. She clutched it with one hand and placed her other hand on her chest. She forced herself to take long, deep breaths to help ease the pain. Radcliffe had taught her that technique during training. Before long the throbbing subsided.

Max dozed with his head on Eliot's shoulder, but the smaller of the two men remained awake. He stared at her as if she were crazy. Beside him Juliette opened her eyes and rubbed them, then glanced at Charlie.

When Juliette saw the troubled expression on Charlie's face, she asked her if she was alright, if something had happened.

Charlie assured her she was fine. "I just had a bad dream, that's all…"

Juliette looked worried. Charlie realized that saying she had a bad dream could upset the others, since sometimes her dreams came true. She shook her head and tried to explain.

"No, it wasn't a dream like that. It was… I was in a cave…" Charlie's words hung there as she thought about it. Was it a prophetic dream? Was she going to end up in a cave all by herself? But she had heard the giant's voice. That wasn't real, so the dream couldn't have been real. "It…. It was just a dream," she hastily finished.

Juliette still looked worried but didn't say anything else to Charlie.

Pepper zipped close just then. She told Charlie about the sweet berries she had found on some plant that hung off the cliff way up high.

Charlie nodded, but barely heard her tiny friend. Her mind focused on her dream, and about sneaking past the group of miners around the bend.

The sky darkened while Charlie thought. It would soon be time to move. She shared a meal of dried meat and nuts with the others. She didn't say much.

Soon enough it was time to move on. Charlie wanted to say something to encourage her friends, but she didn't know what to say. She stumbled over her thoughts, and finally blurted out, "Everyone ready?" Her voice felt a little high. Hopefully no one else had noticed the concern that laced the edges of her words.

Charlie followed the brownies with Juliette right behind. Pepper flew alongside Charlie. Whenever things got serious, Pepper always returned to Charlie's side. Radcliffe brought up the rear.

They walked quickly to the bend in the ravine wall, and then slowly stepped around the corner. The huge camp spread out along the width of the ravine floor. Tents dotted the space, and every so often a fire pit brightened the surroundings. Some had caldrons of boiling things, probably stews. Others had spits of meat being turned slowly by a miner. The smell of food and dirt and sweat overwhelmed Charlie's nose as they inched closer toward the camp.

Stars dotted the now dark sky, and a nearly full moon hung to the south.

Most of the men had gathered around the fires to eat and talk. It wasn't as noisy as Charlie had expected. She had hoped for some kind of party or ruckus to mask their movements. But the ambient noise from their mealtime would probably drown out any noise her group made well enough. Plus, it's not like they seemed to be on the guard or anything. The men clearly didn't expect visitors or an attack.

The brownies led the way carefully along the base of the ravine. They skirted around the outermost tents and kept to the shadows. Charlie wanted to just run through and be done with this. Poking along in the dark was excruciating and she could not wait to get to the other end of the camp and be on their way.

The brownies paused when they were about halfway

along the stretch of the miner's camp. The others quickly caught up.

"What's going on?" Charlie whispered to the short men.

Radcliffe took a minute to catch up. He looked worn out. His restless feet never stopped tapping the ground as he tried to find a comfortable place to rest his hooves.

Max motioned toward a huge pile of round boulders that blocked their direct path. "I don't think we can climb over it and going around it will bring us very close to the camp. See how the tents are pitched so close? We will have to be careful."

Charlie nodded. She followed the little men around the enormous, smooth boulders.

They picked their way around the rocks.

The ground rumbled. The rocks trembled. Dirt trickled from between the precarious mounds.

"What was that?" Pepper asked in a loud whisper. She still flew close to Charlie.

The rumbling grew louder. The boulders began to move. They scraped against one another.

"They are moving." Juliette's whisper held a tone of panic.

Charlie and the others stopped their progress and held still. The boulders slid against one another and piled into an upright position.

"Is that a…" Max started to ask a question.

Radcliffe finished the sentence. "Golem," he stated matter-of-factly. He unsheathed his battle axe and sword. "We need to run."

Chapter 19

The rocks formed themselves into a huge man made of boulders. It stood as tall as the tallest giant Charlie had ever seen. It had huge hollows on its rock face where eyes should have been. It rumbled, like a growl, from within. Even without real eyes, it could see them... somehow.

"Run!" Radcliffe yelled.

Shouts rang from the nearest campfire.

The entire camp had been alerted to their presence. Now thousands of men stirred in front of them, and a huge stone giant blocked the path behind them. Where were they supposed to run? Charlie stood frozen to the spot.

Radcliffe grabbed her arm as he charged past her from behind, which compelled her to move. Once she was in motion, he let go of her so he could fight off the men that now charged toward them.

Charlie's head cleared. She removed her dagger from her ankle with one hand, and her sword with the other. She hated fighting.

She saw Pepper glow bright out of the corner of her eye. The men had no idea what they were about to get themselves into with her. She zipped out of sight and took out as many of the men as she could.

Charlie saw the two brownies underfoot of the humans. What were they doing? A group of ten men crashed to the ground, a rope tangled in their feet. The brownies had woven it amongst them as they ran, then pulled it tight, immobilizing a whole group of them at once.

One of the miners came at her from the side. Charlie slashed at him, then jumped out of the way of another attacker. She skirted around a campfire.

She tried to keep Radcliffe in sight as he cut his way through the camp. The rumble of the golem followed close behind. The ground shook with every heavy footstep it took. It would catch up with them in no time. Where could they go to escape?

"This way, Eliot has an idea," Pepper shouted at Charlie. She zipped by again and ignited the tents with her flame to distract the men and hopefully confuse the golem.

Charlie dodged more attacks as she followed the pixie. Pepper lit men and tents on fire, which cleared the way for Charlie. It was easy to follow her trail of fire, even if she couldn't see the bright light bobbing to and fro ahead of her. She could hear Juliette close behind her.

Soon they had outrun the mass of men. But the golem steadily gained on them. Charlie looked over her shoulder. It did its own share of damage to the camp, not caring where its feet landed while it did the one thing it was bewitched to do: take out the intruders.

She caught up to the brownies. Max had a bunch of random stuff in his hands. He passed things back and forth with Eliot.

"What are they doing?" She panted for breath as they wove through the camp.

"I don't know," the pixie shouted. She zipped away, took down another man, then returned to Charlie's side. "...but they said they have a plan, so..."

Radcliffe took up the rear again. He would protect them as long as he could.

They neared the other side of the canyon floor. How were they going to get out of this mess?

"There," Max called over his shoulder. The brownies led them up a narrow trail that had been carved into the side of the cliff.

"Where are we going?" Charlie called back.

"Just trust me!" Max yelled.

Up ahead, Charlie could see a timber structure that jutted out of the side of the hill. They were now well above the camp. One wrong step would send them falling a long distance. She wondered how Radcliffe managed on the skinny trail. She didn't have time to worry about that now, though, because the golem was practically on top of them.

The golem swung its massive stone fist toward them. Charlie threw her arms over her head and ducked. She still ran as rocks and dust rained down on her from above. The golem had missed its target, but the debris bruised her arms and shoulders. Juliette shrieked behind her, but still followed.

"Quick, in here!" Max yelled. He motioned for them to enter the mine through the timber entrance. He stood at the opening and made sure everyone streamed in. "Pepper! I need fire! Now!"

Charlie stopped and turned. She breathed heavily from

their race through the camp and up the hill.

Radcliffe turned in the mine entrance to fight off the golem. Its fist slammed into the cliff. The ground shuddered. Dust and rock dropped from above.

Radcliffe yelled at everyone to run further into the cave as he prepared to fight the golem in the mine entrance.

But then Pepper shot past Charlie and lit something that Max held, then the same with Eliot.

"Get away!" Max yelled at Radcliffe.

The golem pushed its way into the mine. The golem's head and arm forced their way into the cave. The timber structure broke into pieces with a crash.

"Move!" Max yelled again at Radcliffe. He threw the now burning object at the golem.

The brownies took their own advice and scurried away from the entrance. Charlie followed, as did Radcliffe and Juliette. When the brownies threw themselves to the floor and plugged their ears, Charlie followed suit. What had the brownies done this time?

An explosion rocked the cave. A thunderous sound echoed through the mine. Even with her fingers in her ears, the sound was deafening. The whole mine would collapse on them at any second.

Aftershocks followed the initial explosion. The shaking stopped and the raining debris slowed. Charlie pushed herself off the ground.

She turned to look at the entrance where the golem had been only moments before. All that remained was a pile of boulders, plus wood from the mining structure. The entrance had totally collapsed. The golem had been severed in two, ending its magic.

Charlie coughed a couple of times from all the dust in

the air. Juliette still huddled on the ground. Pepper hovered in the air between the brownies. Max and Eliot looked triumphant.

Radcliffe, however, did not.

Charlie rushed to Juliette's side but jumped when Radcliffe started to shout at the brownies. Her ears rang as his voice echoed off the wall.

"WHAT DID YOU DO?" Radcliffe's voice shook more dust loose from the ceiling.

Charlie placed a hand on Juliette's back. The Princess uncurled herself. She looked scared and relieved at the same time. She reached for Charlie and clutched her arm as they both turned to see what took place between the centaur and the brownies.

Max and Eliot exchanged a shocked look and said at the same time, "What??"

"You have trapped us inside this tomb! How do you expect us to get out now?" He pointed at the entrance with his sword.

"We saved everyone!" Max retorted. "We were being chased by a giant man made of stone, in case you hadn't noticed. Even if we had out run it through the camp, it would have just kept chasing us until it had squashed us all!" Max didn't hold back.

Charlie guessed Max wasn't as intimidated by the centaur as he used to be. She hoped that was a good thing.

"So, you saved us from one terrible death only to lead us toward another!" Radcliffe sheathed his weapons and threw his arms in the air. His tail swished back and forth, and Charlie saw his face twisted with anger.

"Hang on," Juliette tried to intercede. "The brownies are right. We would have been doomed if we had stayed in the canyon."

"Be that as it may, we are just as doomed in here as we were out there," Radcliffe steamed. "At least out there I could have fought…" His respect for Juliette kept him from shouting at her, but only just.

"Radcliffe, calm yourself," Juliette said. "Take a look at your surroundings. All hope is not lost. We are not trapped."

Charlie didn't know what she meant by that. It sure looked like they had been trapped in this mine and their only way out had been destroyed. Even though they escaped the men and the golem, how *would* they get out of here?

"Centaurs don't like to be underground," Max whispered to Pepper, which invited a growl and a glare from Radcliffe. That meant that Max was probably right.

Pepper's fire was the only light that they had. It cast long shadows behind everyone. The light shifted as the pixie hovered in the center of the cave. The movement made Charlie feel a little sick, but she pushed the nausea down and focused on Juliette's words.

"Do you feel the breeze?" Juliette asked Radcliffe. "That means there is another way out through this mine, somewhere." Juliette stood still and waited.

Charlie did notice the airflow. It had blown the dust back toward the collapsed entrance and cleared the air. She took a calming breath and focused on the positive. There must be another way out of the mine.

The constant shift of Pepper's light made Charlie feel dizzier now. Her breath started to come faster. The air still held a hint of dust. It filled Charlie's lungs. It was dark, so dark in the cave. The darkness closed in on Charlie.

"Charlie, are you alright?" Juliette's voice came from far away.

Before Charlie could answer, the floor rose and smacked her in the head.

Christine Marshall

Chapter 20

The blackness seeped into Charlie from all around. She shivered. She tried to lift herself off the ground, but her arms and legs felt heavy like stone. She could faintly hear her friends' voices, but muffled. She tried to move again but could not budge. Soon the sounds of her friends faded completely until she was alone in the darkness, unable to move.

She broke out into a cold sweat. What would happen now? Where was she?

"Charlie…"

She closed her eyes against the darkness and focused on the deep, calm voice.

"Charlie…"

The voice did not belong to one of her companions. But she recognized it right away.

She opened her eyes and looked for her giant friend. She expected darkness but found sunlight surrounded her. Her body felt light again. The air around her shimmered.

She shifted into a sitting position. She felt soft grass beneath her. Oversized ferns lined a small river that gurgled to one side. Sunlight sparkled off many tiny water droplets in the air. To her left, the waterfall and the wall stretched high above. Warmth enveloped her. Not just from the air, but from a sense of home.

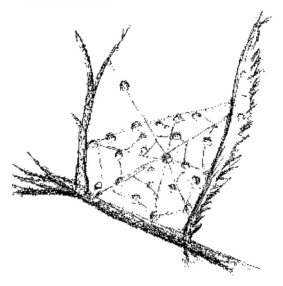

"Charlie," she heard the voice again.

She turned to her right, and there, leaning against one of the gigantic mossy trees, nestled between two enormous ferns, rested her guardian.

"You have done well, Charlie."

His voice permeated deep inside of her. Peace wrapped around her like a warm blanket.

"Your dreams have become more specific. You have followed them even when they didn't make sense to you. You have learned to focus." Pride lit up his face.

Charlie's heart settled. She smiled back at him. She had worked so hard to let go of her fear and let her dreams guide her. The giant was right, she had learned to focus better and dream more. Things would go well now.

But then she remembered the plight of her friends at the moment.

"Thank you, friend. But we are at a dead end. We've become trapped in a cave." Charlie rubbed her forehead to try to release the tension that gripped her head.

"Things happen for a reason, Little Dreamer. Find the right path and you will discover the reason."

Charlie nodded. He always sounded so calm. It helped to calm her, too.

"Eliot has been having trouble with his map. I need my dreams to become... more. So I can lead." She worried about her little friend, and that she may not be able to step up now that no one else had their abilities anymore. How would they find Jessamine without the map?

Like he could read her mind, the giant interrupted her thoughts. "It is *your* time. *You* will stop Jessamine. *You* will restore the balance. You have what it takes."

Amazingly, Charlie believed him. No doubts tickled her mind.

"You have done well to let go of your desire to be with your father."

A pang squeezed her heart, just for a second. But she willed it away.

"You will be required to let go of more before your journey is through. Keep on the path you are traveling."

Charlie's heart swelled. She looked up at her dear friend. She reached out to touch his leg, and to tell him thank you. Before she could make contact, the world faded back into darkness.

She knew right away that she lay on the ground of the mine. The warmth had gone away with the vision. Coolness surrounded her.

Pepper hovered above her face. Juliette held Charlie's head in her lap.

"She's awake!" Pepper called to Radcliffe and the brownies, who must have been waiting a little further away.

Charlie heard Radcliffe's hoofbeats as he hurried to her side. She saw fear in his eyes as he gazed down at her. His shoulders were tense, and his arms folded tight across his chest.

"Are you harmed? What happened?" Radcliffe tripped over his words.

It touched Charlie to hear and see the concern in him, and to see the brownies rush to her side to check on her.

"I'm fine." She struggled to sit up.

"Careful!" Juliette supported her with an arm across her back and her hand clutching Charlie's waist.

"No, really, I'm alright," Charlie said. She really felt it now.

She smiled at those huddled around her. She took Radcliffe's outstretched hand to help her stand.

"Slowly," Juliette warned.

"No, she'll be fine." Radcliffe sounded a little surprised, but sure. He must have been able to see the change in Charlie that she felt in herself.

For the first time since her journey began, she felt complete. She had full trust in herself. Confidence gave her courage. She knew she would find Jessamine. And she would stop her.

Pepper's light barely lit up the space in which they had gathered. Small streams of dirt poured from the walls and ceiling in short bursts. Everyone looked totally exhausted. And scared. Even Radcliffe, a little.

"We need to find a safe place to rest." Charlie gave the brownies a playful grin. "I don't think this part of the mine is so stable anymore."

Max winked back and a smile quivered at the corners of Eliot's mouth.

"This way," Charlie beckoned for the others to follow. Somehow, she knew exactly where they should go now. Something had changed during her vision. For the better, for sure.

They were supposed to be in this mine. For what reason, she didn't know yet.

But she couldn't wait to find out.

They made their way down the tunnel away from the entrance. It was like leaving their troubles behind them. Charlie had a new bounce in her step and didn't feel very much like she needed to rest. But it was the middle of the night, and she knew that some of the others, at least, needed to sleep before they continued to travel through these mines.

They walked single file down the low-ceilinged mine shaft. Unlit torches hung in holders in even intervals on the wall. She reached up and took one, then beckoned Pepper to light it. The others soon did the same. Pepper no longer lit the way.

Light bounced off the solid rock walls and the old, wooden support posts and beams. Some had been reinforced by newer wood beams. The tunnel stretched straight for a long way. Just beyond a nearly right-angled bend Charlie found a side cavern.

It looked well supported and large enough for the group to make camp. As some kind of supply room, it had torches fixed to the stone walls.

The group made their way around the room and lit the torches. The stench of burning fuel from the torches filled the air for a moment, but then it rose to the ceiling and dissipated. A track ran down the center of the room and out a tunnel on the back wall.

Miscellaneous mining equipment appeared to have been carelessly tossed into a handful of carts that had been pushed along the tracks and into the room for storage.

Stacks of rough wooden crates lined one wall. Straw poked through the slats, and lids that had once been secured with nails rested askew atop many of the crates. Plenty of dented shovels and dull pickaxes with broken and splintered handles had been hastily piled in a corner. A dozen hard hats dangled from hooks above the pile of tools. The brownies wasted no time digging through the carts and crates looking for who-knows-what.

Radcliffe promptly curled his legs underneath him and leaned against one wall. He tried to make himself comfortable in the cramped space. He had stooped the entire time they maneuvered along the shaft. He massaged his neck and stretched his back before he folded his arms and leaned his head against the wall. He closed his eyes.

Juliette huddled in a ball near one of the torches.

Pepper observed Max and Eliot for a few moments, then drifted away from them to inspect the opening on the other end of the room. She poked around, then settled on a shelf that held metal buckets full of rusty nails and brackets.

Charlie hated seeing her friends in this place. They had to get out of here. She allowed her body to relax. With each breath she focused on something that she needed to solve: the mine shaft and manufactured tunnels around them; her dad and Alder; stopping Jessamine and restoring the balance. These were the most important things.

After a few hours, Charlie awoke. She knew exactly where to go. They would make their way to a cavern of underground dwellings. This would lead them to their escape from the vast tunnel network. And from the miners that she now knew had begun to track them.

She impatiently waited for the others to wake from their slumber. She wanted to be on the move as soon as possible, but she also wanted to give her companions as much time as possible to rest.

Thirty minutes later, Radcliffe awoke. He stretched, grunted, and looked around at the others. His eyes finally rested on Charlie.

"I know where to go." She didn't bother to keep her voice quiet. It echoed off the stone walls. Soon the others sat up.

"Well, then," Max looked at Charlie with sleepy eyes. "Let's get going."

They packed quickly, grabbed their torches, and Charlie led them down the tunnel which broke into several different offshoots. Two of them led deeper underground, and two continued on level for some time.

Charlie did not hesitate. She chose one of the level tunnels and walked on. When the tunnels split again, she chose one that descended slightly. She hoped Radcliffe would be able to maneuver down it alright. She could hear him grumble under his breath behind Juliette and the brownies, but she pressed on anyway.

The tunnel became shorter and steeper as they descended lower into the mines.

"Aren't we supposed to be finding a way *out*?" Max complained. "It kind of feels like we are just going deeper…"

"Trust me, this is the right way," Charlie assured him. She had no doubt.

After hiking in silence for a long time, the tunnel leveled out and opened into a overly large natural cavern. The darkness hid the ceiling from view. Enormous stalactites and stalagmites cast long, dancing shadows away from the torches that the group carried. The floor of dry, red dirt spread mostly flat in all directions. The cool, dry air came as a relief in contrast with the warm humidity they had been experiencing outside.

This was exactly what Charlie had expected. She told the others to take a break, eat a snack, and rest for a bit, as they still had a long way to go. They had been walking through the tunnels, Radcliffe hunched over, for the better part of two hours. Charlie's own feet and legs ached. They all needed a break.

She found a quiet place, secluded from the others, and closed her eyes to concentrate. She could almost-dream in this state. She had done it before.

The layout of the cavern opened before her eyes. She clearly saw the way through.

She stood and stretched, then joined the others. Her confidence in her dreams had increased higher than ever before. She couldn't wait to get out of these caves and find Jessamine. That evil woman would be no match for Charlie now.

"We need to be on the move." Charlie rejoined the others. "The miners are looking for us. We need to tread quickly, but carefully, through these ruins."

"Ruins?" Pepper looked confused.

"Yes," Charlie pointed at the vast cavern. It was hard to tell from their vantage point, she knew, but she was a little surprised no one else had noticed.

She showed them the details as they made their way through the abandoned underground village. Pillars of rock had been carved hollow and fitted with window openings and doorways. Many even had winding staircases that stretched all the way to the high ceiling. Flat stones had been stacked carefully to create low walls. A courtyard filled the center of the cavern in a wide circle; low stone benches lined at least two thirds of it. A long unused firepit lay in the center.

In the darkness, the dwellings and outbuildings had been camouflaged. The flickering torchlight cast long shadows like the spokes of a tire around the travelers.

"This place is creepy…" Pepper whispered in a dramatic tone. "I swear I saw something move over there." She flew low to the floor, close to Eliot.

"It was probably just the shadows…" Max did not sound certain of his explanation.

In other circumstances, Charlie would have been uncomfortable in this place, too. She did not like dark places. She hated going under the mountains near the City of Giants. She had seen enough strange things to know that even if ghosts weren't real, ghostly beings certainly were.

But the dreams had shown her this place. She felt calm and confident as she wound her way between the structures and toward the back of the cavern.

They passed a place with a stone basin that had probably once held water. Several low stone stools circled the basin. Broken vessels and stone utensils littered the floor.

"This must have once been the dwelling place of some people," Juliette commented. "But it is clearly abandoned. And has been for some time." She bent to inspect the piece of one of the shattered vessels. She set it back on the ground, exactly where she had found it.

"These buildings are small, though. The ceilings are pretty low," Pepper pointed out. "Who would have lived here?"

"Dwarves," came Radcliffe's simple reply.

"Why would they have left?" Pepper wondered out loud.

"Hard to say," Radcliffe replied. "But it must have been a very long time ago."

Layers of dust covered the top of every surface and the floor of every dwelling place. Cobwebs decorated the window-openings and rooftops.

"I wonder what the dwarves were like?" Charlie added to the conversation. "What their lives were like? Why would they want to live so far underground?"

Radcliffe snorted. "You can say that again…"

Charlie recognized a detail from her dream. A cobblestone path led out of the stone village and curved to the right. She beckoned the others to follow her down the path until they reached the back wall of the cavern.

The light from the torches reflected off smooth red stones striped with layers of sparkly quartz and shiny marble. The effect mesmerized the others. Charlie recognized the place from her vision. Her eyes roved over the lines and sparkles. She walked to her right as she ran her left hand up and down over the cold stone.

"What is she doing?" Max whispered loudly to Pepper.

His voice echoed more than he must have expected. When Charlie looked back at him with a smile, he looked sheepish.

"You'll see." She kept walking, left hand on the wall and right hand holding her torch.

"Here." She reached into a small crack.

Something inside the wall thumped.

The wall trembled and grumbled.

"What have you done?" Radcliffe began to ask, but stopped short when a large crack, like a doorway, opened in the side of the cave.

She turned and smiled at the group. "See?"

Then she disappeared into the dark, secret passage.

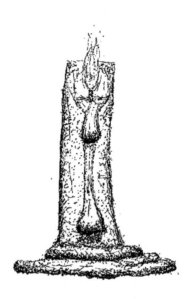

Chapter 21

The others followed Charlie into the darkness one by one. The light from their torches danced on the walls of the narrow passage. Charlie glanced over her shoulder and saw that Radcliffe barely fit. She felt bad, but they had to go this way.

She could hear the brownies whisper to one another, wondering if Charlie had lost her mind. But she was confident in the route. As contrary as it seemed, they would find the exit down here.

The passage opened into a small room. The ceiling was just high enough for Radcliffe to stretch to nearly standing. They all crowded into the room after Charlie. No one spoke as they turned in a circle to take in the space. They all barely fit.

Their torches filled the room with flickering light. This cavern was natural, not dug out like the tunnels had been.

And it was a dead end.

Confused, Charlie walked around the perimeter of the

room. She felt the walls, searching for another secret door or hidden tunnel entrance. She only made it part way around when she came across a natural bowl in the uneven wall. A small amount of water filled the bottom of the bowl. And it shimmered in the torchlight.

"Look at this." Though she spoke quietly, her voice filled the small space. They crowded around her.

Pepper hovered above the bowl, while the brownies stood on tip toes to try to see into it. Juliette and Radcliffe peered from above the small men.

"So… it's some water…" Max drew out the sentence. He looked disappointed.

"Look around, there's no source for the water. No drips. No water running down the walls." Charlie waited for the others to understand.

"What does it mean, Charlie?" Pepper asked, clearly just as confused as everyone else.

She looked at each of them in turn. None of them knew what she had figured out.

"It's the Deep Spring water. Like the water at home. It heals and prolongs life. This must be another source for the water." Charlie stared into the bowl. Her mouth watered. She couldn't take her eyes off the sparkles. It would be sweet.

She wanted so badly to reach in and take a drink. But there wasn't very much there. And the sides were dry, as if this had been the amount in the bowl for a very long time.

"I wonder if this was why the dwarves built their home here," she said to no one in particular.

"And probably why they left," Juliette commented. "The Deep Spring dried up. They no longer wished to stay."

"Or they knew they would age and die, so they

abandoned this place to search for another source," Radcliffe speculated. "This is most likely what Jessamine is searching for in these mines. The desire for some stone is a ruse to hide her true intentions."

They were quiet as they stared at the water.

The silence stretched on until Pepper blurted out, "Drink it, Charlie!" Her face turned pink.

Charlie was startled by the outburst. "I was actually thinking of taking it and finding my father. It would save him to have some of this water until we can defeat Jessamine and go back home." She swallowed the lump that filled her throat.

"Charlie, there isn't time for that." Radcliffe didn't even give Charlie time to decide for herself. "It would only take longer to find him and then continue to search for Jessamine."

"Besides," Juliette added in a gentle voice. "The water from your home did not work for your father. This would likely have the same outcome."

Charlie wiped the wetness from her eyes and swallowed again. The confidence leaked from her eyes with her tears. Her head told her that her friends were right, but her heart would not surrender. "Maybe we could split up. Radcliffe could take it, or Pepper. Max and Eliot probably know a way…"

The brownies shook their heads. Pepper's wings drooped and she frowned.

"We must stay together, Charlie," Juliette said in a soft voice. "You know that."

Charlie nodded. But her eyes never left the water that could save her father's life.

"You should drink it," Pepper said again, quieter this

time.

"Why?" Charlie snapped. She took a deep breath to calm herself. "If we can't take it to my father, then Radcliffe should be the one to drink it. It would enhance his strength and make him nearly invincible for a long time."

"You need it more. You will soon begin to age faster, as your father has." Radcliffe folded his arms. A stubborn look clouded his face.

"You already look different from when we first met, Charlie. You are growing and changing before our eyes." Juliette placed a gentle hand on Charlie's back. "Radcliffe and Pepper are right. You should be the one to drink it."

Charlie shook her head. She started to protest. But then a low rumble came from beyond the passage. Shouts echoed through the abandoned dwarf settlement. Jessamine's men had found them.

"Charlie, there's no time to argue this further. Drink it. Now," Radcliffe insisted.

Charlie hesitated. Her heart felt as though it would split in two. If she drank it, then wouldn't that just secure her father's death? There was no way he would live much longer.

But the others were right. Even if she managed to get it to him, it would not ensure anything. It would only prolong their task. She struggled with herself as the shouts and rumble of many running feet echoed down the passage.

She hated herself for doing it, but she dipped her hands into the bowl and scooped the last of the water into her mouth.

The sweet taste blossomed on her tongue. The cool liquid slid down her throat. The magic of the water coursed through her body. Her achy muscles healed at once. Her arms and legs felt stronger, tighter. Her mind cleared. She had let go of her own wants, just like the voice had told her to. She had done the right thing.

She knew at once, without any dream or vision to help her, what to do next.

The shouts of the men rang in her ears as they reached the entrance to the passage.

"Follow me," she commanded.

Across the room, Charlie pushed another secret lever. A steep, wide passage opened in the narrow wall. She motioned for everyone to go through. Radcliffe led the way, while Pepper waited for Charlie. Charlie pushed the lever again, then slipped through. The entrance closed itself just as the light from Jessamine's men flooded the room. She heard their shouts of protest as they watched their prey slip away, not knowing how to follow.

Charlie and her friends hurried up the passage. The steep ascent required almost no effort with the added stamina from the Deep Spring water. How had she gone so long without its magic to help her? She felt like a new person, like she could do anything. She wanted to shout with the power that coursed through her veins. But the others would probably not appreciate the echo. She followed them out of the tunnel and through a tight cave entrance that opened right in the middle of a pine forest.

Bright sunlight cast long shadows beneath the thick canopy of fragrant pine trees. Charlie welcomed the sharp scent after the stale air from the tunnels. A thick layer of long brown pine needles covered the ground. Clusters of ferns hugged the tall, straight trunks of the long needle pines, and shrub-sized silverleaf oak rounded out the sparse vegetation.

Charlie closed her eyes for a moment to get a sense of which direction they should travel. Her head turned to the northeast, almost of its own accord. Something pulled her in that direction.

Max and Eliot spoke quietly to one another as they walked behind Charlie. Their voices sounded muffled and far away after the echo of the caves. Were they working on another map? What might it lead to? It really didn't matter anymore. She may not know their destination, but she knew which direction to go.

Pepper darted to little patches of bright goldenrod and vibrant colorful bunches of tiny blossoms to drink the sweet nectar. Between jaunts to new blossoms, she hovered beside Charlie and chatted about the flavors of the different flowers.

Juliette gathered bouquets of fern leaves mixed with stems of goldenrod and aster. She tied a string around the bunch and attached it to the outside of her pack. She gathered small reddish-orange-topped mushrooms and larger mushrooms with brown caps. She warned Max away from a patch of flowery looking white mushrooms. Max said he knew not to eat them, but that they glowed at night, and he wanted to harvest them for "other reasons."

Radcliffe walked just behind the Princess, silent as

usual.

The sound of a woodpecker tapping on a tree came from Charlie's right, while of a pair pine warblers called back and forth to one another with clear, steady trills. A squirrel bounded across Charlie's path, then skittered up the trunk of a pine and froze to watch the group walk past. A sense of peace settled over Charlie.

After several hours, Max suggested they stop to rest for the remainder of the evening. Charlie didn't feel tired at all. The Deep Spring water still worked its magic within her body. She agreed, for the sake of the others, that after their long journey through the tunnels and subsequent trek through the woods, it would be a good idea to stop and rest.

Juliette prepared the curled-up fern fronds and both kinds of mushrooms into a hearty, delicious stew with a nutty flavor.

After they ate, Charlie settled near Juliette.

"I miss my dad," Charlie started the conversation.

Juliette nodded.

"I know you miss Roxi, too."

"Yes. I do. But that is not the only thing on my mind." Juliette sighed. "I am worried about what may happen when we find Jessamine. It would break my heart to lose her forever."

Charlie knew that Juliette felt this way. She didn't think there was anything left of the old Jessamine to save, but she had avoided saying that to Juliette.

"It will work out, I'm sure. I wonder if Alder has found the forest people yet? Hopefully they are safe." She steered the conversation away from Jessamine.

"Alder is very capable. He will take excellent care of your father."

Charlie knew that, too. She actually felt confident now that she would be able to stop Jessamine before she lost her father. She itched to continue their journey. The pull toward the northeast did not stop, even though her progress had. It was difficult to ignore.

Pepper plopped onto Charlie's shoulder. "Radcliffe asked if he could talk to Max and Eliot *alone*. As if I care about anything he wants to talk to them about." She folded her arms and glared at Radcliffe.

Charlie chuckled. She glanced at Radcliffe and the brownies. Radcliffe had his canteen in front of him and looked like he was asking the brownies questions about it. What was he keeping from her? And why?

Her mind brushed those thoughts away, and the pull that Charlie had felt all day pulsed. Like it tried to tell her that none of this other stuff even mattered. She couldn't wait for morning so they could be on their way.

Heat and glowing flames surrounded Charlie. The smell of boiling sap and burning pine assaulted her nose. Smoke filled her lungs.

Charlie pulled her tunic up over her nose and mouth. With wide eyes, she turned in a circle. Where were the others?

"This way!" Radcliffe's voice came from behind.

She spun on her heels and ran toward it. A tree branch snapped above her and crashed to the ground. She jumped out of the way. Sparks and flames shot high above her head from the impact. Her way had been blocked.

A strong hand grabbed her arm and pulled her to her left. She followed Radcliffe as fast as she could go. She saw that the others raced ahead of her.

Flames licked at the trees and saturated the carpet of pine needles. They maneuvered through them, changing direction in a snap when new fires erupted.

The forest opened onto a field of knee high clumpy brown grass. The fire followed them. The field ignited in an instant. No matter which way she turned, the fire surrounded Charlie and her friends.

In the midst of the flames Charlie saw a red fox, nearly as large as Roxi. It had at least a dozen tails. It winked at Charlie, then turned and scurried away into the flames.

Christine Marshall

Chapter 22

The farther to the northeast they traveled, the stronger the pull on Charlie. She walked at a brisk pace. Max and Eliot had a difficult time keeping up. Radcliffe mentioned once that they might need to slow down, but Charlie dismissed his suggestion. She couldn't explain why, but they had to hurry.

The forest remained much the same. The images of the trees and ground on fire haunted Charlie, but she had not told the others about the dream. There was no reason to frighten anyone. But she wanted to get out of the forest as soon as possible.

She agreed to stop and rest late in the afternoon, but insisted they travel further before they set up camp for the night.

Dusk turned into darkness. They walked on.

Max loudly complained about his tired legs and sore

feet. Charlie ignored him and continued her march.

"Can't we stop to rest now?" Max finally hollered at Charlie from a fair distance behind.

Charlie was about to tell him no, but Radcliffe beat her to it.

"No, we must keep going." Radcliffe hurried past Charlie, who had paused to address Max.

"Come," he commanded.

Radcliffe's jaw muscles bulged on the sides of his face. His knuckles turned white around the handle of his battle axe. His eyes were hard and alert.

Charlie's heart rate increased. What could Radcliffe smell or hear that the others had missed?

"But we're tired and hungry," Max whined. "We've been walking for ages and we need to rest." Eliot nodded beside his brother.

"What is it, Radcliffe?" Charlie ignored the brownies and caught up with the centaur.

"Nothing. I just think it would be safer if we kept moving." Radcliffe avoided eye contact with her. He skimmed the shadows around them. What was he looking for? Or at?

A shiver ran down Charlie's spine. She knew that the brownies, Juliette, and Pepper were ready for a rest. Perhaps Pepper would last longer if she continued to slurp the nectar at the pace she had been going. But she didn't know how much longer the other three really could travel without burning themselves out. She knew that, overall, they still had a long way to go before they found Jessamine. Keeping a steady pace and resting as needed would be important to their journey. She didn't want to push anyone harder than necessary.

But the pull was so strong. She hadn't paid attention to the needs of the others. Guilt gnawed at her.

Now the look on Radcliffe's face and the way his hooves shifted on the ground told her that they were in danger.

"I agree with Radcliffe," she announced. "Let's keep moving."

"But…" Max started to argue.

Eliot placed a hand on his brother's arm and gave him the slightest shake of the head. His eyes had locked onto Radcliffe's face. Juliette nodded in agreement. They followed Radcliffe through the forest.

"Does he know where he's going?" Max whispered to Eliot.

"He's keeping us safe," Charlie answered in a low voice. She did not want to disturb the silence. She wanted Radcliffe to be able to hear any threat that might be in the forest.

From the edge of Charlie's line of vision, she thought she saw one of the shadows move. She whipped her head around. The forest was still. Charlie squinted to peer through the trees and into the canopy. She searched the darkness for anything out of the ordinary. There was no wind, not even a slight breeze.

Then she saw a shadow move again.

Her heart raced. What was in those trees, watching them? Stalking them? She reached down and gripped her sword with her sweaty hand.

A branch snapped beneath Charlie's foot. She jumped but managed to stifle a cry.

Radcliffe gave her a worried look.

She mouthed, "Sorry," at him, but stayed silent.

He led them at a careful pace through the forest. He

paused often to listen. Charlie watched her own footsteps closer.

Time slowed. Moisture beaded on Charlie's forehead and neck. The hand that gripped her sword ached. Memories of the dark creatures tickled her mind. It had been a while, a long while, since they had seen any. She shivered.

Pepper, hair alight and skin dark red, hovered close beside Charlie's face. "What do you think is out there?" Her voice barely came out above the whisper of butterfly wings.

Charlie glanced at her tiny friend. Her orange eyes were wide and her mouth turned down. She had her own toothpick of a sword steady in front of her.

Juliette's breath came fast. "I have no idea..."

Charlie had not heard the Princess sound so afraid before. Juliette normally would be able to tell what else moved within the forest. But with her connection to the animal kingdom severed, she was as in the dark as the rest of them.

Max and Eliot scurried, arms linked together, in front of Charlie but behind Radcliffe. Max had his canteen of dragon's blood in one hand. Smart, but hopefully it wouldn't come to that. Because if it did, then they were all doomed.

Radcliffe motioned for everyone to stop. They were near the center of a small clearing. Ferns and pine needles covered the ground. A large gap stretched between the pine trees on the opposite side.

Radcliffe's body stood still as a statue. He turned his head slowly, listening intently to something Charlie could not hear. His grip tightened on his battle axe. With careful movements, he reached up to unsheathe his sword.

Charlie's vision blurred around the edges. She squeezed her eyes shut, and then opened them again. Now was not the time to panic or pass out. She had to keep it together. She steadied her breathing and concentrated.

The brownies huddled together near Radcliffe's feet. Juliette stood close beside Charlie, her sword at the ready. Pepper hovered near Charlie's head. Her light had gone out, making her almost invisible in the darkness.

"What is it, Radcliffe?" Charlie tried to keep the fear out of her voice. She didn't do a very good job. Radcliffe's reaction to the situation was enough to grip Charlie's chest with fear.

"The moonlit hunt." He answered just loud enough for them to hear. His eyes did not stop searching the shadows.

"What is..?" Max started to ask, but Radcliffe shushed him.

"I must listen," he told the others.

They all stayed silent. Charlie strained her ears to hear something. She couldn't hear anything.

Whatever the moonlit hunt was, it didn't sound good. If it was a hunt, and they were the ones being hunted, then who- or what- was the hunter?

A moment later, Charlie found out.

A wolf emerged from the trees.

She had never seen a wolf that big before; as big as Radcliffe at least. It made no sound as it slipped out of the shadows. The grey, wiry hair on the back of its neck stood on end. A low snarl escaped from its long muzzle. Huge, sharp teeth gleamed below curled lips in the moonlight.

It took careful steps as it entered the clearing on four legs. But when it took a step closer, it transitioned to stand on its hind legs. Its eyes were eerily human-like. Its front legs hung beside its body like arms. Huge nail-like claws extended from its fingerlike toes at its side.

It tipped its head back and let out a long, haunted howl.

A chill ran down Charlie's spine.

At the same moment, Juliette took in a sharp breath right behind Charlie. Charlie turned her head. Another one of these strange wolves skulked to their left. It, too, entered the clearing on four legs, then stood on two.

Sweat trickled down Charlie's back. She turned the other direction where she saw two more.

"Werewolves," Max mumbled at her feet in a high voice.

Radcliffe stood tense beside her. He did not make the slightest move to defend himself. If he wasn't raging forward and going for the kill, then they must be in more danger than ever before.

Charlie's hands trembled. She had to hold her sword with both of them to keep it steady.

"How many are there?" Radcliffe asked the others without flinching a muscle.

Charlie dared not move. She heard Max and Eliot shuffle below as they counted.

"At least ten, that we can see," Max reported with a wavery voice.

What were they going to do? Radcliffe would not be able to defend them from a huge pack of enormous werewolves. On their hind legs, they stood head and shoulders taller than him.

Two of the wolves within Charlie's line of vision inched their way closer.

They bent forward at the waist with arched backs. She could see their skeletons beneath their scraggly fur. They held their arms out on either side and spread their finger-toes out.

Saliva flew from their mouths as some snapped their jaws. Others curled their lips and bared their massive mouths full of sharp teeth. They lurched forward, awkwardly walking upright on two elongated hind feet.

"They are coming closer," Juliette whimpered beside Charlie.

Charlie and Juliette squeezed against Radcliffe.

Radcliffe remained solid.

"What do we do?" Charlie whispered so quietly that she wasn't sure anyone heard her.

No one answered.

Moisture soaked through Charlie's clothes. She shivered in the chill night air. Her heart felt like it was going to burst out of her chest. Her stomach clenched tight. Her legs shook. Her mind raced to find a solution to their problem.

Even with her enchanted strength and regenerative ability from the Deep Spring water, she could not survive this kind of attack, let alone defend the others.

More wolves emerged from the forest.

Juliette pressed into Charlie's side. Her body shook, too.

Charlie could feel Radcliffe's heavy breaths behind her. He still had not made a move or issued a command.

Where was the voice now? She willed herself to have a vision. Or for a wood nymph or giant or something to break through the trees to rescue them!

The werewolves took slow predatory steps toward the

group. What were they waiting for?

The largest werewolf, closest to Radcliffe, let loose another howl. The haunting sound hung in the air longer than Charlie thought it should.

The others echoed their leader. Charlie saw several lick their lips with wicked gleams in their human-like eyes.

Charlie could feel Juliette shiver beside her. The brownies had never been so silent. Radcliffe had never looked so angry or stood so still.

This was it. They were all going to die.

The entire pack of werewolves lowered their stances, ready to spring forward. Their growls grew deeper and louder. They crouched low.

Then suddenly, something blinded Charlie.

She let go of her sword with one hand and shaded her eyes with her arm. The white-hot light moved so fast it left a trail of light behind it. It circled the group and zigzagged to the location of each werewolf.

A split second later, it stopped right in front of Charlie.

"THAT was annoying!" Pepper folded her arms and rolled her eyes. Then her flame went out.

Charlie shot her hand out just in time to catch Pepper before she fell to the ground.

Charlie's jaw dropped. Each of the werewolves lay in a crumpled heap on the ground. Each had a glowing spot on its chest. The smell of smoldering hair drifted through the clearing.

Radcliffe left the group so abruptly that Charlie nearly fell over. She hadn't realized how heavily she had leaned on him. She stumbled and regained her balance.

Radcliffe hurried around the circle. He inspected each werewolf body before he moved on to the next.

"It's safe. They're dead," he stated matter-of-factly. He returned his weapons to their sheathes on his back. "Thank you," he said to Pepper.

Pepper smiled wide with tired eyes. "Happy to help!" She sounded almost... cheerful.

Charlie tried to process what had happened. From what she could tell, Pepper had burst into white hot flame and flown at such a fast speed that she was able to kill the entire pack of werewolves almost instantly. Charlie had no idea

how she had had the guts to do it. Good thing she had been wearing her fire-impervious dragon armor, or else there'd be nothing covering her pale skin.

"It worked!" Max whispered.

Charlie whipped her head around. "Excuse me?" she glared at the brownie.

Max gulped. "Um, nothing?"

Pepper piped up. "Don't get mad, Charlie." Her voice was weak. "They gave me some fireweed powder. It's supposed to enhance flames. We thought it would increase the heat of my flame. You know, just in case." Pepper tried to sit up, but she dropped onto her back.

"What's wrong?" Charlie was worried about her tiny friend.

"It, like, burned too hot. Or something. I have no energy. I can barely lift my wings."

"Maybe... *don't* eat that again..." Max offered.

Pepper gave a weak nod.

Radcliffe huffed. "You could have caused serious damage."

Max started to protest.

Radcliffe interrupted. "But under the circumstances," he spoke over Max's whines. "This turned out to be a very good thing. Charlie, keep a close eye on the pixie."

Charlie wasn't about to take her attention away from Pepper. She had to make sure her tiny friend would recover.

"Let's get out of here," Max announced. The others agreed and they followed Radcliffe away from the carnage.

Only a few moments later, Juliette spoke in a worried voice. "Do you smell smoke?" She lifted her nose into the air and took a deep breath.

"Whoops…" Pepper sounded guilty.

"Fire!" Max yelled from behind Charlie.

Charlie turned around.

Fire engulfed the clearing.

"Run!" Radcliffe ordered.

Christine Marshall

Chapter 23

"**This** way, quick!" Radcliffe yelled at them.

Behind her, Juliette, and the brownies raced away from the fire.

Charlie stood frozen to the spot. Pepper propped herself on one elbow on Charlie's outstretched palm. The pixie's eyes looked like orange balls, they were so wide at the sight of the flames.

"Charlie, come on! Run! NOW!" Radcliffe grabbed her arm and pulled her in the direction the others had gone.

He let go of her arm and pushed her forward. "Faster!" he growled in her ear.

She snapped out of her daze and ran after the others.

The fire spread through the forest fast. The dry pine needles that blanketed the ground served as perfect fuel. In no time at all, the fire surrounded them.

Radcliffe galloped ahead of the group and led them on a crooked path through the trees. When the fire blocked their path, he maneuvered them in a different direction.

The smoke burned Charlie's throat and lungs and stung her eyes. She coughed behind the tunic that she held against her face.

Juliette stumbled in front of Charlie and fell onto both knees. Radcliffe circled back and picked her up. He looked at Charlie for a second, and she nodded. She was fine.

He carried Juliette's limp body in both arms and galloped even faster.

Charlie looked behind her. Max and Eliot struggled now, too. She maneuvered Pepper onto her shoulder and scooped up the little men. Pepper clung to Charlie's neck.

They had to get out of this death trap! Charlie willed herself to feel which way to go, but the pull toward the northeast hadn't changed. That may be their ultimate destination, but the fire raged in that direction.

They raced through the forest. Charlie dodged hot spots, ducked beneath low hanging branches on fire, and leapt out of the way of limbs falling from burned out trees. Her lungs burned from the smoke and heat, but the magic of the Deep Spring water dulled the pain to a manageable level.

The brownies both passed out in her arms before long. If only she had more of the Deep Spring water to give them!

If it hadn't been for the magic that coursed through Charlie's body, she never would have made it to the huge meadow of tall dry grass.

Radcliffe slowed, ready to set Juliette down and check on her.

But Charlie recognized this place from her dream. This was where she had seen the fox. With a ton of tails. That winked at her.

The flames would engulf this place.

"No, we have to keep going!" She ran past Radcliffe and entered the trees on the other side of the meadow.

The flames reached the meadow just as they exited. The fire spread so fast through the dry grass that they would not have been able to outrun it.

Radcliffe and Charlie raced through the trees on the other side of the meadow. There had to be some way to escape the inferno. If they didn't find it soon, then they would all die... except maybe Charlie. That's not how this was supposed to end.

Radcliffe sidestepped another flare up and took a sharp turn to the right. Another clearing opened in front of them, just past the smoldering trees. The ground in the clearing squished beneath Charlie's feet. Her boots sunk deep into the muck. Milkwort and pitcher plants grew in groups. Cattails huddled together in the center. Flora or fauna... or both? It didn't matter just then.

"Stop!" Charlie shouted to Radcliffe. "We'll be safe here."

They had stumbled upon a marsh. The sedges grew low. No trees or shrubs sprouted out of the ground except around the perimeter.

It didn't take long for the fire to reach the marsh. Flames licked the edges but did not come any closer. The wetness of the ground kept the fire at bay. The air filled with smoke, but neither the heat nor flames threatened them. The smoke rose above the cool air from the water. Near the ground the air remained clear enough.

Radcliffe paced in circles. The fire agitated him more than it did Charlie. His tail swished too much, and his jaw clenched tight. Soot had collected on his bulging muscles. Sweat dotted his forehead.

Charlie administered to Juliette and the brownies. She poured cool water over their faces and wiped them gently with her spare tunic. She dribbled water into their mouths. Instinct forced them to swallow a little. She held her breath and waited.

Juliette woke first. A wet cough shook her petite frame. Charlie rubbed her back as her lungs tried to expel the ash that had polluted them.

When Juliette's breathing cleared, she looked up at Charlie with red, watery eyes. "What happened?"

"We're safe, for the moment."

Max rolled onto his side and coughed up black gunk from his own lungs. Eliot joined him. They recovered quickly, as well.

Pepper watched the suffering of the group. Her wings drooped. "This is my fault." She hid her face in her hands.

"No, this is definitely not your fault." Charlie scooped Pepper into her hands. She held the pixie in front of her face and looked directly into her eyes. "You saved our lives back there."

Pepper shrugged. "But I set the forest on fire. I didn't mean to!"

Charlie smiled. "No one could blame you for this. Your flame may have started the fire, but it also rid the woods of the werewolves. Because of you we are safe. And countless others who would have become victims of the werewolves are safe, too. The fire is a small price to pay."

Max interrupted their conversation. "It's still safe, isn't it? From the werewolves, I mean."

"Yes," Radcliffe said, but offered no other words of reassurance.

Max let out a sigh of relief.

Everyone else settled down and, before long, drifted off to sleep. But Charlie stayed up the long into the night. The Deep Spring water still coursed through her. The pull to the northeast kept her from relaxing.

The fire burned its way past them and continued to smolder until Charlie couldn't keep her eyes open any longer.

Charlie found herself in the battlefield facing Jessamine.
Again.
In this dream, everyone on Charlie's side died.
Only Charlie survived.
Her heart broke.
Jessamine won.
"The balance must be restored."

She forced herself awake. These dreams of watching her friends die did not help her to understand how she was supposed to stop Jessamine. But she knew where they needed to go. Maybe she'd be able to end this before it came to people fighting and dying.

Anxiety to continue their journey warred within Charlie with concern for her friends. But they needed to rest. In the morning they all slept later than usual. When they awoke, they each stretched sore muscles and let out wicked coughs, their movements slow and stiff.

Charlie handed out dried berries and nuts for breakfast. She had already eaten as much as she wanted. She didn't have much of an appetite. The Deep Spring water provided her body the energy she required. She tried really hard to not be impatient, but her foot tapped on the ground while she waited to be on the move.

They were lucky to have survived that fire. And the werewolves, for that matter. And if it hadn't been for Charlie's dream the night before, they may have stopped in that first meadow and been consumed by fire.

What had that strange fox in her dream meant? She hadn't seen anything like it in real life, not before her dream, and not during their mad dash away from the flames.

"I didn't think there were any werewolves left in the world," Max interrupted Charlie's anxious thoughts.

The brownies huddled close to Juliette while they ate. Juliette didn't seem to mind. In fact, she looked like she needed their closeness as much as they needed hers. They were all pretty shaken from the night before.

Pepper had enough energy to hover but couldn't even manage to make her hair smolder let alone light. Charlie watched her try over and over as the others spoke.

"There aren't," grunted Radcliffe. "Or at least, there weren't supposed to be."

"Well, there aren't anymore, now, are there?" Max grinned at Pepper.

The pixie turned pink. "Where do werewolves come from anyway?"

Max shrugged. Eliot shook his head.

Charlie had no idea. Honestly, she didn't even know they existed until last night.

Juliette explained. "A long time ago, someone performed dark magic on a man. The night of the next full moon, the man turned into a wolf. He turned on those he cared for. As the last human thoughts raced through his mind, and before he could harm his loved ones, he fled into the surrounding wood."

Eliot had a nervous look on his face. Pepper rubbed her arms and shivered. Max had a gleam in his eyes and rubbed his hands together, like he couldn't wait to hear the rest.

"A few days later, someone found him lying on the ground, and, thinking he was dead, did not stop. But the man groaned, and the stranger moved nearer to see if he could help. He found the man with deep lacerations all over his body. The stranger took the man home and nursed him back to health.

"Nearly a month went by before the man became well enough to travel again. He thanked the kind stranger and departed to make his way home. But the trip took some time because of his injuries.

"After three days, there was another full moon. Thick, wiry hair sprouted across his entire body. His fingernails grew into claws. He could feel his arms and legs change shape. He felt his face as it stretched and changed into that of a wolf, with large canine teeth protruding from his jaws. He felt his mind slip away."

"Dun, dun dunnnnn..." Max hummed an ominous tune.

"Shhh!" Pepper scowled at him, then winked.

Juliette looked back and forth between the tiny people. She had a haunted look on her face.

"Sorry," Max looked sheepish. "Continue."

Juliette swallowed. "When he regained himself the following morning, he was horrified to discover that he lay in a sweaty mess on the ground. His clothes hung in loose strands on his body, torn to shreds and covered in blood. He could not remember what he had done or where he had gone while he was in the wolf form."

"Fearing what may happen if he did return home, he fled deeper into the forest until he happened upon an abandoned hunting cabin. Among the belongings he discovered within he found books. He tore out pages so he could document his experience."

Now Charlie shivered. She couldn't imagine how awful that would be. To feel yourself change, and then wake up knowing you had done something terrible but not knowing what you had done.

Juliette paused, then continued. "Sick about what he may have done, he wrote everything down that he could remember. The last words he wrote in his experiment journal were, 'Beware the full moon.'

"The next person to happen upon the cabin read his notes and took them to the nearest city. He asked if anyone knew about this, or had known the man, but no one had. They all believed that with his death the threat was gone."

"That makes sense! How could there have been more?" Pepper puzzled out loud. She gasped. "Unless…"

Juliette nodded. Her eyes stayed downcast. "Several months later, on another night of full moon, a young man and woman walked through the forest together. They were attacked by a wolf-like creature that stood on its hind legs. The woman managed to escape. No one believed her account. But then her friend appeared a few days later. He looked a little worse for the wear but seemed to be alright. Until the next full moon, when he turned on the woman and nearly killed her."

"How awful!" Pepper cried.

At the same time Max mumbled, "Wow!"

"Only then did the townspeople believe her story. They soon learned that all it took was a single bite from one of these creatures, that was not lethal, to turn the person who had been attacked into a werewolf. All month long the person who had been bitten would appear normal, but on the night of the full moon, they would transform into a hideous creature with only animal instincts, and attack anyone nearby."

"What did they do?" Radcliffe spoke in a low voice from behind Charlie. She would have thought that he had known about all of this already. But he was as engrossed in the story as everyone else.

Juliette met Radcliffe's gaze. "They learned how to protect themselves. Eventually they drove the werewolves from their own town. Years and years passed. Many worked to eradicate the world of these unnatural beasts. It has been a very long time since I have heard of any reports of werewolves in the land. I had believed them to be gone myself." A pained look crossed her face.

Charlie took a deep breath. Pepper had rid the forest of the werewolves. Even if more existed, the full moon had passed. At least they would be safe for now.

"That…." Max had a somber look on his face, "was an excellent tale. Well done, Princess." He stood and shook Juliette's hand to congratulate her.

Christine Marshall

Chapter 24

"We should get going." Charlie stood and shouldered her bag.

The others stood and stretched, then packed their own belongings to prepare for the day.

Charlie led the group northeast. Instead of a thick pine forest, though, they tromped through smoldering ashes and blackened tree trunks. Charlie could see far into the distance, which made it easier to find the path of least resistance.

The more Charlie thought about her friends suffering, the lost abilities of so many, the creatures captured by Jessamine, and the entire world out of balance, the angrier she became.

She allowed her anger to combine with the effects of the Deep Spring water. The added strength and stamina carried her along at a fast pace.

Juliette and the brownies had a difficult time keeping up. Their lungs were still raw from the smoke exposure.

Radcliffe had no trouble, of course, but he lagged behind with the others to ensure their safety.

Pepper rested on Charlie's shoulder when she grew tired of flying alongside Max and Eliot. "They're not talking much. It's kind of boring…" she had explained when she joined Charlie.

She left Charlie now and then to inspect the landscape for anything edible. She returned empty handed every time.

After several hours, Pepper zipped up to Charlie and told her that the others needed to rest.

"No, we can't rest now. We are almost there." The further they went, the stronger the pull. She had to keep going. She did not pause or slow her pace.

"Charlie," Pepper gestured at the others. "Look. They are tired. They can't keep going like this."

"Radcliffe can, they can ride him," Charlie stated without thinking.

Pepper paused in her flight and gasped.

Charlie turned her head to look at the pixie.

"Don't say that, Charlie. He's not a horse, you know," Pepper spoke softly.

Guilt poked at Charlie. She rubbed her temples and closed her eyes. The pull was so strong now. Charlie's head pounded. Stopping felt like torture.

She opened her eyes and looked back. She could barely make out the others through the burnt forest. They had stopped. Juliette sat on a fallen tree trunk. Radcliffe stood nearby. His sharp eyes stared right at her. Hopefully he hadn't heard what she said.

Charlie looked at Pepper. "I'm sorry, Pepper. You're right. We should take a break. And please, don't tell Radcliffe what I said, alright? He doesn't deserve that."

Pepper nodded.

Even though she didn't feel like she needed to rest in the slightest, Charlie sat next to Juliette on the charcoal log.

"How are you doing?" Charlie asked Juliette.

"Oh, fine," Juliette smiled weakly. Charlie knew that the Princess would never admit that she wasn't fine, but the weak smile told Charlie that she was exhausted.

Charlie examined the brownies who had stretched themselves out along the sooty forest floor and appeared to be asleep. Max made quite a show of snoring, at least Charlie knew some of it was exaggerated, at least for Max's part, but that the brownies must be exhausted, too.

Even Radcliffe leaned against a blackened tree with his eyes closed.

This trip was now much easier for Charlie than for everyone else. They wouldn't be able to keep her pace.

"I will go alone." She stood and brushed the black dust from her backside.

They met her statement with protests, gasps, and shaking heads.

Charlie held up her sooty hands. "Look, it's not that much farther. After we leave the forest, there's a small hill to climb, and in the valley beyond is a city. She's in there, somewhere. With the water giving me a boost, I can get there in no time."

"But what will you do once you're there?" Pepper's face turned red. "It's not like you can stroll through the gates and ask around for Jessamine. And even if you could, what would you do once you found her?" She looked at Charlie with pleading eyes. "If you know where to go, then we'll make our way there together. We don't have to rush!"

"The pixie is correct." Radcliffe opened his eyes and

stared at Charlie. "You are too well known by now to go into the city looking for her. She must have spies everywhere. And many of them are probably not human. Or kind." Radcliffe growled the last part.

Charlie hadn't really thought the whole thing through. But the pull was *so strong*. And she was tired of struggling against it. She was tired of all the suffering in the world. She wanted everything to go back to normal. She wanted to stop growing up too fast. She wanted to rescue her dad. To go home. She wanted Jessamine's power over everyone to end. She wanted her friends to have their abilities back. She couldn't stand waiting for her friends to rest and recover, and then need to rest again. Not when she had so much bottled-up energy. Not when she was so close.

"I don't know what I'll do when I get there." The words rushed out of her. "But I'll figure it out. I know I will."

"You could wear the hat." Eliot still lay flat on the ground, his arms folded beneath his head, face toward the sky, ankles crossed, and eyes closed. She hadn't even realized he had woken up.

"What?" He always spoke in riddles. She didn't have time for this.

"The hat," Eliot said again. "You could wear it. And then no one would see you."

Max sat up. "That's a great idea!" His eyes shone with excitement. "Can you imagine how far you could go and all the things you could swipe... I mean... see... if no one knew you were there?" His voice rose and a smile spread across his face. "I'll do it, if you don't want to..."

Charlie's mind whirled for a second. What were they talking about? Then she remembered. The small, leather hat they had stolen from the City of Giants all those months ago.

She had tucked it into her bag and hadn't given it another thought. Not with everything else they had been through since then. But Eliot was right. If she wore the hat and was invisible, she could easily sneak into the city and pinpoint Jessamine's location. With any luck, she could defeat her, too, without putting any of her friends in harm's way. It was the perfect solution.

Charlie dug the hat out of her pack and held it out in front of her. It shimmered slightly in the afternoon sun, nearly weightless in Charlie's hands. She turned it around and inspected it from all angles. What was it made from? How did it work?

"Just put it on." Max's eyes gleamed and he bounced on his feet. His hands twitched, like he wanted to wear it himself.

Charlie held the hat over her head. She slowly lowered it into place. She could still see her hands when she held them out in front of her, but from the gasps and the way everyone looked at slightly the wrong spot, she could tell that she had become invisible. A subtle warmness trickled from the top of her head. It tickled her back and arms as it spread over her entire body. Combined with the effects of the Deep Spring water, Charlie felt invincible.

She didn't want anyone to try to talk her out of what she meant to do. She didn't make a sound.

Everyone still looked fleetingly at the place where Charlie stood.

Charlie's heart thumped in her chest. Without a word of farewell to her friends she jogged on light feet away from the camp.

As soon as the others realized what she had done, they

called out to her.

Her heart broke a little. If things didn't go well, she may not return. But what else was she supposed to do? She had to protect them.

Her dreams always showed a huge battle. And her friends, either some or all of them, always died in the fight. She couldn't let that happen. She couldn't lose anyone else.

It didn't take long to make her way out of the forest and across the remaining grasslands. She crested one final hill and viewed the valley below. There at the bottom of the wide gulch rested a city. From the view of the grasslands, one would never know it was there. It was only visible from the surrounding hilltops. It would be easy to miss.

Why had Jessamine chosen this particular place for refuge? It would be easily defeated in an attack. Charlie could only assume that not many people knew of its location.

Charlie gazed down on it for several minutes. She oriented herself to the layout of everything. She could easily see it all. The valley stretched out all around the city. It hosted farms and grazing pastures for sheep and goats. A central road went from one end to the other. The farms skirted the perimeter, with more huts and small houses closer together nearer the city gates.

A low wall, maybe only twice as tall as Charlie, built out of smooth stones, surrounded the city. Within the wall, two-story buildings created a circular pattern around a central courtyard, divided by more cobblestone roads. Charlie imagined the buildings to be shops and boarding houses. On one side of the courtyard stood several larger buildings that most likely housed the governing individuals. That's where she would find Jessamine.

The city bustled with activity. More than just humans lived within its walls. From this distance, she couldn't make out distinct shapes, but she recognized the forms of half-goat-half-human fawns, tall nymphs with flowy cloaks, squat hairy shapes with pointed hats, and plenty of beasts of burden of a variety of species. How many of them were under Jessamine's control? What dangers lay below for Jessamine's enemies?

The ability to sneak around unseen gave Charlie confidence that she wasn't used to. She would be able to stroll right through the heart of the city, undetected, march right up to Jessamine, and cut her down where she sat.

She didn't want to kill anyone. The thought made her stomach turn. But how else would she stop Jessamine?

Charlie slid sideways down the steep hillside. She jogged through fields and hopped over fences and made her way toward the city gates.

Once she arrived, she paused. She thought about her father aging and dying far away; about her friends who had lost their homes, their abilities, and their families. She thought about the creatures being kidnapped and their souls being used for evil, never to be restored. She allowed the sadness and anger to well up inside of her to a whole new level.

Then she rushed through the city gates. She didn't care that she bumped and pushed others out of her way. She wasn't concerned by the frightened cries and curious questions of those around her. She just pressed forward.

She zigzagged through the shops and buildings. She avoided the busiest roadways and alleys, and easily changed directions when she encountered crowds too large to maneuver through.

In no time she stood at the edge of the circular courtyard. She faced the large government building that loomed over the center of the city. The front was lined with enormous stone pillars. Arches stretched between each one. In the center two wooden doors with gilded trim, almost tall enough for a giant, stood firmly closed.

This was it. The pull led right to that building. Right inside those doors. Jessamine would be in there. Charlie could end everything.

The balance was about to be restored.

She took a deep breath and let it out slowly. Just as she took a step forward, a hand clenched her arm. Tight.

She stopped short. She whirled around and wrenched her arm free. At the same time, she unsheathed her sword.

Chapter 25

"**Don't** hurt me!"

In front of her stood a guy about her age with his hands out in front of him. An easy smile spread across his face. "I didn't mean to startle you!" His golden eyes sparkled, and his reddish-golden, wavy hair shone in the sunlight. He chuckled. "I'm Beau." He stretched his hand toward her.

Charlie's eyes darted from his face to his hand, and back again. She kept her sword pointed at him. Should she fight or flee?

But then a thought struck her like lightening. How could he see her? Had the magic of the cap worn off? Was that even possible? She could still feel its warmth envelope her, so she should still be invisible. The brownies didn't say anything about the effects wearing off. She gripped her sword tighter and swallowed hard.

The confusion must have shown on her face, because Beau leaned a little closer and stage-whispered, "It's alright, no one else can see you…"

Charlie jumped at his movement. She almost stabbed him with her sword, but just as quickly he backed a step out of her reach.

"How… who…. How can you…?" Charlie stammered. Who was this guy?

"I can see the invisible. It's a gift," Beau shrugged and kept smiling at Charlie. His perfect, white teeth shone, and his eyes crinkled at the corners.

Charlie shook her head. She would not let him distract her from her task.

"Nice to meet you," she said coolly. "I've got to go."

She returned her sword to her side and turned away from Beau. She was about to take a step toward the large building across the courtyard when she felt a hand on her arm once more.

She turned back toward Beau and snapped, "What?" as she yanked her arm free again.

"Don't go," he pleaded. "I haven't even learned your name." The charming smile had not left his face.

Charlie wondered how someone could smile that much without their face hurting. But it also reminded her of Juliette a little. Well, the way she used to be, when Charlie first met her. She had smiled that much, too. Maybe Beau could be trusted.

She took a deep breath and glanced over her shoulder at the building.

"I'm Charlie." She kicked herself inwardly for giving him her real name. Too late, though. "Nice to meet you. But I really do need to go…"

"What's the hurry? No one's there right now, anyway." Beau pointed at the government building.

Had Charlie been that obvious about her destination?

Well, yes, she supposed she had been, since she had assumed that no one could see her. She would have to have a little talk with Max and Eliot about the fact that this hat wasn't fool proof.

She wanted to rush into the building, find Jessamine, and get this all over with. She was so close. But if Jessamine wasn't even in there, then what was the point? And if she left Beau behind, there was the chance he might let slip that he had seen her. She had no idea who he was or who he might talk to.

She groaned inwardly. She pasted a fake smile on her face. She would have to gain his trust in order to feel safe. She couldn't have him talk about her to the wrong person. The invisibility cap would be useless if Jessamine found out Charlie was here. If some random guy could see her, then Jessamine surely had a way to detect Charlie's presence.

She stuck out her hand for Beau to shake.

Beau's smile grew unbelievably wider.

Charlie inwardly rolled her eyes. Who did he think he was, anyway?

He shook her hand.

A strange tingling traveled up her arm. She allowed his hand to linger.

Their eyes locked. Charlie's cheeks warmed. She slid her hand from his and averted her eyes. Butterflies fluttered in her stomach. The tingling spread down to her toes.

"Shall we?" Beau stretched his arm toward one of the streets that led away from the town center.

Charlie nodded and followed him, just a half step behind.

After a few moments, the butterflies had gone, and the

tingling had stopped. Who was this outgoing, handsome young man that could see her even though she was invisible? How could he even tell she was supposed to be invisible? And where was he leading her?

A small voice in the back of her mind told her that maybe she shouldn't blindly follow him. Maybe it was a trap. But then her heart sped up. That feeling she had when he had gazed into her eyes. And when their hands had touched. She blushed again. Her lips twitched at the corners as if they wanted to smile.

"Are you hungry?" Beau tossed the words over his shoulder. His golden eyes flashed when he looked at Charlie.

"Uh, sure." Every time he looked at her like that, it was just a little harder to concentrate. And breathe.

Beau led Charlie to a little bakery with tables and chairs lined up in front of the brick façade. Words had been etched and painted on a wooden sign that hung perpendicular to the building, just above the door. *Sally's Oven.* Below the words, a drawing had been etched into the wood: two bread loaves on two crossed oven peels that looked like flat shovels on poles.

"Sal makes the best spiced honey biscuits I've ever tried. You'll love them!" Beau walked to the counter and ordered two buns.

Charlie wasn't sure what a spiced honey biscuit was, and she wasn't sure how she was supposed to sit and eat one with Beau without it looking strange. She already wondered how it might look for him to be talking to himself as they walked along the street and into the pastry shop. Her clothes were invisible under the cap. Would the biscuit turn invisible when she took it from him?

Beau took the paper-wrapped pastries from the petite, red-headed girl behind the counter. He winked at her instead of paying for them. The girl blushed and fluttered her eyelashes when Beau said he would see her later.

Charlie's heart somersaulted. How could Beau flirt with that girl when he liked Charlie? Charlie was prettier than that girl had been, right? If anything, she was stronger. And she could heal fast, and run fast, and fight really well, and...

Charlie stopped herself. Why was she jealous about a guy she had just met? What was her problem, anyway? She had a job to do and couldn't afford these petty problems to distract her. It's not like she was sticking around here. But maybe Beau would join her and her friends as they traveled back home? Maybe...

She jumped slightly when Beau poked her in the side with his elbow. "You coming?"

She vaguely nodded and followed him outside. When he was about to take a seat at one of the little tables, Charlie found her voice again.

"Wait," she said, still standing. "Won't it look strange for you to be sitting here talking to an empty seat?"

Beau's eyes flashed again. He smiled up at her with that smile she was beginning to really like. "Why, you are absolutely right! What could I have been thinking? We do need to find somewhere a little more private to talk, don't we?"

Charlie smiled back at him and nodded. "Where should we go?"

Beau looked thoughtful for a moment, then said, "Well, where are you staying? Perhaps we should return there?"

This caught Charlie off guard. She had expected him to think of an out of the way corner, or a secluded park beyond the city center. Now she had to decide how much she wanted to tell him. She stood there dumbfounded as she tried to figure out what to say.

Beau watched Charlie with an easy smile. He draped an arm across the back of the chair next to his. One ankle rested on the opposite knee. His relaxed posture and comfortable disposition calmed Charlie. She decided to trust him. At least a little.

"I'm not... well, you see... I'm not staying..." It was hard to lie to him. She swallowed and started again. "I'm not staying in the city. I'm... passing through." She settled on a little bit of truth at a time for now. "My camp is outside the city, beyond the farmlands and into the grasslands a ways. It's kind of far..."

Beau stood up. "What are we waiting for then?" His smile never faltered.

He handed Charlie her biscuit. She hesitated. "Will it be, you know, invisible, too?"

"Sure, it will." Beau waved his hand in the air as if to wave her worries away. "You have nothing to fear. Your secret is still safe." He winked at her.

Charlie relaxed a little more. Her stomach grumbled. She took the first bite of the biscuit. She hadn't realized how hungry she had been. She was so focused on her task, that she hadn't thought much about food. And the Deep Spring Water gave her energy, so she hadn't needed to eat.

The biscuit was sweet on her tongue, but then as she chewed it, a hint of spice spread around her mouth. The bread was soft and fluffy; it melted as she ate.

"This is amazing!" She took another bite and chewed slowly to savor the flavors.

"Told you!" Beau let out a hearty laugh.

His laugh danced around her. That tingling sensation returned. There was definitely something about Beau that made her feel good.

They walked through the city toward the gates, back the way Charlie had come. Beau pointed out things Charlie had missed on her way in. The merchant guild district was to their left.

"That's where the court houses are located, and political meetings are held. The tax collectors are down that way too. Better steer clear!" Beau laughed and pulled Charlie's arm, like he wanted to protect her from the tax collectors.

Charlie laughed and playfully pushed back.

"The craft guilds take up most of the streets that way." Beau pointed to their right.

Charlie saw street signs with names like *Makers Street* and *Crafters Lane*. The bottom floors of each building down the cobblestoned streets held markets, while the upper stories that jutted over the dirty road must have been apartments for the shopkeepers. Various signs of simple ironwork hung above the different doors. She saw large scissors, a cauldron with a stirring stick, a shoe, a wagon wheel, and a horseshoe. Smells of burning wood and heated metal wafted around her, and her ears rang from the hammering, grinding, and sawing being done. The herby scents of the apothecary nearly made her sneeze.

Down the next few streets her mouth watered at the smells of fresh baked bread, cooking meat, and a sour yet sweet smell of the brewery.

Merchants and craftsman called to one another, some taunting, some jovial.

Several large inns and guildhalls framed the city gate. The bathhouse stood in between two of them, steam pouring from vents in the roof. Taverns occupied a corner of each of the buildings.

"The church district is that way," Beau said, pointing to the left.

Charlie nodded. A steeple with a bell tower rose above the other, shorter buildings.

"And the storehouses and stables are around back that way." Beau leaned across Charlie and pointed behind the public buildings. Charlie could just make out the sounds of animals.

She grew more fascinated with her surroundings, and with the boy who walked beside her. When she asked him questions about himself, his funny answers came quick. Charlie laughed. A lot. She hadn't had a reason to laugh in so long. What a relief to let go of her worries as the afternoon melted into evening.

The sun sunk below the horizon. The sky over the grasslands turned brilliant shades of red, orange, and pink. They blended with the blue of the darkening sky behind them into lavender and indigo. Charlie marveled out loud at the beauty. She delighted in the good day she had had, and the good luck in finding someone who could help them.

Chapter 26

Radcliffe and Juliette had made a good camp with a small fire in the center. Charlie took off the invisibility cap. The warm, safe sensation peeled away from her. She took in a sharp breath, surprised at the chill in the air and the uneasy feeling that now settled over her. She swallowed hard a couple of time. Her hands grew clammy.

"Are you alright?" Beau reached out and pulled her to a stop with one of his big, warm hands. Her arm tingled where he touched her. She sighed.

"Yeah," she said. "I'm fine. Really, I'm good."

He looked at her doubtfully.

She smiled at him which eased his worried expression.

"Good, you seemed… surprised by something," he prodded.

"No, it's fine. Let's go meet my friends." Charlie grabbed Beau's hand and pulled him toward the camp.

"Hey guys! I'm back!" Charlie rushed forward. She smiled wide at all her friends, very aware of Beau's presence beside her.

Her friends' reactions weren't what she wanted. Juliette gave a polite smile to Beau, then looked at Charlie with a question in her eyes. Radcliffe looked up from the food that cooked over the fire. His face wrinkled into an angry scowl. Max and Eliot eyed her from where they were huddled over a piece of parchment, surprised at the presence of an outsider. Charlie didn't see Pepper around at all.

Charlie had been welcoming to each of them when she had met them. But they didn't want to accept Beau? She frowned at the group.

She introduced them to her new friend. "I met him in the city. He can help us."

Radcliffe stretched himself to his full height and crossed his huge arms. Juliette walked over to Charlie and gently wrapped her hand around Charlie's arm to pull her aside. Away from Beau.

Charlie glanced back at him. She gave an apologetic smile. He kept on smiling and shrugged.

Juliette whispered to Charlie, her voice strained. "We were worried about you when you left so suddenly. What has happened? Who is this?"

Charlie shook off Juliette's hand. "I'm fine. And I told you, his name is Beau. He knows stuff."

"But how do you know that he can be trusted? You have only just met him…"

"So?" Charlie didn't let her finish. "We've trusted other people we've 'just met.' I trusted you and you trusted me. Why shouldn't we trust him?"

Why was Juliette so worked up about this? It wasn't that big of a deal.

"I apologize." Juliette rubbed Charlie's arm and gave it a squeeze. "You are right. We shall give him a chance."

Charlie noticed she still looked concerned. She rolled her eyes inwardly but smiled back at her friend.

Juliette approached Beau and held out her hand to introduce herself. Even though he stood right in front of Juliette, he just waved awkwardly. Juliette dropped her hand to her side and gestured toward the fire.

She introduced him to Radcliffe and the brownies. Charlie followed close behind. Radcliffe did not relax his aggressive stance. Max gave him a short "Hi," and a polite wave. Eliot just stared at him for a long second, then continued to work on the parchment laid out before him.

Charlie wanted to brush the paper aside and shake Max and Eliot for being so rude. She took a deep breath.

"Ignore them," she whispered to Beau. "They're not worth your time. Come on, let's get something to eat."

As she returned to the fire with Beau, she dismissed the hurt look on Max and Eliot's faces. And the anger that rolled off Radcliffe in great waves. She also ignored the small gasp that Juliette gave. She pretended not to notice Juliette lean down and apologize for her own rude behavior. But they deserved it. They should be treating Beau as a guest, not as an intruder. Which he wasn't.

She handed Beau some of the vegetables and meat that Radcliffe had cooked in the fire. He took it graciously.

Then she remembered Pepper. The pixie hadn't appeared since she returned. Where was she? Still annoyed with everyone, and not ready to make amends, she didn't ask for Pepper's whereabouts.

As they ate, Beau leaned close. "What's going on? You seem upset."

"Yeah." Charlie slowly chewed her food and thought about her feelings. It was kind of weird for her to be so annoyed with everyone. But when she thought about letting it go, it didn't want to go away.

Beau rested a hand on her arm. Warmness spread up her arm. It was a strange sensation, but it pushed away her negativity.

"Don't worry," he said, "everything will be fine." He lifted his hand and the good feelings stayed.

Her stomach flipped a little and her heart sped up. She was a great judge of character and there was no way she would fall for someone she couldn't trust. Wait, was she falling for him? She must be because she had never felt like this around anyone else before. Well, maybe Alder. He was also very good looking and made her laugh and feel happy. She had known him for a long time. But that was different. They were just friends.

This feeling with Beau, it was so much more. Butterflies fluttered in her stomach again and she suppressed a smile that wanted to take over her face. She scooted a little closer to Beau on the ground in front of the fire until their knees touched.

Charlie avoided the others as the evening passed. She didn't look at anyone and only spoke with Beau. Her friends still looked at him with suspicion and huddled together from time to time. To talk about Beau, she was sure.

Evening bled into night. One by one the others lay down to sleep. Except Radcliffe. He continued to sit on the other side of the fire and stare at Charlie and Beau.

Eventually Charlie spread out her blanket and stretched out on it to try to sleep. Beau stayed by her side.

She only thought of him as she drifted off with a smile on her face.

In the middle of the night, someone prodded her awake. She opened groggy eyes and saw Max's blurry face right in front of her. He held his finger to his mouth as she rubbed sleep from her eyes. He motioned for her to follow him.

She reluctantly complied. He led her out of earshot of the campsite where she found Juliette, Eliot, and Radcliffe. Still no Pepper.

"What is this?" She kept her voice low.

"We need to talk," Radcliffe stated evenly.

Charlie looked up at him. His face still looked angry.

"There's nothing to talk about." She still didn't believe that Beau was a problem that needed to be discussed.

"Charlie, at least tell us what happened when you left yesterday," Juliette urged.

Charlie sighed. She had only been away from them for the daylight hours of one day, but it felt like ages ago when she took off without saying goodbye. She recounted her snap decision to go in search of Jessamine herself, at which Radcliffe let out a snarl that Juliette silenced with a stern look. He rolled his eyes and folded his arms but stayed silent.

Charlie told them about the journey through the city and to the city center, where she believed she would find Jessamine.

"But before I could make my way across the courtyard to the building, Beau saw me."

"Why weren't you wearing the cap?" Eliot spoke like he was talking to an idiot.

"I *was* wearing the cap. Beau saw me even with the cap on." She had to admit to herself that it felt kind of good to be noticed like that. Her mouth twitched with a smile. "He said he has the ability to see the invisible. Or something like that." She shrugged.

"Something about him feels... off," Radcliffe said. "And how can he see invisible things? This doesn't sit right."

Charlie huffed. "I don't know why he can see stuff he shouldn't. Why can Eliot make maps, or Juliette talk to animals?" Charlie defended her new friend.

"Well, actually there are very good explanations..." Max began, but Charlie wouldn't let him finish.

"I don't care," Charlie spat. She rubbed her forehead.

"Look, all I know is he knew where I was going, and he told me that Jessamine wouldn't be there. All the leaders of the city have gone off somewhere, and she's with them. So, my whole trip into the city was pointless anyway. I figured he might have more information that we can use to locate Jessamine."

"How much does he know about us?" growled Radcliffe.

"I didn't really tell him much," Charlie replied. "Just that we are travelers. That's all."

"Good. Don't tell him anything," Radcliffe commanded.

Charlie rolled her eyes. "I don't know why you guys don't trust him, and why you felt like we had to have a sneaky conversation about all of this. You could have just asked me before. I'm not going to tell him everything. I just think if we are strategic, we can get some information out of him."

"That's all, huh?" Max elbowed Eliot and winked.

Charlie blushed. "Yes, that's all." Had her blushing and butterflies been that obvious?

"Whatever you say." Max wiggled his eyebrows at Charlie.

Charlie looked around at her companions. She knew she should be cautious like they wanted her to be, but she also felt different than she had before. She wanted to see where it would go. That wasn't so wrong.

She wished Pepper was here. She always took Charlie's side on things. That reminded her... "Where's Pepper?" she asked Juliette.

Juliette bit her lip, as if she was afraid to answer the question.

Had something happened to Pepper? It couldn't have, or

they would have told her right away. Charlie took a deep breath and stopped her mind from inventing a worst-case scenario.

"Well," Juliette finally said, "after you left without telling anyone what you were up to… Pepper tried to follow you."

"Oh," was all Charlie could say.

"I imagine it was probably impossible to actually follow you, since she could not see you. She has not returned." Juliette had worry lines around her eyes.

Charlie knew part of this was her own fault. She had done enough to make Juliette worry, and now she had led Pepper on a wild goose chase, too.

"When will things start to go right?" Charlie asked, mostly to herself.

"Um, how about, the day after never?" Max laughed at his own joke.

"Why do you crack jokes about everything?" Charlie snapped at the brownie.

"What else am I going to do?" He scowled at her. "I can either laugh or cry. Who wants to cry all the time? So, I choose to laugh." He rolled his eyes at her. "You should try it sometime." He then gestured for Eliot to follow him back to the camp.

Radcliffe went next, not speaking again.

Juliette stayed with Charlie.

"Seriously, though, Juliette. Nothing goes right. It feels useless to even try anymore. Jessamine is always one step ahead of us. And who are we against her armies, anyway? I don't even know how we're supposed to find her now. I really felt a pull to the city, and then I find out she's not even there?" Charlie shrugged at Juliette.

"All hope is not lost. As long as we keep trying, keep fighting, we have the chance of victory. You will see." Juliette gave Charlie a sad smile and a quick hug. Then she pulled Charlie by the hand toward camp.

Charlie tucked herself back into her makeshift bed and fell asleep.

Jessamine stood alone on the dry grassy battlefield. Charlie saw no sign of the army she usually saw in these dreams. Jessamine looked lost and scared.

Charlie heard movements from behind. She turned around. An entire army stared daggers at Jessamine. Humans, dwarves, animals, giants, weapons at the ready, all on Charlie's side. They geared up to charge. The woman did not stand a chance.

Charlie's heart raced. This is what she thought she wanted. Jessamine would be stopped. The balance would be restored.

But instead of joining the army, she raced ahead to stand between the warriors and Jessamine.

"Stop!" She held out her hands in front of her. What was she doing??

Jessamine cowered behind Charlie as the fighters rushed toward them.

"No!" The cry escaped Charlie's lips.

"The balance must be restored."

Christine Marshall

Chapter 27

Charlie sat up. Stars dotted the night sky. Beau breathed in a steady rhythm on the ground beside her. The others remained asleep, too.

She stood and slipped away from the group. She needed to clear her mind.

She analyzed every detail from the new dream. The battlefield had been the one she had seen in many of her previous dreams: the distant mountain, open space, dry clumps of grass that blanketed red soil.

But why the change? Why was the army on Charlie's side now? And why in the world did Charlie try to stop them? It made no sense! Their whole mission was to stop Jessamine. Why had Charlie tried to save her?

Fear gripped her heart. She had been acting strange toward her friends. She defended a guy she barely knew. And now she saw herself protect Jessamine? What was wrong with her? Was she turning bad or something?

She tried to focus on her breathing and see something again, but nothing came. Before she knew it, the sun began to lighten the sky. Morning had come.

She returned to camp, where Beau waited for her near the freshly stoked fire.

"Are you alright?" His amazing smile lit up his face.

She blushed. He was good looking and everything, but why had she brought him here? A funny feeling knotted her stomach.

She sat on her blanket to pack her bag. He reached a hand to her arm. That same warm, tingly feeling tickled her. It calmed her. She met his gaze and returned his warm smile. She needed him. That's why she had brought him back. How could she have forgotten? Her other worries slipped away.

She teased Beau. He poked and tickled her. Beau helped her pack her things. She brought him some breakfast.

The others kept a close eye on him. When no one noticed, she rolled her eyes at them. Beau chuckled and she giggled back. What was so wrong about having fun even in a difficult situation, anyway?

When Beau left to help gather firewood, Charlie offered to go with him. But Radcliffe asked her to stay.

Beau gave Radcliffe an almost-annoyed look.

Radcliffe glared icy daggers back.

Charlie urged Beau to go without her. She didn't want anything worse to happen between Beau and Radcliffe. She shuddered.

"We need to discuss…" Radcliffe began.

Charlie interrupted. "I trust him. You should too." She crossed her arms.

Max smirked and elbowed Eliot. "Told ya!" she heard

him say to his brother.

She ignored the brownies.

Radcliffe answered Charlie between gritted teeth. "*I* do not trust him. But that is not the purpose of this conversation."

Charlie sighed.

"We need to discuss our next move. Do we stay and wait for Jessamine to return? When will that be? We need guidance." He looked at Charlie expectantly.

Charlie no longer felt a pull in any direction. She hadn't had any dreams about where they should go next. Eliot still couldn't draw a map for them. And Jessamine should return to the city any day now. She shared her thoughts with the group.

"We need to obtain further information about Jessamine," Juliette noted.

"Maybe you can ask your 'friend' for help." Max poked fun at Charlie some more.

"Yes. See what you can find out from him." Radcliffe paused to give Charlie a serious glare. "And do not tell him anything he does not absolutely need to know, do you understand?" Radcliffe sounded like a parent scolding a misbehaving child.

"Yes, sir." Charlie bit back a snappier comeback.

What had come over her? She never treated anyone this way. "Sorry," she mumbled to Radcliffe.

The centaur nodded, then stalked away. "I am going to hunt." He did not look back.

"Still no sign of Pepper?" Juliette asked Charlie.

Charlie was glad for the change of subject, but also worried to death about her tiny friend. The last time Pepper had disappeared, Charlie had assumed the worst. She would not allow herself to sink down that hole again. She pushed the negative thoughts from her mind and shook her head at Juliette.

Max and Eliot scampered off together. To make mischief, no doubt.

Beau came back a little later with a small armful of firewood. What had taken him so long? That wasn't much wood for the amount of time he had been gone.

He set the wood down and slung an arm across Charlie's shoulder. Where his hand touched the skin on the back of her neck, warmth blossomed.

It felt good to have him by her side again.

Charlie tried to get Beau to tell her something important that could help them. He always answered with some witty or funny comment that made Charlie laugh. She would forget what she had asked. Later she would realize that she never did get him to tell her anything. She would feel frustrated and defeated. The cycle repeated itself over and over.

The behavior started to annoy her. Couldn't he be serious for one conversation? But then he would do or say something cute or funny, and she would forgive him.

He asked her a lot of questions about what she was up to, what she seemed worried about, and why she traveled with such an "interesting" group of companions.

Charlie guarded her answers, but also found herself relieved to talk to someone about everything. Gradually she revealed more and more of their plans to him, but without ever actually naming Jessamine. She talked about her father aging too fast and how scared she was that she would never see him again. She told him about how her home had been destroyed, though she didn't tell him exactly how. She didn't specifically talk about her friend's abilities, but she did allude to the fact that Juliette's sadness stemmed from the fact that she didn't feel as connected to the world as she used to. She had been vague enough to not have to worry that he knew too much.

She constantly waited for some sign of Pepper's return. Her head often turned the direction of the city. Had something bad happened to Pepper? If she hadn't known Jessamine was gone, she would be worried that Pepper had been caught, and had her soul sucked out of her. The thought made Charlie shiver. She held on to hope that her friend would return at any time.

At night Charlie snuck away from Beau to give her report to the others. She told them that she hadn't learned much but that she would keep trying. They didn't say anything about him to her anymore, but she could tell from the looks they gave each other that they still thought of Beau as a threat.

The others asked about her dreams. She didn't know how to tell them that her dreams had changed. Instead of fighting Jessamine and losing, she helped Jessamine instead. In one dream Jessamine collapsed with fear. Charlie reached out a hand to help her stand. In another, Charlie stood between her own army and Jessamine to protect her. Jessamine's army either didn't appear or else they retreated when things escalated between the two women.

No matter what, though, everyone on Charlie's side survived. Because they did not fight. She chose to not tell the others. If she didn't understand her dreams, they certainly would not. She kept her new dreams to herself.

"How do you plan to solve your problems, Charlie?" Beau sat beside Charlie on a log a little away from the others. "It sounds like that is what you and your friends are trying to do. You are trying to find a solution, right?" He rested his hand on her knee.

How should she answer him?

She stumbled over her reply. "Well, I think that if we... I mean, there's probably someone... or something, that's connecting everything. Together. You know? Some underlying problem that is causing all these things to be happening..."

As she tried to spit out something coherent, she heard Juliette let out a cry behind her.

"Pepper! You have returned!" The Princess rushed away from camp.

Charlie turned and stood, excited to see her little friend again. The pixie flew straight toward Charlie. Charlie smiled wide and called the pixie's name. Pepper must have missed her as much as Charlie had missed the pixie.

"What do you think you're doing, Charlie?" Pepper's voice rose and that's when Charlie noticed the pixie's crimson body and her glowing hair.

Charlie stopped dead and stammered, "What do you mean??"

"Why are you talking to a kitsune?? You know they can't be trusted, right?" Pepper waved her arms wildly at Charlie.

"A... what?"

"A kitsune. That creature that you sat next to on the log? The human sized fox with a dozen tails?"

What was Pepper talking about?

Juliette's eyes were wide.

Charlie turned to look at Beau. He was gone.

She rushed over to the log. She searched the tall grass for some sign of where he had gone. There was no sign of him. No trail into the grass, no indication that he had been there at all.

"Uh, guys... I think we may have a problem. Again." Max interrupted the tense exchange. He pointed.

Smoke rose into the air just beyond their camp.

Radcliffe hurried over. He grabbed Charlie by the arm and growled. "We have to move. Now."

"But where's Beau??" Charlie's voice rang with panic.

The brownies threw their supplies into their packs. Juliette tossed things at Radcliffe.

Radcliffe hoisted Juliette, and then Charlie, onto his back. He shouted for the brownies to climb on.

Radcliffe took off at a gallop through the grasslands, away from a fire.

The flames spread quickly across the dry grass. Not again! They had barely escaped the last fire. They couldn't be so lucky twice. And where was Beau?

She looked over her shoulder, afraid that he had somehow become trapped in the flames. Her stomach curled at the thought. She turned forward as Radcliffe carried them away from danger. Pepper flew right alongside, hair and skin bright.

Radcliffe carried them through a river and far away from the flames. When he stopped, Charlie slid off his back and thudded to the ground. She brushed herself off. Her lower legs and feet were still wet from the river crossing. She slogged to a huge river rock along the bank of the river and plopped herself down. Head in her hands she choked back

245

tears and tried to steady her breathing.

It didn't take long for Juliette to settle beside her and Pepper to alight on her knee. Her heart ached at the concern for her closest friends. She was embarrassed to ask but had to know what had happened.

Her face burned. She asked Pepper about what she had said about a "kitsune." She didn't even know how to pronounce it right, but just tried to imitate the word Pepper had said earlier.

Pepper sighed. Her skin had paled again, and her hair returned to its normal orange color. She seemed reluctant to have this conversation with Charlie, but Charlie needed to know.

"A kitsune is a giant multi-tailed fox with magical abilities. After they've aged a hundred years, they can take human form. They have many other abilities. They can easily manipulate those around them to see or feel or even remember things. They can become invisible. And they can control fire. You were talking to one when I got back..." Pepper looked at Charlie with concern.

Charlie's heart sank. She had been duped. Beau had manipulated her. But why?

"When I tried to follow you..." Pepper started.

Charlie interrupted with a sheepish, "Sorry..."

Pepper brushed away her apology. "... I ended up in the city. I flew all around to figure out where you would go. I listened to a lot of people talk and spent the whole day trying to find out where Jessamine might be. I mean, I assumed that was your goal. To face Jessamine by yourself? Right? Which, by the way, was a really dumb idea." Pepper gave Charlie a sharp look.

Charlie looked away.

"Anyway," Pepper continued before Charlie could apologize again. "I finally figured out that Jessamine would be in the city center. By then it was dark, so I made my way there, and slept in a tree that night.

"The next day, I snuck into the building and found Jessamine. I was curious why you hadn't shown up yet, and worried that she had captured you already or something. But I heard her talking to a couple of soldiers. I stuck around and eavesdropped for a while.

"They reported on the death of the werewolves in the forest fire. Jessamine said she already knew about that. Then she said your name, Charlie. She knew you were there at the werewolf attack. She tracked your movements and had sent the werewolves to kill you."

Pepper paused and shuddered.

Nausea burned Charlie's throat. Jessamine was insane. Unleashing werewolves on people? How did she even control who they attacked? Charlie had been really lucky to survive the werewolves. And the fire afterwards.

But one thing didn't make sense. "She was there? Beau said the city leaders had all gone…"

Realization sunk in. He had lied to her. Shame weighed her down now that the truth had been revealed.

Chapter 28

"**Let** me continue…" Pepper patted Charlie on the side of her face.

The tears that had stayed on Charlie's cheeks evaporated in a tiny cloud of steam beneath the pixie's warm touch.

Pepper's emotions about the situation kept her little body heated as she continued to tell Charlie what happened.

"I wanted to take her out then and there. I was so mad about the werewolves." At these words, her hair smoldered, whisps of black smoke rising above her head.

"But the next thing she said sent me back here. She said she had a spy watching out for you in the city. He had found you and he would 'take care of the problem' for her. I knew I had to find you before it was too late. I couldn't risk doing anything to Jessamine that might get me captured or worse. I had to protect you. Besides, my flame is still out." She shrugged.

Pepper settled on Charlie's leg. "I'm so glad you're safe

Charlie. I was really worried." Pepper's skin cooled and paled to a sickly hue.

Charlie barely heard that last part. Beau had planned to kill her. Not before he found out everything he could about their plans. She was so glad she had delayed telling him too much valuable information. But he had escaped and gone back to report what he had learned to Jessamine. She would know about the loss of abilities, and that Charlie's dad was aging too fast, and that Charlie was aging, too. She would know where they were located and that Charlie was trying to stop Jessamine.

Their whole plan had fallen to pieces. All because of Charlie.

She buried her face in her hands. How could she have even thought Beau cared about her at all? She was nobody.

"Charlie, it's totally not your fault. Kitsune's are tricksters. Each does it his own way, but they all have the ability to manipulate anyone unaware of their true identity. He may be handsome, Charlie, but he is also a terrific liar." Pepper tried to comfort Charlie.

"His touch," Charlie whispered.

The feeling she had felt when he touched her hadn't been fondness or attraction. He had manipulated her feelings through his touch. That's why he hadn't touched any of the others. They may have been able to tell what he was. Oh, how could she have been so stupid?

"Please do not be hard on yourself up about this," Juliette encouraged. "You could not have known. None of us could have."

Charlie felt sick. She had delayed their plans, and now Jessamine expected them. They no longer had the element of surprise.

"There's more." Pepper hesitated to continue.

Charlie groaned. Great. What else had she messed up?

"I really hate to have to tell you this," Pepper hurried her words. "The giants have dug up the Deep Spring. They have begun construction of a palace for Jessamine. She plans to leave in a matter of days to go there. To live. Permanently. She will have prolonged life and heal fast. She also has the souls of countless creatures. She will be basically invincible. She will be immortal. Impossible to defeat." Pepper's skin turned orange and her hair smoldered again. "If we are going to have any chance of taking her down, it has to be soon. Like, now."

Charlie's head spun. Her surroundings became blurry. She was aware that her friends talked to her, but their voices sounded muffled, like she had cotton stuffed in her ears. A second later she felt her body relax. She couldn't hold herself upright any longer. Her head hit the ground.

The next thing she knew she stood on the battlefield in front of a huge army of creatures. Jessamine sneered at her from the front line. The restless creatures only awaited her command to attack.

Jessamine beckoned to Charlie to come closer.

Charlie hesitated, but then proceeded. The only weapon in her hands was her small sword. It would be no match for Jessamine's army.

"Are you ready to die today, Charlie?" Jessamine's voice dripped with contempt.

Charlie could not respond.

"Your army is no match for me. Give up now, while you still have the chance."

Charlie turned around. A multitude of dwarves, forest people, and other creatures mingled behind her. It was the same army she had seen in her last dream. Where had they come from?

In rapid succession Charlie saw Jessamine give the signal and her army advance. Charlie saw the same scene over and over. Each time a different one of her friends died in the brutal battle.

Charlie could only watch. She could not help.

Before anyone else could be killed, Charlie interrupted the pattern. She rushed forward just as Jessamine was about to signal her army to attack again.

Charlie stood between the two armies. What should she do? Jessamine was right. Her army would outlast Charlie's. But she couldn't just do nothing.

Jessamine signaled for the attack. As if time slowed, Charlie watched Jessamine's army decimate her own. No one on Charlie's side survived this time. Charlie watched everyone she cared about, and so many she didn't even know, die.

Jessamine won the battle, just as she predicted.

Charlie screamed.

How would she ever win against an opponent like Jessamine?

Suddenly, the scene changed. Now Jessamine stood alone on the battlefield, just like Charlie had been seeing in her dreams the past couple of nights. The woman looked frightened and confused.

Charlie's army geared up to take Jessamine down.

Jessamine huddled on the ground. She looked up at Charlie with wide eyes.

"Stop!" Charlie commanded her own forces.

She approached Jessamine. Just like she had before, she reached down a hand to pull Jessamine to standing.

"You must protect Jessamine. The balance must be restored."

Charlie's friends huddled around her.

"You passed out." Juliette helped Charlie sit.

Charlie tried to control her breathing. She allowed Juliette's gentle touch to calm her.

Max and Eliot exchanged nervous glances.

"I had a dream, or vision, or whatever. I saw her. She has a huge army." Charlie tried to bring her mind back to reality.

The images of the massive army haunted her. She didn't know how to explain her dream. It wasn't so much what she saw, but how she had felt, and that would be too difficult to get across. And she didn't want to scare everyone.

"She's ready for us," was all she could think to say.

"Where, Charlie?" Radcliffe asked.

Charlie still felt like an idiot for being manipulated by Beau, but she couldn't think about that now. If Pepper was right, they had run out of time. Jessamine believed she would win. Charlie couldn't let that happen.

"Look," she made eye contact with each of her friends. "I've had so many dreams about facing Jessamine. And in each one of them some of you, sometimes all of you, die. That's why I snuck off to take care of her myself. I don't want anyone to get hurt. I can't let you get hurt." Charlie's voice cracked.

Juliette wrapped her arms around Charlie and squeezed.

"I don't care what happens to me. I just want that woman gone from this world," Radcliffe growled.

"Same." Pepper's word held an enormous amount of conviction.

"We're in, right brother?" said Max, his voice a little shaky.

"To the end." Eliot sounded as sure as Pepper.

"Charlie, you do not need to do this alone." Juliette released Charlie.

The others nodded.

Charlie shook her head. She wiped the tears from her face. "I'm sorry, you guys. I won't tell you where she is. I don't want you to die. Any of you. I won't let you help me."

"Well, that's the dumbest thing I've ever heard!" Pepper countered. "We've come this far. Why would we turn back now?"

"I will just put the cap on and sneak off again," Charlie started to say.

"Charlie!" Radcliffe barked. "If I don't help you, you will die."

Charlie's jaw dropped. "Excuse me?"

In a slightly less agitated voice, Radcliffe repeated himself. "If I don't help you, you will die. It's what the siren showed me. I cannot let you go alone."

Charlie didn't know what to say.

Radcliffe looked at her in a different way than he ever had before. Like he was scared to lose her.

Everyone else stayed quiet. Charlie thought that they were afraid, like her, that if anyone said anything Radcliffe would stop talking. And she had a feeling they needed to hear what he was about to say.

Radcliffe didn't pay attention to anyone but Charlie. He

took a step closer to her. His hooves pawed at the ground. He moved his hands as if he didn't know what to do with them.

When Charlie looked up at him, she saw his eyes were red and wet. What could have the siren shown him that had upset him so much? It must be really bad.

Her heart raced. Maybe she didn't want to know.

"You remind me so much of her." Radcliffe's voice came out as a husky whisper. He reached a hand out, like he wanted to touch Charlie, but then withdrew and turned his head away.

"Of who, Radcliffe?" Charlie stayed still as she spoke.

"My daughter," he choked.

Charlie's breath caught in her throat. Her own eyes stung again with tears.

"That's why I can't let you go alone, Charlie." Radcliffe spoke in a low, tight voice. "I can't let Jessamine take you away, too. The siren showed me the battle. If I don't fight, you die. With me by your side, you survive. It's that simple."

"But what about you, Radcliffe? I keep seeing you, and everyone else, die." Charlie motioned at the others. "Over and over. How can I let that happen?"

She swallowed the lump in her throat. "You said before that you saw the battle but not the outcome. So, do you know if *you* even survive?"

Radcliffe shrugged. "What happens to me is not important. I have no family, no people. You still have so much life ahead of you. Your life is far more valuable than mine. Send the others away if you must, but I will not leave."

Charlie wanted to argue, but Radcliffe folded his arms

and glared at her. "And do not be obstinate and sneak away." His voice had hardened again.

"Besides," Max looked up at Radcliffe. "You have the dragon's blood. You'll be fine."

Radcliffe glared at the brownie.

Max's eyes went wide. He mouthed "Sorry" to Radcliffe, then crouched to hide behind his shorter brother.

"Radcliffe, is this true?" Juliette sounded hurt. Or was it relief?

Honestly, Charlie didn't even know how she felt about it herself.

Radcliffe nodded. It was the first time Charlie had seen him look as guilty as Max. "I am the one that told them about the dragon's blood. I asked them to test it. After the griffin attack, I knew I needed a way to protect you better. And after the siren saw me 'not as I was', I knew there had to be a way. Max and Eliot's tests proved to be the answer."

Max looked proud of himself.

Images flashed through Charlie's mind. Radcliffe gray and stone-like. Pained cries escaped from him. That's what the dream had meant. She had thought he was dying, but that wasn't it at all. He would drink the dragon's blood to protect Charlie from Jessamine.

"But it doesn't last very long," Pepper interrupted.

"It doesn't matter. It will be enough to take down Jessamine. I won't need long." Radcliffe had still not taken his eyes off Charlie.

"But her army will kill you…" Max pointed out.

Radcliffe nodded. "I have accepted my fate." His eyes softened. "You are worth it."

He may have accepted his fate, but Charlie would not allow him to sacrifice himself for her.

She sighed. "I don't know what to do." She looked around the circle. "I care about all of you too much. I'll think about it, try to dream again. I'll let you know in the morning."

"And no sneaking off again," Pepper chided, her hair brighter than usual, but still not aflame. "I've got my eyes on you!" She pointed at her eyes with two fingers then turned them toward Charlie.

Charlie nodded. "I promise."

But would she keep that promise? She would decide by morning. If the only way to keep everyone safe was to sneak away again, she would.

Eliot cleared his throat. He locked eyes with Charlie and shook his head. How did he know what she planned?

She looked away. She would have to be much more careful the next time.

The rest of the afternoon Charlie noticed everyone keep a close eye on her. Radcliffe even went so far as to station Eliot right beside Charlie's pack, that way she would not be able to remove the cap without someone noticing.

They discussed what their next move might be. Should they go back to the city to find Jessamine now? Or wait until she left and hope that she would travel light and fast? Attacking her in the city seemed foolish. Radcliffe believed their only hope was to ambush her as she traveled.

Pepper disagreed. "She knows we're out here. She'll be expecting something. We should attack now."

A strange feeling overcame Charlie. Words came out of her mouth, but they didn't feel like her own. "We need to wait. I need to dream. We need to protect Jessamine."

Chapter 29

"Are you crazy?!" Max jumped up from the ground and waved his arms around. "Why in the world would we protect her?" He paced back and forth. "She's evil. We have to stop her. We might need some help, but that's what we have to do!"

Pepper zipped around Charlie, as if she expected some unseen force to have a hold on her.

Juliette looked conflicted. She probably did want to protect her cousin, but somehow stop her at the same time.

Radcliffe stomped his hooves. *"What?"* The word came out as a growl.

A sense of peace washed over Charlie. It didn't make any sense. None at all. Protect Jessamine? Why *would* they do that? She had to *stop* Jessamine.

"The balance must be restored."

The words whispered beneath her thoughts.

Pepper gasped. Her hair lit up with a whoosh, then went

259

out again. She dropped from the sky and landed on the ground with a thump. Eliot rushed to her side. Charlie kneeled in front of the pixie.

Pepper's eyes were wide and her breathing fast. She held a hand to her chest. "I saw it, Charlie…"

"Saw what?" Charlie had no idea what Pepper meant.

"I saw the battle." Pepper's voice was barely above a whisper. She had a haunted look on her face.

Eliot rubbed Pepper's back.

Pepper pressed her hands over her eyes. "It was horrible." She began to cry hot tears that sizzled when they hit the ground.

"What is she talking about?" Radcliffe wanted to know.

"I don't know." Charlie hadn't done anything.

Before Charlie had time to think about it, Juliette gripped her arm tight with both hands. A horrified look darkened her features. "Oh, no! This is too much."

"Juliette, look at me. What is too much?" Charlie held Juliette's face in both of her hands.

"I see the battle, as well." The Princess squeezed her eyes shut.

Next, Radcliffe groaned. "I see it, too," he growled.

Max and Eliot each dropped to the ground. Max curled into a ball with his hands over his head. "Make it stop," the brownie whimpered.

What was happening? How could she make it stop? She didn't even know how it was possible for her friends to see what she had seen.

But they were right about one thing, the battle scenes, all of them that she had ever seen, were horrifying. And so real. Her own heart nearly burst every time from the pain of losing loved ones. But she also could tell that she dreamt.

The others had never experienced these dreams.

All at once, everyone relaxed. They each slowed their breathing and cleared their minds. Then they all turned their eyes to Charlie.

"Is that what it's like every time?" Pepper asked. She still sat on the ground beside Eliot, knees pulled to her chest.

"How do you do it?" Max wanted to know.

Juliette threw her arms around Charlie and squeezed. "I am so sorry."

"Indeed. You are stronger than I had thought possible." Radcliffe nodded at Charlie.

"But, how?" Pepper asked.

How had they seen? Was this part of becoming a true Dreamer?

No one knew the answer.

"It doesn't matter how or why." Charlie looked around the group. "The fact is, we must do something to stop the battle from taking place."

"You must protect Jessamine."

"Did you guys hear that?" Max had a scared look on his face.

Radcliffe nodded. Juliette swallowed hard. Eliot and Pepper stared at each other with wide eyes.

Now they heard the voice, too?

"What does it mean?" Juliette whispered. Her eyes shone with hope. Maybe her cousin would survive after all.

None of them knew.

Maybe Charlie would dream. Maybe then they would understand what to do next.

That night, Charlie dreamt of Jessamine leaving the city.

Five mounted soldiers in full armor came out of the city gates first, followed by an elaborate, gilded horse-drawn carriage. The morning sun reflected off of the curved sides and flat roof of the carriage. Dark, thick curtains on the inside hid the passengers from view. Even though Charlie couldn't see into the carriage, she knew that it held Jessamine.

A dozen guards marched on either side, their movements clumsy because of their heavy armor and swords belted around their waists.

Behind the carriage followed the wagons, pulled by more horses, laden with trunks and crates.

Another dozen guards marched on either side of the train of wagons.

Five more mounted soldiers protected the rear of the caravan.

Charlie didn't see any non-human protectors. Was Jessamine's army already at the Deep Spring? Would she gather them along the way? Jessamine could be easily defeated if these men were her only protection.

Before Charlie could even finish that thought, clear words entered her mind.

"Protect Jessamine. The balance must be restored."

As soon as the others woke up the next morning, Charlie wasted no time announcing her dream to her friends.

"She's on the move." She told them what she had seen in her sleep.

"What are we supposed to do?" Juliette looked like she didn't really want to hear Charlie's answer.

"She is under-protected. We must make our move." Radcliffe pulled his battle axe from his back and gripped the handle tight.

"No. We do nothing. We just follow." Charlie packed her things while the others stared.

She shouldered her bag and stood. "I know it's not what most of you want to do, but it is what we are supposed to do. Be patient. Please. Just… trust me."

How could she explain to them that they had to wait? She wanted so badly to put a stop to Jessamine right now, before anyone else had to suffer.

But the voice compelled her otherwise. For now, she would obey.

Radcliffe stomped along behind Charlie. The grassy ground had not seen rain in a while, and little clouds of dust poofed around his hooves each time they smacked the ground. He muttered to himself. A lot. Charlie could make out Jessamine's name, and phrases like "what she deserves" and "this could all be over." He also complained about wasting time following her when she had little protection.

Charlie understood how he felt. Her mind cycled through all the different outcomes she had dreamt about. She felt lost. And frustrated. She was ready for this to be over. She was ready to see her dad again, to be back home.

Instead, they followed Jessamine's entourage south. The dust the horses and wagons kicked up made it an easy task. They stayed far behind. In fact, they waited a half a day to begin their journey. Most of them had the urge to race ahead and finish this. But Charlie held them back.

They trekked slowly over the gentle slopes. Jessamine's caravan left matted grass and tracks in the dirt. The brown grasses had bent and broken beneath the horse's hooves and wagon wheels. Before the end of the day, they crossed the river that snaked through the grassy landscape. It was the same river that Radcliffe had carried them across to escape the grass fire the day before.

The fire that had been set by Beau. It was so obvious to Charlie now. That's why Charlie had seen a fox in her dream in the forest. He had tried to kill them all.

Charlie's throat tingled. Her stomach felt queasy. She had been so stupid to fall for his tricks.

She shook her head. She couldn't dwell on that now. She had to focus on what she had to do next, not beat herself up for mistakes from the past.

By sunset the river was far behind them, and a hazy

forest shadowed the horizon. They would reach the edge of the woods the next day. Then it would be easier to follow, and maybe even spy on, Jessamine and her guards.

Pepper and the brownies snuck close to the camp once night settled. Charlie made the brownies promise not to pull any pranks or steal anything. They could not afford for the little men to be captured. Max nodded with a solemn look on his face, no hint of his usual mischievousness.

The trio returned a short time later. The guards had circled the wagons around the carriage. A small fire burned within the circle, and all the men slept between the wagons and Jessamine's carriage. The curtains of the carriage were still drawn tight. There was no way for the brownies to sneak a peek.

While the brothers had whispered and peered around the wagons, Pepper flitted in the shadows closer to the top. Someone pushed the curtain aside. Beau's face appeared, shadowed in the darkness, but his golden hair had an unnatural shine to it. He locked eyes with Pepper, like he knew she was there. The pixie began to glow and scowl at the kitsune, but Max jumped up and pulled on her foot from below to hold her back. Beau had smirked at Pepper, then the curtain dropped back into place.

Beau was with Jessamine. Jessamine knew they were being followed. She would stay hidden and under heavy guard the entire trip. Even if they wanted to try a sneak attack, it would be impossible.

*"You must **protect** Jessamine. You must restore the balance."* The voice reminded Charlie as she drifted off to sleep.

Charlie did not sleep well. She tossed and turned. Every noise that echoed in the night made her flinch. She was sure

Jessamine would send her soldiers to slaughter them in their sleep.

When she did manage to sleep, her dreams were troubled. Jessamine making alliances with bands of angry looking elves. A crystal golem that looked like it was made of ice joined the woman's forces. A dozen minotaur, a giantess wearing furs and carrying a huge bow, and a pair of creatures that Charlie had to assume were ogres, all flocked to Jessamine's army.

Every day Jessamine stayed in power her army grew stronger. Every day Charlie followed and did nothing, their chances of defeating her shrunk.

How would protecting Jessamine restore the balance? How was Charlie going to stop Jessamine if they didn't fight now, when the odds were in their favor?

When Charlie woke up, she could see her breath. Each blade of grass had white fuzzy spikes up and down both sides. The ground was white and hard. Icy crystals coated all of their supplies. Charlie even felt a little ice in her hair. The grey clouds hung low in the sky. The thick chill of the wintry air pricked her lungs when she took a deep breath. She shivered.

The season had changed overnight. Had that been natural? Or the work of some magical creature, like the mountain guardian? Or was it just the world trying to rid itself of its residents again?

Charlie wrapped her shawl around her shoulders. If winter had arrived early, she would need warmer clothes. So would the others.

Pepper volunteered to scout around for a village or settlement. They couldn't stray too far off course, but they had to find the necessary supplies. And the path that Jessamine's caravan left on the frozen ground was even easier to follow. It shouldn't be too hard to take a detour, and then catch up to Jessamine.

The icy grass crunched under Charlie's feet. She didn't feel uncomfortably cold while they were on the move, but she was worried what night would bring. They would need to have a big fire, which meant someone would have to stay on high alert throughout the night. Hopefully Pepper would return with news of somewhere they could gather supplies

They followed Jessamine south toward the forest. The trees were no longer shadows on the horizon, but a massive forest of evergreen and deciduous trees. The frost extended into the shadowy woods.

Charlie's heart beat just a little faster. Some woods were safe. Others, not so much. What surprises would this forest bring?

Christine Marshall

Chapter 30

Jessamine's caravan took the path of least resistance through the woods, winding around closer growing trees and through more open areas. If only they could just travel in a straight line, it would go a lot faster. But they had to stay back. At least, for now.

They followed Jessamine through narrow pines with short branches packed with thick, short needles. The frosty branches only grew on the top half of the trunks. Charlie had to crane her neck to see through the canopy for a peek at the sky. Other pines had bushy branches full of long needles covered in fuzzy frost that made them look soft and hairy.

The deciduous trees were still in full leaf, but each leaf had been coated in a smooth layer of ice that pulled the branches toward the frozen ground.

The low shrubs had red and orange leaves beneath the layers of frost which created patches of pastel colors beneath the trees.

Thin ice covered each individual blade of grass, fallen leaf, wayward pinecone, and patch of clover on the forest floor.

Pepper returned before long with a report of a settlement to the east, near the edge of the woods. Since their quarry moved so slow, they agreed that they had plenty of time to travel to the settlement, gather the necessary supplies, and continue their trek without losing Jessamine in the woods.

By midday they arrived at the village. Mud-walled homes with circular thatched rooves ringed the perimeter. At the center of the village stood a makeshift market with stands for buying and selling home-grown and handmade wares. Beyond the houses, the grasslands stretched out and Charlie saw herds of fluffy sheep grazing on the frozen grass. The occasional wooly llama mingled with the sheep and kept a wary eye on the intruders.

The villagers stared at Charlie and her friends as they made their way to the market.

Juliette reminded everyone to smile. "A friendly smile can work wonders on one who is wary."

Pepper chirped "Hello" to every person she could.

Max and Eliot waved like they marched in a parade.

Radcliffe's smile looked more like a grimace.

Charlie did her best to appear cheerful.

"We need warmer clothes and better boots." Charlie took inventory in her mind of what else they might need. "And food that we can carry with us."

"We don't have any coin or goods to trade…" Pepper said out of the corner of her mouth, still smiling and waving at the villagers.

"We got you covered." Max dug into his pack and pulled

out a small velvety drawstring pouch.

"What's that?" Pepper zipped down to take a look.

"You probably don't want to know," Radcliffe growled through his teeth.

"It's just plain old gold coin. We carry it for… emergencies. We rarely need it though." Max shrugged.

"Yes, because usually you steal what you require." Radcliffe didn't even look at the brownies when he spoke.

"Borrow… we prefer the term borrow. We always *want* to return it."

"Right," snorted Radcliffe.

"It doesn't matter!" Charlie interrupted. "You two bicker like an old couple. The point is, we'll be able to buy what we need."

Charlie looked at Max. "Thank you."

She stopped and turned to face the others. "We should split up; it will go faster. Juliette and Radcliffe, you find food, you'll know what we need best. I'll take Pepper, Max, and Eliot to get shoes and clothes. We'll meet back here as soon as we can."

"Uh… we just have a quick errand to run…" Max started to say. Eliot looked at Charlie with his serious expression. "Here's the money, see ya guys later!" Max tossed the money bag at Charlie and the two brownies scampered away before Charlie could protest.

Whatever they were up to, she had learned to trust them. She never knew when one of their secretive missions might end up saving her life one day.

Charlie wasted no time finding the weaver and purchasing wool cloaks for each of them. Fortunately, they even had child sized ones that would fit Max and Eliot. Pepper wouldn't need one. If she got too cold, she would either light her hair up or just huddle inside Charlie's cloak.

Next, they went to the leather-smith and purchased better boots for Juliette. She knew Juliette didn't like wearing leather, but her canvas boots just wouldn't cut it on the icy ground. The leather-smith didn't think Charlie needed anything different, but suggested she stuff some wool inside the ones she wore for added insulation. Charlie bought extra wool for the brownies, too.

Radcliffe and Juliette rejoined Charlie and Pepper, and they divided the goods. Radcliffe had purchased dried meat, mushrooms, and potatoes. Juliette had obtained a sack of apples as well as a hefty bag of oats and barley. She promised she could make them pottage that would not only warm them but taste amazing, too.

Charlie gave Juliette her leather boots. The Princess was grateful for Charlie's purchase. She understood that under the circumstances, she must take care of herself. Charlie shoved chunks of wool inside her own boots for added warmth. Her toes instantly felt the comfort.

She handed out the scratchy wool cloaks to Juliette and Radcliffe. Juliette pulled the cloak over her head, then used a cord to cinch it at her waist. Radcliffe let his cloak hang loose, with the handles of his huge weapons sticking out the top. Charlie imitated Juliette and tied hers at the waist.

She tucked the cloaks she had purchased for Max and Eliot underneath her arm and looked around. "Now, where are Max and Eliot?"

They waited for several long minutes before the brownies jogged out from between the market stalls. Eliot had a small cage in one hand. At least, it looked like it might be a cage. It had a thick, wool cloth covering it. A twisty thread of dark smoke snaked out from beneath the cloth. Max had his arms wrapped around a wooden box that clinked as he made his way over.

Charlie handed the brownies their cloaks and wool for their pointed boots, while Pepper buzzed around the pair.

"What'd you get? What'd you get?" Pepper flew circles around them. Her skin was orange and her hair warm.

"Nothing, let's get going." Max said as he pulled the warm cloak over his head and padded his boots. He avoided eye contact with everyone as he walked right past the group and headed for the edge of the village.

"What did you steal this time?" Radcliffe's hooves clopped on the cobblestone street, his voice condescending.

273

"We didn't steal anything. We paid for it." Max called over his shoulder. He didn't seem offended by the question.

Eliot caught up to his brother, donning his own new outerwear, and nodded.

"But you gave us your money. Which, by the way, here's what's left." Charlie held the pouch out to the brownies.

Max waved away the pouch. "Keep it. We can get more."

Charlie and Juliette exchanged surprised glances.

"Are you sure? There's a lot left…" Charlie didn't want to take Max's money.

"I'm sure. We won't need it."

Charlie felt weird about it, but she put the money pouch into her pack.

"So, why was everyone staring at us like that?" Pepper flitted around the others as they followed the brownies out of the village and toward the frozen forest once more.

"Was it because of Radcliffe? No offense or anything, Radcliffe, but you can be a little…." Pepper tapped her chin and searched her mind for the right word.

"You." Eliot stated in a flat voice, just loud enough for Radcliffe and the others to hear.

Radcliffe grunted, but he did not disagree.

Charlie had assumed it was Radcliffe that the villagers were leery of. It usually was.

"But it wasn't him this time." Eliot spoke louder.

"Well, what was it then? Was it me?" Pepper looked excited at the idea of being the one to intimidate an entire village full of people.

"Nope, it was Jessamine." Max turned his head over his shoulder and gave Pepper an apologetic look.

Pepper's wings wilted a little, but she covered up her disappointment before she thought anyone had noticed.

"Is she here?" Radcliffe reached over his shoulder to arm himself.

"No, obviously not, weirdo. We were following her, remember?" Max smacked his forehead and shook his head. "But her soldiers made a detour here. I guess they took all the young men to fight in Jessamine's army."

Christine Marshall

Chapter 31

"**What** do you mean they took all the young men?" Juliette's voice barely rose above a whisper, and she came to an abrupt halt.

"I mean *all* of them. Didn't you notice that the villagers were all either women or older men?" Max and his brother stopped walking and turned to face the others.

Charlie hadn't noticed that the young men had been missing from the village. Guilt gnawed at her stomach.

"What do you mean she *took them*?" Radcliffe's gravelly voice sounded angry. Really angry.

Max looked at Radcliffe like he had asked a stupid question.

Radcliffe stared back.

"I mean…" Max started out slow, but then his words came faster. "Her soldiers came through here just yesterday and *took* all the young men to fight in her army. The people are either too terrified of Jessamine to do anything about it,

277

or too old or weak to try." Max shook his head, but this time in pity.

"We have to help them fight back. I will assist." Radcliffe turned to return to the village.

Charlie moved to block his way.

"What are you doing?" Radcliffe growled.

Charlie held her hands out in front of her. "You will not go back and get them to fight Jessamine." Charlie kept her voice firm.

Radcliffe sidestepped around Charlie. "Yes, I will."

Charlie moved fast and blocked him again. "No, you won't. We are supposed to protect her, not gather an army to fight her." Charlie hated the words as they came out of her mouth, but she spoke the truth.

Radcliffe's eyes squinted; his eyebrows wrinkled his forehead.

"You wanted me to dream. This is what I have dreamt. I don't see how we have any choice." Charlie stepped aside. "But if you feel like you need to go help the villagers try to fight Jessamine, go ahead. Just know, it's not what is supposed to happen. Which means it probably would end really bad."

Radcliffe groaned. He stomped his hooves on the frosty roadway. Little flurries of white flakes swirled around each of his feet. "Fine." His lips didn't move. Charlie barely heard the word.

Charlie turned to look at the others again. "I know it seems wrong to not fight back or to stop others from fighting back. But my dreams showed that if we fight, she wins. I don't understand why any more than any of you." Charlie hoped her face showed how sorry she was. "I want to avenge my village just as much as each of you has your reasons for wanting revenge."

Radcliffe scoffed and rolled his eyes with his arms folded across his massive chest.

Charlie ignored him. They couldn't compare their losses.

"Revenge means battle. And battle with Jessamine means certain death. We *have* to wait." Charlie swallowed the lump in her throat.

Juliette nodded. Max and Eliot exchanged one of their looks that Charlie didn't understand. Pepper zipped around Charlie as if she wanted someone to challenge her. Radcliffe stayed as still as a statue. But at least he wasn't roaring in anger or galloping off on his own.

They quickly made their way back onto Jessamine's trail. By nightfall they were close enough to see the fire from Jessamine's camp through the frosty trees. The ice and thin layer of snow muffled any sounds, so they didn't have to worry too much about being quiet. They were careful to light their fire behind a large boulder so that Jessamine's men wouldn't notice theirs.

Even though Charlie was sure that Jessamine knew she was being followed, she didn't want to make it too easy for Jessamine's men to know their location.

Late the following morning, a group of around twenty work-hardened young women and older men from the village caught up to Charlie and her friends. They said they knew Charlie's group tracked Jessamine, and they wanted to help when the fight came. They wanted to rescue their fathers and brothers.

Charlie explained that they only followed Jessamine for now and had no plans to battle with her any time soon. The villagers agreed to hold back; they were no match for

Jessamine's men on their own. But Charlie could tell they were anxious to put a stop to Jessamine sooner than later.

Over the next week, Charlie dreamt every night about more people and creatures joining Jessamine.

Plenty of men joined the dark woman's cause, with promises of riches and power once she had settled into her new fortress. And plenty of creatures gathered to Jessamine as well. Charlie saw a huge, bony dog creature with tufts of grey fur growing in patches all over its thin body. It looked sickly. And mean. It had sharp teeth that barely fit inside the mouth on its long muzzle. It reminded Charlie of the werewolves. The creatures in her dream, however, did not stand on their back legs like the werewolves had. She awoke the morning after that dream in a cold sweat. Which wasn't good considering the wintry conditions that still surrounded them.

Another night she dreamt of a band of dwarves marching toward Jessamine. Charlie recognized the frosty forest as the one they were in now. And she paid attention to the dream and the landmarks around the dwarves. The short, stocky men, covered in layers of furs and carrying oversized axes and spiked clubs for their size, grumbled about Jessamine and what they would do to her once they found her. The voice reminded her to *"protect Jessamine."*

The following day, Charlie watched for the landmarks from her dream, and even suggested a slight detour so that she could intercept the dwarves before they crossed paths with Jessamine's entourage. Charlie reasoned with the dwarves, and they, too, joined Charlie and her friends.

With the addition of the villagers and the dwarves, Charlie's group now numbered near forty. How many others would they gather along the way? Maybe she really would have an army on her side when the time came to face Jessamine. Maybe Charlie would be able to stop her.

Whenever Charlie thought about fighting Jessamine, the voice would remind her: *"The balance must be restored. Jessamine must be protected."*

It didn't make any more sense now than it had the first time she had heard it. But so far, when she followed her dreams, things worked out the way they should. She had to trust they would this time, too.

By the end of the third week of tromping through the icy woods, Charlie's group consisted of the villagers and dwarves, plus a dozen tiny, white-bearded gnomes with tall pointy hats, a pair of horses with icicles in their manes and tails that tinkled when they trotted, a pack of large but gentle white wolves, and a troll-like creature that was made entirely of crystals... or ice... Charlie couldn't tell.

Each of these groups had been on their way to stop Jessamine. Charlie had dreamed about them and gathered them to her side before they could attack Jessamine's caravan. In a way, she *had* ended up gathering her own army. Much like the one she had seen in her dreams of battling Jessamine.

The dreams where everyone on Charlie's side died.

With each passing day the group grew more restless to put a stop to Jessamine before she arrived at her fortress. Charlie didn't know how long she would be able to hold them back.

It was halfway during the third week that something else happened that surprised Charlie. She and Juliette walked along together. They talked of anything except Jessamine; Juliette just couldn't bear it. Charlie worked to distract her friend. A bright red cardinal landed on Juliette's shoulder. The Princess stopped in her tracks. She made sing song noises at the bird, and the bird answered then flew away.

"Um... Juliette?" Charlie raised her eyebrows at her friend.

A slow smile spread across Juliette's face.

"Did you just talk to that bird?"

Juliette could only nod.

A warmth spread across Charlie's chest and down into her arms and legs. If Juliette could talk to animals again, what did that mean about Jessamine's power? And about the world being out of balance?

"Should we tell the others?" Charlie asked.

"Yes!" Juliette whispered back.

Juliette tried to talk to other animals on their way, but each time the animals scurried away. The hope that Juliette's abilities had been restored began to fizzle, but Juliette's good mood stayed. If the Princess was happy with this development, Charlie should be too. She did her best to echo her friend's positive energy as they continued their travels.

Not many days later, the temperature began to rise. The frost and ice on the flora and ground thawed throughout the day. Water dripped, making pitter-patter sounds as they continued their trek through the wood.

They neared the edge of the wood. Charlie could see tall mountains that loomed over the trees, casting long shadows as the sun dipped behind them.

With the somewhat warmer weather, the group that

traveled with Charlie became more anxious to finish the task they had all set out to do, independent of one another. But the task became more realistic with the addition of each person or creature. The mood around camp became more anxious the longer they traveled. Charlie worried how this would all end.

Charlie's dad looked like himself again; older, but not too old. He shuffled around a workshop that held all new tools.

Charlie turned in a full circle and took in the house with sliced log siding and a cedar shingled roof. She stood in a vegetable garden with tidy rows of cabbage, beans, sweet peas, and patches of strawberries.

The place felt familiar. Like home.

Her dad turned and waved at her. His eyes had wrinkles that radiated from the corners, like he wore a permanent smile.

Charlie leaned over and picked up the basket of vegetables that rested at her feet. Her own hands looked more like a woman's hands than a girl's.

Charlie heard the voice of a child giggle from inside the workshop. "Papa! Papa!"

Charlie stared.

Her dad squatted low and held out his arms, ready for a child to leap into them.

Just when the child was about to come into view, Charlie woke up.

She lay on her makeshift bed on the ground and pulled her cloak tight around herself.

This was the first time she had dreamt of something that wasn't imminent. And dangerous. Ever.

Had that been her future? Was her dad a grandfather? Which would make her a mother.

Warmth wrapped around Charlie's heart.

Juliette had several more encounters communicating with animals. She asked a snowy owl one night to please take a message to her people in the north. The owl hooted and twisted its head around, then returned its eyes to Juliette.

The Princess bowed her head and said, "Thank you." Then the owl took flight.

The Princess smiled more than Charlie had seen in a long time. She behaved more like her old self. But the sadness about Jessamine still clouded her cheeriness when she thought no one was looking.

It only took a few more days for Charlie to recognize her surroundings. The temperature warmed even more, Charlie and her friends left their cloaks near the edge of the forest for some traveler to find and use in the future.

The prairie stretched to Charlie's right. The wall of her home nestled within the forest of oversized trees ahead of them.

If the voice or her dreams didn't tell her to do something soon, they would miss their chance to confront Jessamine out in the open. It consumed Charlie's thoughts.

Those who followed her openly voiced the same concerns on a daily basis. Radcliffe and Juliette convinced them that it was Charlie's decision, but the others murmured when they thought she couldn't hear.

Charlie led the way, far ahead of the others, so she wouldn't have to hear their opinions. The thing was, she agreed with them. She wanted to surge forward; attack Jessamine while she was vulnerable. But when she tried to talk about it, or even think about it, the voice insisted she wait, protect Jessamine, and restore the balance.

She walked alone, caught up in her own thoughts.

A sound to her right caught her attention.

Someone called her name.

Christine Marshall

Chapter 32

Alder rushed toward her. Patches of star-shaped periwinkle flowers burst from the ground with each step he took. A smile stretched across his face.

Charlie's jaw hung open. She pulled herself together and hurried toward his open arms.

He picked her up and spun her in a circle.

"I'm so glad I found you, Charlie." His eyes didn't leave her face.

She blushed and nodded.

She stared into his deep brown eyes for a long moment before her brain caught up with her heart.

Her smile disappeared.

"How is my father?"

Was Alder here because something bad had happened? Was it too late for her dad? Would she ever see him again? A lump filled her throat.

Alder cupped his hand around one side of Charlie's face

and leaned closer.

"He is doing as well as expected, Charlie. He has continued to age rapidly and can no longer stand unassisted. But he is holding on for you. He has faith in you."

The breath she had been holding escaped all at once. She covered her face with her hands and let the tears flow. Alder wrapped his arms around her again. She rested her hand-covered-face against his broad chest and breathed in his earthy, sun-kissed scent. She forced her breathing to slow, and her mind to focus.

She was so close to finishing this. Jessamine was not far ahead. Charlie could easily catch up to her, and with her new army, fight Jessamine and win. She was sure of it.

"THE BALANCE MUST BE RESTORED."

Charlie jumped. The voice had been so loud this time. So firm.

Alder released her from his embrace but kept his hands on her shoulders. He searched her face.

Charlie took a deep breath. She could do this. She would do whatever she must to restore the balance. Especially if it meant she could see her father again. And that her friends would regain their abilities.

Which reminded her… "Alder! The flowers!" Charlie pointed at the ground.

Alder laughed. It sounded like music to Charlie's ears.

"Yes, this is recent. But I'm not complaining. I thought maybe you had defeated Jessamine? But I can see now that I was mistaken." Alder pointed at the mass of people and creatures that had caught up to Charlie and Alder.

Juliette rushed forward and gave Alder a warm embrace. Radcliffe nodded his greeting.

"What's up?" Max tried to sound cool when he gave

Alder a silly salute.

Pepper squealed and circled Alder with pink skin, then settled on Charlie's shoulder.

"I told you he liked you," she whispered in Charlie's ear.

Charlie ignored the pixie. She didn't need to be distracted by whether or not Alder was interested in her. She had a job to do. She needed to focus.

But she definitely didn't mind when she felt Alder wrap his big, warm hand around her own.

Juliette asked the questions that Charlie probably should have thought of, but she had been thinking of her father. And herself. Whoops.

"What are you doing here, Alder? How did you find us?"

Alder told a story about how his connection to the plants had gradually returned over the last couple of weeks, and that through this connection he had discovered their location.

"I've also learned that there are other groups actively opposing Jessamine," he continued. "Whole towns are fighting back against her men, and there are groups of creatures banding together to free her captives. The fear she has spread is being dissolved little by little."

Alder sighed. "There are still many who are afraid. Many who have lost loved ones. It's one thing to push back against Jessamine's men at home, but quite another to face her and her army in battle. She has many vicious warriors on her side."

Alder took a moment to study the crowd gathered with Charlie and her friends. "It looks like you've gathered a small army yourselves, but I doubt we'll be able to find many more willing to fight against her directly."

"That's alright." Charlie knew it to be true. Between the

voice and the dreams, she would figure out what she needed to do.

Alder turned to look directly at her. He didn't understand. How could he? He didn't know anything about her dreams, or the voice.

"We need to let her finish what she has started." Charlie knew it was true, even if it's not what she really wanted.

Alder looked more confused. "Why would we want her to finish what she has started? Shouldn't we try to stop her?"

"That's what I started out to do. But I've had dreams and... other insights... that have told me otherwise. I want to stop her right here, right now. But we're not supposed to. Not yet."

Would he understand? What would he think about her? She waited for the rejection, disinterest, or worse.

"I trust you." He squeezed her hand a little tighter. "Just tell me what you need me to do."

She gave him a sad smile. "Thank you." She spoke low so only he could hear. "I hope the others who follow will do the same."

She had forgotten, though, that Radcliffe, and some of the other creatures in her midst, had exceptional hearing.

"Why should we wait?" called one of the dwarves. His companions rallied behind him. "Jessamine..." the other dwarves spit on the ground when they heard her name. "... is right in front of us. Why don't we attack now, before she settles in her fortress? This is madness!"

The villagers shouted their agreement. The horses and wolves whinnied and howled. The dwarves and gnomes banged their weapons on the ground or shook their fists in the air. Restlessness and frustration rippled through the crowd, picking up momentum as it went.

Charlie had tried to explain about her dreams and the voice to each group as they arrived. They had reluctantly held themselves back from attacking Jessamine on the journey.

But the atmosphere had changed. They egged each other on. They wanted the final battle. She had to stop them.

But how? How could she convince them that she told the truth?

"Think about what you saw in your dreams," a small, quiet voice whispered in her mind.

This wasn't The Voice that she had been hearing. It was different. But she had learned to trust the voices she heard. So, she did what the new voice told her to do.

She pictured the battle where they face Jessamine, and Jessamine's army wipes out everyone on Charlie's side.

All at once the crowd gasped.

Shouts of surprise escaped lips. Groans of pain dropped others to the ground. Many clutched their heads and squeezed their eyes shut.

What happened? How had they seen what Charlie had seen?

"Make it stop!" called one of the teenage villagers.

Charlie looked all around with wide eyes. How could she make it stop when she didn't even know how it happened?

"Now do you believe her?" The tiny voice that Charlie had thought she had heard in her head came from behind her.

As soon as the words had been spoken, the crowd relaxed. They kept alert and frightened eyes on Charlie, though.

A flash of gold glinted in the corner of Charlie's eye.

A pixie, smaller than Pepper, with long, straight, shiny golden hair and pale lavender skin, hovered in the air beside Charlie's ear. She wore a deep blue woolen dress with lacey white edges. She had her hands on her hips and scowled at everyone around her.

Pepper zipped over to her and stuck out her hand. "Hi! I'm Pepper. And you are…?"

The pixie startled. She must not have known that Pepper was there.

She shrunk in on herself a little bit and answered in the quietest voice Charlie could hear. "Oh, um, I'm Skye."

"Nice to meet you! So… did you have something to do with the collective vision that we all just shared? Cause if you did…" Pepper hovered in front of Skye, who floated ever so slightly in a backward motion, away from Pepper.

"I'm so sorry! I wasn't trying to cause any problems! I swear! I just, I saw her struggling with her dreams." Skye pointed at Charlie. "She seemed so nice. And so sad. I wanted to help. So, I started to follow you…" A guilty look spread across Skye's face. "Then I hid and listened, and I saw what she was trying to tell everyone." Now Skye pointed at Charlie, "and I wanted everyone to be able to see it so they would believe her. That's all! I promise!"

Pepper held out her hands. "Don't go, please."

Skye did look like she was about to bolt.

"I was going to say, because if you did, that was amazing! I mean, I can light my hair on fire, but you can make people see stuff? So cool, right?"

Skye nodded. "So right!" She smiled wide.

The makeshift army had pulled themselves together to watch the exchange between the two pixies. Most of the humans looked dumbstruck. How many of them had ever seen a pixie before they joined Charlie's group?

"The question is, how did you do it?" Max called from below. He whipped the cap off his head and gave Skye a low bow. "Maxwell, at your service."

His name was Maxwell? How had Charlie not known that before? After all the time they had spent together? Wait, was he even telling the truth?

While Charlie tried to figure out Max, Eliot elbowed his brother.

"And this is my fine brother, Eliot. But I'm more fine, I can tell you that!" Max hurried to add.

Eliot rolled his eyes.

"The tiny man is correct to ask," Radcliffe interrupted Max's performance.

Max shot him a dirty look.

"How *did* you do that?" Radcliffe ignored the brownies.

Skye had stopped trying to slip away. She flew down to stand beside Pepper and the brownies. Charlie was glad that Skye had chosen to stay. And she was dying to know the answer for herself.

Skye looked like she was trying to figure out how to explain, when Juliette answered for her. "She is a midnight dewdrop pixie, born in the blossom of the midnight dewdrop flower."

Skye looked at Juliette with awe. She nodded slowly. "That's right…"

Juliette kneeled beside the tiny group. She introduced herself, then continued to explain to the others.

"The midnight dewdrop pixies are also known as 'sweet memory pixies.' They have the ability to put thoughts into others minds. They are known to give troubled souls sweet memories to ease pain and suffering."

Skye nodded again. "But…. Sometimes…. the visions *I* give aren't so sweet. Sometimes people need to see the truth, you know? That's all." She shrugged and looked at the ground.

"That is very wise, little Skye. It is a pleasure to meet you." Juliette stood again.

Skye looked pleased with her interaction with Juliette.

And the explanation made sense. She had taken Charlie's memory and shown it to everyone else. And they certainly needed to see the truth right about now.

The pieces came together. Charlie spoke to Skye. "It was you! You are the one that showed my friends the battle before, aren't you?"

Skye nodded. She looked away.

"Thank you." Charlie wouldn't have been able to convince her friends to hold back from facing Jessamine if they hadn't seen the battle. And she would definitely not have been able to convince the others to refrain for this long if it hadn't been for the help of her friends. Especially

Radcliffe. When he told someone to do, or not do, something, they usually listened.

"I am so glad you decided to tag along. I only wish we had known you sooner. Please, join us." Charlie invited Skye to follow the others as they continued their journey.

Christine Marshall

Chapter 33

They spent the next three days making their way through the massive forest of oversized flora, fed by the Deep Spring water flowing from the wall Most of those that traveled with Charlie had never seen this place before.

The dwarves seemed unimpressed. They pretty much kept to themselves. Their emotions, hidden by their bushy eyebrows and beards, were hard to read. They marched through the forest in silence.

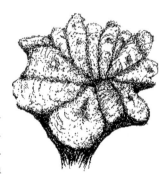

Charlie caught the gnomes studying their surroundings with wide eyes. They nudged each other and pointed out oversized flowers, mushrooms taller than themselves, and ferns that were large enough for several of them to hide bencath.

The horses trotted alongside the teenage girls from the

villages. The girls showered them with attention and offered them bouquets of enormous magenta daylilies and branches from star magnolia shrubs.

"Oooh! I *love* daylilies! Which is me, Skye!" The pixie also charmed the girls from the villages.

One of the girls held a blossom and Skye settled into the center. Did she like to drink the sweet nectar as much as Pepper?

The pack of wolves followed at a fair distance behind the others. They sniffed the air, scouted the underbrush, and kept ears and eyes on their surroundings.

Charlie could hear the crystal troll's heavy steps far

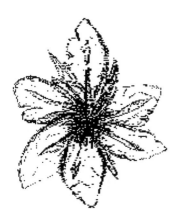

behind the wolves. It reminded her so much of the sounds Charles and the other giants had made when they maneuvered through the three-times-too-tall bushy pines and towering oak trees.

The sweet, humid air filled Charlie's lungs. After the frosty forest, the warmth and humidity of this wood lifted Charlie's mood.

Alder walked along beside Charlie, never straying from her sight. She shared easy conversation with him. He told her more about the place where he had taken her father. He was being cared for by another group of Juliette's forest people. Alder promised he was safe, and Charlie tried not to worry. But she felt guilty almost enjoying herself in Alder's company when her dad and so many others were suffering and in hiding.

Pansies of every color imaginable blossomed in each of Alder's footprints. Even though everything else here was bigger than life, the pansies that sprouted and bloomed instantly were their usual size. Charlie had never seen such a variety. Alder told her that pansies symbolize change. She loved listening to him talk about the plants and flowers.

Forest animals of all kinds began sidling up to Juliette. Before long birds fluttered above, rabbits and squirrels circled her feet, and a porcupine plodded along beside her. She beamed as she conversed with the animals non-stop.

In the evening, the villagers asked the dwarves to give them some advice for battle. The teenaged girls seemed more nervous than the elderly men, but they all looked afraid. The dwarves gave some good pointers, and before long Radcliffe joined the group. In no time almost everyone had gathered around to watch and learn what they should expect from the battle.

The atmosphere in camp changed from frightened and unprepared, to almost confident. Instead of each group keeping to themselves like they had been, they mingled and chatted long into the night.

Charlie had to keep them all safe. The weight of it pressed heavy on her shoulders.

The problem was her dreams continued to show her army face Jessamine's. The outcome stayed the same. If they fought, they lost.

But her dreams never showed her an alternative. How was she supposed to know what to do if the dreams, or the voice, didn't tell her?

Whenever her train of thoughts headed that direction, she reminded herself that everything had worked out so far. She had to just keep going.

She had managed to let go of her own need for revenge. Her blood no longer boiled when she thought about Jessamine. If anything, she felt pity for the woman.

They finally reached a point where they could see the wall to Charlie's home, even though it was still a day away at their pace. Enormous glacier boulders had been carefully placed by the giants long ago to create a barrier between the Deep Spring and the villagers within, from the rest of the world. Leafy ivy and creeping-wire vines covered huge sections. Charlie couldn't see from here, but she knew of at least three places where the wall had been partially destroyed. It wasn't as impenetrable as she had once thought.

Charlie wanted to give the all-clear to rush forward and finish Jessamine before she made it to the Deep Spring. But the voice firmly disagreed. She surrendered and helped set up camp for the night, instead.

Jessamine would go through the wall during the night. She would establish herself in her new fortress. She would drink the Deep Spring water, if she didn't have a supply of it already. She would be stronger and heal faster.

This really felt like a now or never situation.

After everyone had settled and they had eaten their evening meal, Max regaled the camp with one of his tall tales. At least, Charlie believed they were exaggerated. She didn't see how such a little person could have had such big adventures. And survived.

Skye loved listening to Max's storytelling as much as Pepper. She shrieked and clapped in all the right places. For the first time, Max seemed a little nervous. He kept glancing at Skye, like he wanted to make sure she was still listening.

When Max had finished telling the camp, or at least, those that had stayed to listen, about his narrow escape from a band of pirates, Skye clapped and cheered right alongside Pepper.

Max looked pleased.

"I love pirate stories!" Skye flew circles around Max. She mimed sword fighting and running away from a bad guy while she hovered above the ground.

Max laughed out loud.

Eliot gave Pepper a smirk and a nod.

Pepper grinned wide.

Skye landed in front of Eliot. "That was a great story, right Eliot?"

She waited for the brownie to answer. But Eliot didn't say anything.

"Right, Eliot?" Skye folded her arms.

Eliot glanced at Pepper. Pepper nodded and encouraged him to answer.

He returned his eyes to Skye.

"RIGHT. ELIOT?" She enunciated every letter in his name.

His eyes grew round like saucers.

Pepper jumped in. "Right, Skye! So good!!"

Skye relaxed and nodded. Then she flitted around Max a few more times.

Alder chuckled beside Charlie. "They are quite the entertainment, aren't they?"

Charlie agreed.

Alder leaned back and gazed at the sky through the incredibly high canopy. The view was limited, but what they could see was clear and the stars twinkled bright.

Charlie stretched out on the ground and placed her hands beneath her head. She thought about Alder beside her, and her stomach did a small flip.

But then, murmurs from the various groups reached Charlie's ears. They wanted to trust her. They believed what they had seen in the shared vision. But they didn't see any other way to handle the situation.

Charlie's head would burst if she battled with the voice anymore about this. She couldn't take it. She stood.

Alder quickly stood beside her. He reached for her hand. "Don't listen to them, Charlie. You're doing everything you can."

"I know. It's just… I don't know."

She sighed. She slipped away from Alder and walked away from camp to clear her head.

Alder didn't follow. She was a little disappointed, but at the same time she needed to think. Alone.

She settled herself on a log that faced her home. She closed her eyes and relaxed her body. She focused on the task at hand: protect Jessamine; restore the balance.

If there was a time for answers, it would be now.

She waited.

And waited.

She opened her eyes and let out a frustrated yell. "Just tell me something!"

Everything went black.

A beam of light shone from above, between the branches of the trees. It illuminated a patch of moss dotted with tiny white flowers. The flowers glowed yellow from the light.

Dust particles sparkled in the light.

Charlie stepped toward the spot.

"Hello?"

Where was she? She didn't recognize the area at all.

Moss wrapped around the tree trunks like a soft, green blanket. A slight breeze rustled the leaves of the oak and aspen trees. The pine needles scratched against each other.

She took another step forward. "Is anyone here?"

"Just me."

Charlie recognized that voice.

A chill ran down her spine.

She turned in a circle.

"Where are you? Come out!" Charlie hollered.

Her heart raced.

A shadow moved off to one side.

Charlie spun on her heels to face it.

Jessamine stepped out from darkness.

Charlie couldn't see Jessamine very well in the shadows. But could tell that the woman's eyes had dark rings around them. Her sharp cheeks left harsh shadows on her face. Her dark hair hung limp over her shoulders. She had her hands hidden behind her back. The hem of her loose, dark dress puddled on the mossy ground.

Jessamine avoided the beam of light. She tried to look casual about it, but Charlie could see that she intentionally didn't allow the light to touch her.

"I see you have gathered quite the reinforcements." A false sweetness laced Jessamine's words.

Was this a dream? Or something more?

Charlie stepped further into the light.

Jessamine circled Charlie with slow, careful movements.

Charlie gulped.

"But it's too late, sweetheart. I've already begun to drink the Deep Spring water. I've already felt it's effects. I have gathered a formidable host that will fight on my behalf. You might as well surrender while you still can." Jessamine continued to move in a circle around Charlie and the beam of light.

"You must restore the balance." The voice whispered from every direction.

A look of panic flashed across Jessamine's face, but she composed herself in a blink.

"Don't listen to that voice." Her words were harsh. Her hands balled into fists at her sides. "All it's done so far is keep you from any attempt to defeat me. And now, you don't stand a chance. No matter what you do at this point, you will fail."

A wicked smile pulled on the corners of Jessamine's mouth. "I have won."

All at once the beam of light expanded. It filled the entire clearing. Jessamine screamed and covered her head with her arms. She tripped as she ran back into the shadows. She disappeared.

"The time has come. You must face Jessamine. The balance will be restored."

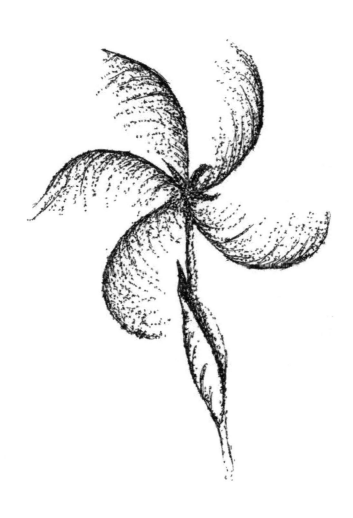

Christine Marshall

Chapter 34

Wait, now she was supposed to face Jessamine?

Charlie found herself on the ground next to the log. She sat up and held her head with her hands.

What had been the point of waiting all this time if they would end up in battle anyway? Was Charlie's side supposed to *lose*? How would that restore the balance?

Her mind raced while she tried to make sense of the vision.

If she fought Jessamine and lost, wouldn't that just make everything worse? Then she would have all the power. There would be no one to oppose her.

"Charlie? Charlie!" Juliette's voice interrupted Charlie's thoughts.

How long had Charlie been out here by herself? It had only felt like minutes, but it must have been much longer. The sky to the east had lightened a bit. Sunrise was on the way.

"I'm here!" Charlie stood. She brushed the moss, twigs, and bark from her clothes and hurried to meet the Princess.

"There you are! We have been worried sick! Alder told us that you needed time to think. But Radcliffe is sure you have put the cap on and snuck away to fight Jessamine. He has threatened to ride off to find you. We must hurry back before he does something rash."

Charlie nodded and the two women rushed back to camp.

Most of the small army slept soundly in groups away from the middle of camp. Charlie's friends, however, stood near the fire. Radcliffe paced back and forth. Pepper's hair burned warm. Even Max and Eliot looked concerned. Alder watched the woods where Juliette had gone to look for Charlie.

"There she is!" Alder jumped up and pointed.

"Charlie!" Pepper buzzed around Charlie's head. Her skin and hair cooled to a faint glow.

Radcliffe looked like he wanted to scoop Charlie up in his arms. But he glanced around and held himself back.

"It's fine, I'm here. I didn't sneak away." Charlie reassured everyone. "Actually, I had a vision."

Skye joined Pepper near Charlie. "Want me to show them?"

Charlie had forgotten about the pixie and her gift. Did she want them to see? It felt strange to share her visions with others. The others looked nervous. They didn't want to see. "No, I don't think so."

Her friends gathered close, and Charlie gave them a brief explanation of what she had seen.

"I don't know what has changed. Why we need to face her now? I guess I need to think about this some more. But, either way, the message was clear. It's time to face her. We shouldn't wait any longer."

It took too long to wake everyone and wait for them to gather their belongings. Some chose to leave everything except their weapons in the camp. They would return for them. If they survived.

The villagers that wanted to free their fathers and brothers milled around one another and spoke quiet words of encouragement. The dwarves didn't want to wait for anyone else. They smacked the ground with their axes and clubs. The icy horses and white wolves waited to follow the group and the crystal-ice troll looked to Charlie for direction. The gnomes huddled together so their pointed hats touched. They linked arms and hollered things like, "Who got this? We got this!" and "This is where we fight! This is where they die!"

Charlie watched everyone gear themselves up for battle. This was it. She took a deep breath. Would they win?

Maybe she *should* just slip the cap on and sneak away. She could surrender to Jessamine and finish this.

But then all of these creatures would still want to fight. It wouldn't solve anything. It wouldn't restore balance.

The only way forward was... well... forward.

Alder joined Charlie. He put his arm across her back and rested his hand on her shoulder. "We all have your back, Charlie. You are not alone."

Charlie swallowed hard and nodded. "Thank you."

He squeezed her shoulder. "We are ready. Are you?"

Was she?

She didn't know.

But everything had led her to this.

It was time.

Charlie led her small army down the hill and toward the wall. They hiked between the massive pines with long, thick needles and the towering oaks with leaves almost as big as Charlie. They pushed their way through laurel and ferns that were larger than life. Patches of enormous fox gloves and tall coneflowers became trampled beneath their feet. Even the blades of grass as wide as her arm and as tall as her waist didn't stand a chance. The army carved a nearly straight path through the forest toward Charlie's wall.

Before the sun fully rose, a giant stumbled into their midst. Several of Charlie's army cried out in surprise and fear. But Charlie recognized this giant.

"Willem!" She rushed toward him.

Willem was out of breath. He bent over his knees and held up a finger. He took several deep breaths, then stood tall.

He removed an animal horn of some kind from a loop on his waist, brought it to his lips, and blew into the small end. A sound, not unlike the sound of the Battle Horn that Charlie had activated some time ago, reverberated through the forest. It shook leaves and needles from the trees. It scared a flock of black birds from the canopy.

Those that followed Charlie had stopped and gathered around Charlie and the giant.

"What's going on?" Charlie asked Willem.

"Wait." Willem turned the direction that he had come.

A horn sounded from a long way off. It matched the sound of Willem's. Upon hearing it, Willem faced Charlie again. "They're coming."

"Who's coming?" Charlie asked. Was this good news, or bad news? The look on his face didn't offer any clues.

"The giants. And others." Willem didn't say more.

Instead, he waited for the others to arrive.

The sun had come up and moved above the horizon by the time the "others" caught up to Willem.

Charlie couldn't believe her eyes. Neither could anyone else.

Willem's "others" consisted of thirteen giants and giantesses. But that wasn't all. Charlie saw at least fifty elk with huge racks of antlers; several enormous black and grizzly bears, as well as one enormous white bear that Charlie didn't recognize; a dozen porcupines; five large spotted cats with rounded ears; at least twenty red and brown foxes; and a huge basilisk.

"Orrin!" Alder spoke behind Charlie.

She looked where he was headed.

From another direction, Orrin and around fifty forest people arrived. Juliette rushed to greet them alongside Alder.

The forest people had villagers from several other villages with them. They totaled at least four dozen more people.

"What's that smell?" Radcliffe wrinkled his nose.

"Be nice," Charlie admonished. He hated the giants.

"No, I'm serious. I don't recognize that smell." Radcliffe looked around for the source of the unknown scent. "Oh."

Charlie hadn't seen him surprised very often. But she saw why he was now. A tall, upright, apelike creature broke through the trees. It had pale hair all over its body matted in a layer of mud, twigs, and leaves. Its hairy arms hung well below its knees, and its feet looked like hands. Its wrinkled forehead made it look angry. And Radcliffe

311

wasn't joking. It smelled really bad.

The white wolves that had already joined Charlie before began to howl. A return howl came from another direction of the forest. A moment later, another pack of wolves, grey ones this time, came out of the forest. A woman rode one of them. She wore a long white cape with flowy sleeves. Her white hair was pinned close to her head in tight swirls. A trail of frost followed behind along the path she had traveled.

"The Winter Queen," Max said with awe from below.

Juliette, who had greeted her people, rushed to where this "winter queen" dismounted the largest wolf. The two women embraced and spoke in quiet voices to one another.

"She's related to Juliette, somehow. Her aunt, maybe? She is a protector of animals, just like Juliette." Max gave Pepper a brief explanation.

The pixie rushed over to meet the queen.

A twinkle of white lights floated around the edge of the group. "And what are those?" Charlie asked Max.

"Winter wisps." Max didn't sound as excited about those, though.

"Wisps, like the one in your wisp lamp?" Charlie asked.

"You mean my *alleged former* wisp lamp." Max corrected Charlie. "No, they're different. Those were wisps that led people into the mouth of a giant toad. These guide people through frozen nights to warmth and safety."

Charlie wasn't sure how that would be helpful in a battle, but she wasn't about to complain.

She couldn't believe what she saw. Her army had just more than tripled in size. Where had everyone come from? How had they found Charlie?

She asked Willem.

"We have come to fight Jessamine. The others followed." He motioned at some of the other groups.

"You do not need to face her." Willem spoke to everyone. "This is not your fight. Let us handle it. The weak need not lose their lives."

Willem and the other giants wore thick, shiny armor and wielded massive swords, clubs, and maces. They definitely looked like they could take on Jessamine and her army all by themselves.

But as soon as he said this, the other groups shouted their protests.

"She has stolen our men!" The villagers shook their weapons in the air.

"She has ruined our homes!" The dwarves banged their weapons on the ground.

The wolves barked and howled. The smelly ape-creature roared and waved his arms. The crystal troll shot icicles out of its back. The other animals stomped their feet, screeched or roared, and refused to be held back.

Willem looked to his people. The other giants nodded and shrugged. "Very well. We will face her together!"

The entire army roared as one.

How was Charlie going to stop them from surging forward and fighting Jessamine? She still didn't know exactly what they were supposed to do.

Radcliffe walked beside Charlie. He looked like he was ready to finish anyone or anything that threatened her safety. She could tell that he didn't like the sudden swell of fighters any more than Charlie did. She was grateful that they had come to help, but she didn't know how she would control them.

Alder returned to Charlie's side, too. He reported that the forest people would only fight if she asked them to. Juliette had called them here. They were not looking to battle anything or anyone.

That was a relief. Not everyone was anxious to fight.

Charlie knew which way to go. Just like the pull that had led her to the city where she had met Beau, something led her to the section of the wall that had collapsed near her house. The place where Charlie had led her own villagers away from the battle of the giants.

They were getting closer to Jessamine. They would have to face her army.

The dreams had shown Charlie's side losing every single time. How could she change that? What was she supposed to do?

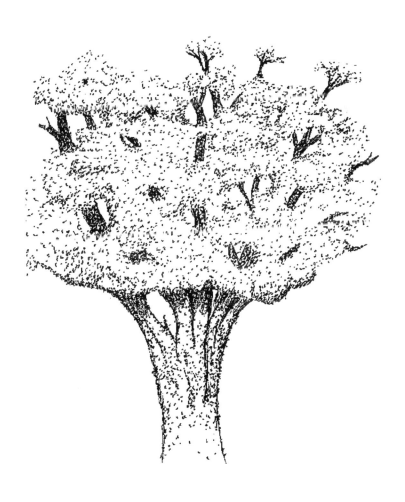

Christine Marshall

Chapter 35

The larger members of Charlie's army cleared the glacier boulders out of the way, creating a much easier passage to the other side of the giant-made wall.

Charlie remembered gazing up at the wall all her life. She had often wondered what had been on the other side but had never thought she would see it for herself.

Now the barrier between her home and the world had disappeared. Her people hid from the world. Their homes had been destroyed.

Charlie led her army past where her house used to be. It was nothing but rubble now. Her father's tools lay broken and scattered. Her house had been flattened. Shingles from the roof littered the ground. Bricks and stone from the front of the house and chimney had been trampled and crumbled to bits. Even the logs that made up most of the structure of the house had been split, broken, and squished. Nothing of the yard or garden remained.

All of Charlie and her father's hard work over the last several hundred years had been ruined in one day. She ached to dig through the rubble and search for their belongings, but now was not the time. She must press on.

Evidence of the battle of the giants surrounded them. Would they find bodies? She wasn't prepared to see the remains of those that had fought for or against her and her people.

Deep impressions pitted the ground, but no bodies were in sight. Charlie could almost see in her mind's eye the battle that had taken place here. The giants from the City of Giants, led by Charles, had fought against the dark giants loyal to Jessamine. Not many had survived. Deep gashes striped the landscape. Trenches from where giants had skidded as they battled one another led to huge mounds of earth. Enormous, broken arrows stuck out of the ground. Helmets, shields, body armor, all larger than seemed possible, littered the area within the wall.

Alder looped Charlie's hand through his arm.

Radcliffe looked sideways at them but didn't say anything.

The various groups that had joined them sprawled along behind. The troll, ape-thing, and giants took long, steady steps beside the others. The humans hurried their steps as they maneuvered over the battleground. The dwarves and gnomes had to jog to keep up. The other animals trotted, loped, or skittered among the rest.

The pull led Charlie past the remains of the village. Husks of burned-out buildings surrounded the now destroyed village center. The stonework that had made up the gathering area had been torn up and pieces of it scattered all around.

Nothing was recognizable. If she hadn't lived here for so long, she would not have known that these ruins had once been a bustling village. Now, nothing remained.

They continued to the fields around the outskirts of the village. What had once been tidy rows of crops and lush green grazing grass for farm animals had been wiped out. Now it was bumpy, trampled ground with patches of weeds. No fences remained standing. No farm implements could be seen. The ground was littered with oversized weapons and giant armor.

A sword five times Charlie's height stuck out of the ground at an odd angle where it had been dropped, it's point buried and the handle reaching high into the air. Charlie kept her eyes on it as she passed.

No one spoke as they passed through the destruction. The overwhelming size of the battle that had clearly taken place here was not lost on anyone. Besides that, Charlie thought most of those who followed were busy focusing on the battle they were about to fight. Would they end up the same as the giants who had fought here before?

Charlie marched across the dry, unkempt fields until Jessamine's hastily constructed fortress loomed in the distance. The wall that had stood for centuries circled around and right up against a tall, spiky mountain. The Deep Spring originated from deep within. Jessamine's fortress jutted out the side of the mountain. Massive rough-hewn stone bricks formed the walls. Enormous wooden beams- probably taken from the forest just outside the wall- supported the structure at odd angles from beneath. The structure looked like it would collapse at any moment.

A makeshift barrier with spiked portcullis stood just in

front of the fortress. A moat of some kind had been dug around the perimeter.

Charlie imagined herself sneaking in, finding Jessamine, and ending this on her own. But the place would be heavily guarded. And Charlie had seen the kinds of creatures Jessamine had recruited to her side. Even with the magical cap that made her invisible, it wasn't likely she'd get very close. Especially with Beau in there. He could see her when she wore it. How many other creatures might be able to do the same?

The idea of Pepper winging her way in and taking Jessamine out had crossed her mind as well. She knew the pixie would be more than happy to comply. But, again, Jessamine had a way of spotting and capturing all kinds of creatures. Charlie just couldn't risk it.

And storming the fortress would be totally pointless.

The only option was to march forward, draw Jessamine and her army out, and let things play out the way they were meant to.

A loud battle horn sounded. It echoed across the ruined fields and bounced off the massive, damaged wall that encircled them.

Charlie stopped in her tracks. Her army fanned out to either side of her.

Radcliffe remained to her left, while Alder and Juliette stood to her right. Pepper and Skye hovered on either side.

Max and Eliot stood near Juliette. The little men looked nervous. Fighting made them uncomfortable. Charlie wanted to tell them that they didn't have to stay, but she knew her offer would fall on deaf ears. Besides, those two usually had something up their sleeves, or in their packs, which made up for their size. Like the dragon's blood.

321

That reminded her... she looked at Radcliffe. Sure enough, he had the canteen of dragon's blood out and ready to swallow. The image of him writhing in pain and turning into what she had thought had been stone, but turned out to be literal dragon scales, flashed through her memory. It better not come to that. That would mean Charlie was in grave danger. That would mean Jessamine was about to win. She swallowed hard and faced forward again.

She could feel the presence of those who had joined the fight behind her as well as hear their movements and conversations. The dwarves were more than ready to battle. They didn't want to wait. The gnomes sounded a little more reserved. They hoped it wouldn't come to death, but they would fight to the end. The villagers talked of bravery, but fear hid behind their words. They would not give up, no matter how bad it became.

The Winter Queen looked fierce. Charlie wouldn't want to face her in a battle! Who knew what abilities she possessed? The animals flocked around and behind her and gathered among the forest people. The big cats prowled the line just in front of the others. Juliette's people appeared ready, but they really didn't want to fight anyone.

The remaining creatures pawed at the ground, sounded encouragements to one another, and waited for Charlie's signal.

The enormous, scaly basilisk slithered into a coil and raised its head at the end of the line. Its long fangs protruded from its mouth, and its red eyes glowed in the sunlight. It gave Charlie the creeps, but she was glad it was on her side, at least.

The giants, troll, and ape-thing stood ominous behind everyone else. Their massive weapons would be no match for creatures smaller than themselves, but Jessamine had plenty of huge beings on her side as well.

A sound from the sky drew Charlie's attention. Above Charlie's army, hundreds of enormous birds of various species circled.

"They are here to help," Juliette leaned around Alder to inform Charlie.

It was hard to tell since there were so many of them, but Charlie thought she saw what looked like a handful of griffins, and maybe even a flock of Pegasus, among the birds.

A familiar feeling settled over Charlie.

The dry fields that were once farmland. Her friends and allies beside and behind her. Even the winged help in the sky.

And the shadow that poured out of Jessamine's fortress and moved steadily forward. The gap between herself and her enemy would close fast.

She had seen it in her dreams. In all of the dreams where she did not survive. The ones where Jessamine won.

Charlie's stomach tightened. Her skin became clammy. The back of her throat tingled like she was going to be sick.

This wasn't supposed to happen. They weren't supposed to fight. It would end in disaster.

How was she supposed to change this?

The line behind Charlie flinched. Some wanted to rush forward, others to retreat.

"Ready yourselves!" Radcliffe shouted.

She almost jumped out of her skin.

He armed himself with his massive, double bladed battle axe and sharp twin edged sword.

The others followed his lead. Clinks of weapons being

unsheathed came from either side. War cries traveled down
and back the line like a wave. Feet and weapons pounded
the ground in anticipation.

The volume increased.

Pounding. Shouting. Clanging.

Charlie covered her ears with her hands. Her head
throbbed.

If they fought, they would lose.

She had to do something!

She closed her eyes.

She focused on her breaths.

In.
"The time has come."

Out.
"Let go of the anger, the fear."

In.
"You must face Jessamine."

Out.
"The balance will be restored."

Charlie gasped.

Her eyes popped open.

She knew exactly what she needed to do.

Chapter 36

Jessamine led the charge from atop a massive grizzly bear. Her army, ten times the size of Charlie's, followed in a wide V.

Several hundred human soldiers on horseback rode just behind Jessamine. The hooves of the horses kicked up a cloud of dust that hung in the still air. Sunlight glinted off the armor of the men.

Close behind the calvary, the pack of giant rats the size of Roxi spread out to either side. Their strange gate and snake-like tails spurred the horses faster. Charlie remembered from her dreams that they also had huge, sharp, yellow teeth that protruded from their mouths beneath big pink noses and long, wiry whiskers.

Charlie could just make out the packs of hairless coyotes. They snapped at the larger dog-monster things that Charlie had seen, with tufts of hair that made them look sickly. Even among Jessamine's own forces, the creatures fought with one another.

The larger creatures were easy to see from this distance: the pack of half-bull half-human minotaur, armed with two huge spiked clubs each; a pair of ogres with fists so large they didn't need to carry weapons; the giantess archer, no longer donning a fur wrap; at least two dozen of Jessamine's dark giants that had managed to survive the previous battle.

A crystal golem sparkled in the sunlight, a dozen trolls with arms that nearly touched the ground, and the lion-goat-snake creatures that Charlie had seen in her dreams, which outnumbered the minotaur and trolls combined.

Charlie couldn't make out the elves that had joined Jessamine's army, but she knew they were there.

Jessamine's army grew as it advanced, like water from a broken dam filling the valley.

They were vastly outnumbered and outmatched. Even with the number that had bravely taken up the fight on Charlie's side, they could not hope to conquer this foe.

Charlie didn't plan to try.

She marched forward.

Radcliffe roared at her to stop.

She ignored him.

He galloped ahead of her and skidded to a halt to block her path.

"What do you think you are doing?" He yelled at her, his face crimson.

"It's fine Radcliffe. Go back." Charlie sidestepped around him.

Ahead, Jessamine urged her mount faster.

"You can't do this!" Pepper zipped around Charlie's face. "She'll kill you!"

"No, she won't." Charlie hadn't even armed herself.

Radcliffe and Pepper followed close on Charlie's heels. Radcliffe had his canteen out, ready to drink the dragon's blood. Pepper flew hot, ready to burn molten through the enemy.

Charlie didn't make it very far before Jessamine's bear skidded to a stop. Her dark curls flew around her head, like snakes. She slid off the bear's back and stomped toward Charlie.

The bear stayed put. Jessamine's army didn't move past her mount. They lined up to face Charlie's army.

Charlie could hear her people steel themselves for battle. They clanged their weapons against shields or armor. The creatures shouted or neighed or grunted or growled. Jessamine's army did the same.

The noise was too much. Charlie needed Jessamine to hear her.

"I can make them stop," Skye's voice whispered in Charlie's ear. Charlie nodded.

A second later, the noise died down. The battlefield was silent but for the sounds of feet milling on the ground.

Radcliffe mumbled something behind Charlie about the new pixie being a pest. Charlie ignored him.

Pepper retorted to Radcliffe that he wasn't exactly easy to tolerate. Charlie ignored her.

She only had eyes and ears for Jessamine.

And the voice.

"I told you not to come, little girl." Jessamine stood straight, her hands folded in front of her.

Charlie had wondered about the vision with Jessamine. Had she really been there? It turned out that it *had* been a shared vision after all. But that didn't matter now.

Jessamine continued to taunt Charlie. "Look around. You don't stand a chance. I have already won." Jessamine looked confident. Triumphant.

Charlie removed her bow from her back.

Jessamine's eyes widened and her smile disappeared. She stiffened.

Charlie didn't break eye contact. She didn't speak.

She tossed her bow on the ground.

Jessamine gave Charlie a wary, questioning look. But she didn't speak, either.

Charlie unsheathed her sword. She dropped it with a thud beside the bow.

She removed the dagger from her ankle holster and added it to the pile with a clang of metal on metal.

Jessamine looked confused. And a little scared. She tried to hide her emotions, but Charlie had already seen.

"You're right," Charlie said in an even voice.

She heard Radcliffe hiss. Pepper's hair lit up. But Charlie kept her focus on Jessamine.

Jessamine looked surprised.

"You win." Charlie turned around. She cupped her hands around her mouth.

"Stand down!" She hollered to those that stood with her.

Radcliffe's jaw dropped. Pepper zipped around in a frenzy.

The others exchanged confused looks. The dwarves glared at Charlie. The animals called to one another. The giants kept their faces neutral.

Juliette and Alder were the first to disarm themselves. They actually looked relieved. Their people followed right away.

It took longer for the others to comply. Would they listen

to her? Many were clearly terrified of fighting. But most seemed more worried about not being able to defend themselves. Plenty looked at Charlie like she was crazy. Some with contempt.

After what felt like forever, every last person or creature had laid down their weapons of war. The animals stood or sat in submissive positions.

Radcliffe was the last to lay down his weapons. "I hope you know what you are doing," he growled in her direction.

She pleaded with her eyes for him to trust her.

He nodded, then dropped his own weapons with a clatter at his feet.

Charlie faced Jessamine again. "We surrender."

A toothy smile spread across Jessamine's face. "Big mistake."

She raised her arm to signal her side to attack. Her army bellowed in response. They barely held their line, but they waited for their commander to signal for them to attack. The noise shook the ground.

This is exactly what Charlie had seen in her dreams. What Skye had shown the others.

Charlie's people quivered but held their line. She willed them to not pick up their weapons.

"I got you," Skye whispered.

Charlie felt the pixie's voice in her head. *"Trust Charlie."*

It was a plea, not a command.

Good. Charlie did not want to compel anyone to do anything. She wanted this to be each of their own choice.

Jessamine's arm twitched.

Before she could lower it, Charlie spoke.

"I don't think you understand, Jessamine." Charlie kept

her voice quiet.

Jessamine managed to hear above the ruckus her army made.

Perhaps Skye had something to do with that, too?

Jessamine held her hand high in the air but did not drop it. "What do you mean?" Her words were edged with barely masked panic.

"We are not surrendering to *you*." Charlie kept her voice calm.

The ground rumbled. Jessamine widened her stance.

"The world is out of balance." Charlie stood firm.

The ground shook again. Harder. Jessamine's army did their best to brace themselves.

"But we're done cowering to you and your power." Charlie lifted her chin.

Shouts of agreement came from behind Charlie.

Jessamine's eyes widened. She scanned her opponents. Her eyes returned to Charlie.

Charlie took a step toward Jessamine.

"*You're* the only thing out of balance." Charlie spoke with force now. "And the balance *will* be restored."

The shaking intensified. The less sentient beings on Jessamine's side panicked and fled. That took care of the rats, coyotes, and scraggly looking dog-monsters.

The minotaur, elves, and men took the chance to break their line and surge forward.

Charlie stood her ground. She was close enough that she could see the lines appear on Jessamine's face. The woman's dark curls grayed. Her posture shrank, just a little. As if she had aged many years in a single moment.

The ground shook harder. The fields rippled like water. The waves originated from the place Charlie stood. They radiated away from her to the front but did not move behind. The ground her army stood upon stayed still.

Jessamine's face alternated between terror and fury. She lunged at Charlie.

At that exact moment, the ground ripped open between Charlie and Jessamine. Jessamine teetered at the edge, then managed to regain her balance and stepped away from the chasm. A crooked line carved itself between Charlie's army and Jessamine's army.

Cries of fear and shock rose from Charlie's side. But the crack in the ground did not venture near them.

Many of Jessamine's fighters, however, fell into the crevasse before they even had time to register its appearance.

The human soldiers that had not been swallowed up by the earth threw down their weapons and galloped away on horseback.

The remaining forces seemed buoyed by the challenge. They looked even more angry.

So did Jessamine. "What is happening?" she screeched.

"The world is about to restore the balance of power..." Charlie pointed at the chasm "...by removing you from it."

The ground fell out from beneath Jessamine. Her scream hung in the air as she disappeared into the darkness. The ground swallowed up the remainder of Jessamine's army. None had been spared.

A moment later, the ground knit itself back together. Like when Charlie's people healed.

The rift was gone, like it had never been there.

Like an afterthought, the earth trembled one more time. Jessamine's fortress toppled to the ground in a cloud of rubble and dust.

Christine Marshall

Chapter 37

"The balance has been restored."

The voice whispered in Charlie's head. She couldn't take her eyes off the spot where Jessamine had been standing only moments before.

Silence surrounded her.

It was over. Their enemy had been defeated.

Jessamine, and those she had recruited, were gone.

All at once the silence broke. Ecstatic cheers, whoops, and whistles echoed across the landscape.

Charlie turned around.

Animals flocked toward the handful of forest people that had joined the group. Green grass, patches of clover, and a rainbow of various blossoms sprouted like a blanket being unfurled across the field.

Those who had chosen to stand with Charlie danced in groups and celebrated. They hugged one another, slapped backs, and threw their hats in the air. Some collapsed on the ground in tears. All the hostility, fear, and anger evaporated. Nothing but relief and joy could be felt from the crowd.

Charlie still didn't move.

She watched the various groups as the celebrations died down. A buzz of conversation remained. One by one those that had thrown down their weapons retrieved their clubs, swords, and shields.

"Do you want to explain what just happened?" Radcliffe's voice startled Charlie. She had forgotten that he and Pepper had been right behind her the entire time.

She blinked a couple of times. "Yeah. In a minute."

Alder and Juliette rushed to Charlie. Together they wrapped her in a tight hug.

"You did it!" Alder said into Charlie's ear.

Juliette wept. This was not the outcome the Princess had hoped for, but it was the one that was best for the world.

The three stayed together for several long minutes, before separating. Alder stayed by Charlie's side. He wove his fingers between hers and held on tight.

Max, Eliot, and Skye joined the group. Max held a small bottle in each hand. One held a bright purple liquid, the other a thick silvery substance. These must be some of the elixirs he had retrieved from the village. Charlie would probably never know what he had intended to use them for. But she was glad that she hadn't needed to find out.

Eliot already had a small parchment in his hands and his charcoal pencil out. His map-making ability had returned. He didn't look thrilled about the idea, though. Perhaps he had hoped that it had been taken away for good.

Skye flew circles around the pair of brownies. "Did you see the way those minotaur got sucked into the ground?

They were like…" She made a strange gurgling sound, and her body shook, then she collapsed at Max's feet.

Max grinned at his new friend. She sprung up and continued. "Or how about that golem thing. It just… crumbled!" She mimicked crumbling into pieces then imitated a pile of rocks.

Eliot looked at Skye, then returned his eyes to his parchment. Max, though, clapped his hands. "Encore! Do more!"

Skye continued her performance. "This is what the soldiers looked like when they ran away, cowards!" "This is what the rats looked like when they almost got trampled by the bigger things." "This is what the giants looked like…" Max rolled on the ground with laughter.

Charlie chuckled and shook her head. That little man had met his match.

By the time the crowds had settled down, some had slipped away. The dwarves and gnomes were nowhere to be seen, and the basilisk had vanished. The big cats, the crystal troll, and ape-thing had disappeared. Most of the birds had scattered back to their homes. There was no sign of griffins or Pegasus. Charlie would never know if she had really seen them or not.

The humans had gathered into groups and sat in circles. They shared the food they had brought along and wondered what had happened to their friends and loved ones who had been taken by Jessamine.

The forest people mingled with the animals. They appeared to thank the animals for their assistance. Charlie saw Orrin hug a huge grizzly bear. Another tickled a porcupine behind one ear.

The ice horses and white wolves gathered around the Winter Queen. She touched each on the head and said some words that Charlie didn't understand but sounded like a blessing of some kind. When she was finished, the horses galloped away in one direction, and the wolves ran low the opposite direction. The Winter Queen pulled Juliette aside. The two women hugged and spoke in low voices. Then the Winter Queen left the crowd as well.

The dozen giants that had stood with Charlie hung back, away from the others. They didn't speak to one another. They looked somber.

While Juliette joined her people, and the brownies and pixies kept themselves busy, Charlie approached the giants. Alder stayed beside her, and Radcliffe followed. Would these two ever let Charlie leave their sight again? She smiled to herself. She'd be fine if they didn't.

Willem stepped forward and knelt to face Charlie. The other giants stood behind him.

"Willem... I don't know what to say. Thank you." Charlie held her hand to her heart. It was obvious he had not found his family. His face had no trace of happiness. His demeanor was that of someone who had lost everything and suffered.

"Yes," Radcliffe added. "Thank you." He nodded at Willem then stepped back.

This was... huge. Radcliffe had thanked a giant. One that he had not really trusted from the beginning. But out of all of them, Radcliffe knew how Willem must feel more than anyone. And the other giants, too. They all looked the same as Willem. Broken.

"You have done it, Charlie. You have restored the balance." Willem nodded at Charlie.

She blushed. "I didn't really do anything..."

What *had* she done? Stood there and let Jessamine be swallowed up by the earth? Anyone could have done that.

One of the giants behind Willem seemed to have read her thoughts. He spoke in a deep, slow voice. "It was you, Charlie."

Willem stepped aside. The giant who spoke looked older than the others. His hair was graying, and skin wrinkled around the eyes. his posture bent. And his voice... Charlie recognized that voice.

"*You* had to be the one to restore the balance."

Charlie could only stare as he spoke. It was *the voice.*

"You followed the dreams and let go of your feelings about Jessamine. No one else could have done what you did. Others would have let her go or ended her too soon."

Charlie's mind raced. She hadn't known why at the time, but she had known that she had to lay down her weapons and surrender. But like she had told Jessamine, she had not surrendered to the woman, she had surrendered to the world.

"Jessamine was the only thing out of balance. By amassing your own army..." this new giant started to explain.

Charlie protested. She hadn't *meant* to amass an army.

But the giant held up his hand for her to stop. "... you had the potential of defeating Jessamine. This began to restore the balance. She had an army. You had an army. And though they were mismatched, your side fought for their families and freedom. That is a battle that is won more often than not."

Juliette joined Charlie and Alder. Radcliffe listened carefully to this wise giant's explanation. Charlie let it all sink in.

"If that had happened, she may have survived the fight. The balance would still not be restored." The giant paused.

"But by surrendering, you forced the world to take her. It has been trying to even things out for a long time. At the time you faced her, her power was greater than ever. By surrendering to the world, you were allowing the world to see who is good and who is evil. You allowed whatever outcome would be best to happen."

This was all too much. She didn't fully understand the explanation, but she had done the right thing. Jessamine was gone. Her followers had been removed from the world. Things would be balanced once more.

Again, this giant seemed to know what she thought. How did he do that?

He shook his head. "No, Charlie. The balance is restored... for now. But there is still one thing that needs to be done."

More? Charlie's heart sank a little. She thought she had finished her task.

The giant interrupted her thoughts. "Jessamine used the giants to gain power many times. We are a feared race. Our power is too great. We are diminished. This is nearly all of us that are left." He gestured to the eight giantesses and four giants behind him.

"But our race will rebuild. We will become strong again. And someone will try to use that power for evil, eventually."

Willem stepped forward again. He knelt before Charlie. "That's why we have decided to return to the earth. We will sleep. Forever. Never to be awoken again. Any giants who may be in hiding will succumb. The rest of us have agreed that it is better for the world this way. We will become one with the landscape. No one will be able to use us ever again."

Charlie choked back a sob. Alder wrapped an arm around her shoulders. Tears streamed down his cheeks. Juliette cried quietly on her other side.

"But that's not fair!" Charlie looked at Willem. His eyes were as red and puffy as hers. "You have done nothing wrong!"

One of the she-giants joined the conversation. "We never want anything like this to happen again. It is a small price to pay."

Another added, "We will not die. We will live as one with the world."

"You'll be able to recognize where we lie, Charlie. You will still be able to feel us. Maybe even speak to us in your dreams. This is how it must be." Willem closed his eyes and took a deep breath. Then he stood.

Charlie looked from one giant to the next. They had all accepted this fate. What they said made sense logically, but her heart protested. How could she live in a world without giants?

Chapter 38

The sun neared the horizon. Night would fall soon.

While the humans talked and made plans, Charlie saw the giants slip away, one by one.

Willem was the last to go. He nodded at Charlie. He looked so sad. Charlie's throat tightened. Her eyes stung. She waved at the last of the giants that she would ever see again.

Juliette, along with Orrin and Alder, gathered the forest people. After watching Willem disappear beyond the mountain, Charlie joined them.

Juliette received reports from the various leaders. Charlie's father was safe. One of Juliette's people would send word to bring him home at once. The people from Charlie's village had settled fairly well in the north lands. Some would probably choose to stay. Others would come home to rebuild.

Would Charlie recognize any of them? Would they

recognize her? She had grown and aged almost three years in the time they had been separated. When she had left the first time, she had appeared to be a fifteen-year-old. Now, she looked at least seventeen. Her body had changed, her face looked more mature. And she had grown on the inside, too. She was a different person than she had been before.

Orrin took his group of forest people to meet up with Charlie's villagers. They would receive the message that it was safe to return by morning. It would take some time, a couple of weeks, maybe, for them to make the return trip. And it would probably be just as long for her father. What would Charlie do in the meantime?

The remainder of Juliette's people decided to set up camp where they were. The villagers joined them.

A huge fire burned bright, and all the people surrounded it. They cooked and shared food. They talked and laughed as they acquainted themselves with one another. Juliette's people, who had all regained their abilities, shared their skills and knowledge with the villagers. They would return home better able to care for their gardens, lands, and animals.

Many of the villagers still worried about missing loved ones. Not long after nightfall, a scraggly group of men, young and old, wandered into the camp. They looked confused, tired, and hungry. Charlie soon learned that they had been prisoners of Jessamine's. When the fortress fell, they had miraculously survived. They saw the campfire and made their way slowly across the newly green fields to the camp.

Joyous cries of reunion rang out. Tears fell, hugs exchanged. The men were given food and warmer clothing. Plans were made to return them to their homes as soon as possible the following day.

For those that still had missing family, Juliette's people offered to assist in a search. They, too, would depart the following morning.

Charlie observed things from the sidelines. She had been a leader that morning. Now she felt like an observer. With all the plans being made for travel, would she be left nearly alone to wait for her father?

Radcliffe stood still as a statue nearby. At one time he would have looked disgusted by the lowly humans, but now he watched with longing. Did he miss his own people? He had no one to return to, either.

Max, Eliot, Skye, and Pepper huddled together in the dancing firelight. Eliot showed them the newest map he had been drawing all day. Pepper and Skye pointed at the parchment, Max laughed heartily, and Eliot nodded and drew something. What were those four up to now? Charlie smiled to herself.

The fire died down as the groups began to settle for the night. It wasn't long before Radcliffe and Charlie were the only two still sitting beyond the firelight.

Charlie sighed.

As if he could read her mind, Radcliffe grunted in agreement. "Do not worry. I will not leave you." He didn't turn to look at her. His body stayed still.

Charlie swallowed. Her eyes filled. Tears leaked out.

She rushed to his side and flung her arms around his human torso. His muscles tensed. Then softened. He slowly wrapped his arms around Charlie and held her for a long time.

She broke free, wiped the tears from her eyes, and looked up into Radcliffe's face. He had tracks on his cheeks from his own tears! She didn't even know he was capable of crying.

She shook her head to clear her thoughts. "Thank you."

He nodded once, then looked away.

She settled beside him on the now lush grass dotted with various fragrant wildflowers.

She gazed at the stars for as long as she could keep her eyes open, then drifted off to sleep.

No dreams troubled her mind. Her body rested fully. By morning, she felt fresh and healed. Almost like she used to when she drank the Deep Spring water.

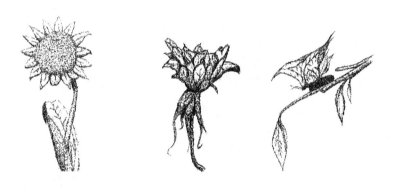

After most of the people had left, Charlie's group had returned almost to its original size: Juliette, Alder, Radcliffe, Max, Eliot, and Pepper. Roxi and Charlie's father were not with them, but they would be soon enough. Willem, though, was gone forever. And they had added Skye to their group. She was a welcome addition, adding more laughter and joy that was desperately needed.

Charlie had thought she would feel complete once her

task was finished. But now she just felt like she had no purpose. Was she supposed to go back to dinking around the village? What about the others from her home? Would their memories cloud again? Would they still have prolonged life, or age as normal? No one knew the answers to these questions.

A group of Juliette's people, including Juliette herself, had decided to remain at Charlie's home to help them rebuild. They would blend their separate groups into one people. At least Charlie wouldn't have to figure this all out on her own.

By the time Charlie's father and the villagers returned, the rebuilding had already begun. They had spent the days cleaning up the broken places, sorting supplies that could be reused from those that could not. With the addition of those who had fled, Charlie's village would now be home to twice as many people.

Evidence that the world was no longer out of balance was everywhere to be seen. The invasive vines and noxious weeds had disappeared. Native plants and animals had returned and thrived. Things were back to normal.

Mostly.

Max and Eliot had left a few days after the battle. Max just said they had "things to take care of," and Charlie saw the new parchment rolled up and sticking out of Eliot's pack. Pepper and Skye both wanted to go with them, but the brownies insisted they would be back in no time. They trotted away from the new town center under construction, waving over their shoulders as they went.

"They'll be back," Charlie reassured a droopy Pepper. "They always come back."

Pepper nodded, then zipped away to assist with the rebuild.

Alder worked side by side with Charlie. The two spent almost all of their time together. They laughed and shared memories. Alder couldn't help but talk about every plant he saw anywhere. Charlie loved it. She loved the idea of being with someone who would not forget her when a year had passed. And his dark brown eyes were easy to get lost in, too.

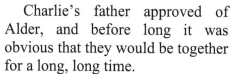

Charlie's father approved of Alder, and before long it was obvious that they would be together for a long, long time.

Charlie's dad's aging had reversed somewhat. He looked older, and felt it, but had salt and pepper hair instead of all white, and his posture was tall instead of bent. His forehead and eyes had more wrinkles than she was used to, but she kind of liked how wise they made him look.

It became clear that they would begin aging faster than they had before, but not too fast. And after a year, Charlie was relieved that she wasn't the only one who remembered the things that had happened.

When Jessamine had been defeated and her fortress

collapsed it sealed up the Deep Spring. This had ended the prolonged life. But it had also broken the other protections that had been put into place. Her village had no wall, no enchantments, no Deep Spring water. Her people were normal now. They had just been around for a very long time.

Charlie opened her eyes to find herself in the clearing. The air sparkled. The sun shone. The giant was there.

Charlie couldn't speak.

The giant smiled at her. "Come closer, Little Dreamer."

Charlie obeyed.

"You have done it. The balance has been restored. At last."

Christine Marshall

Epilogue

Charlie kneeled in her vegetable garden. She pulled the weeds that tried to grow in her patch of tiny carrot seedlings. The sun shone bright, but her wide brimmed straw hat shaded her neck and face.

Laughter came from inside the house that had siding made from sliced logs. The raw edges against the light wood made the house glow.

She stood and studied the tidy rows of her garden. The beans had grown fast, the cabbages would be ready to eat soon. The sweet peas twisted up their frames and many of the pods were plump.

She stretched her back. Standing up after gardening was a little harder than it used to be. She sighed and smiled. The joys of growing older. But she wouldn't trade it for anything.

She made her way toward the house. She could see her father through the window, sitting in his favorite chair. A cute little girl with brown skin and a head full of tightly curled hair sat on his lap. He read to her from a picture book that he had drawn himself. Charlie knew the story. It was about a girl that had dreamed about giants.

The little girl interrupted. "Papa, there's no such things as giants!" She giggled at the pictures.

Charlie's dad chuckled. "Don't be so sure…"

"There you are," a deep voice came from behind her.

Charlie turned around as Alder walked toward her. "Sometimes I think you like this garden more than you like me." Alder teased Charlie and poked her sides.

She shrieked and dodged out of the way.

"You know that could never be true," she said.

He stopped in front of her. Her heart beat like it had the first time she had met his eyes.

"I know." He wrapped his strong arms around her and lifted her feet off the ground. He swung her in a circle then set her down.

"You know, I can help you out here. I have a pretty green thumb." Alder grinned wide.

Charlie rolled her eyes, but smiled. "No way! This is MY garden. I'll do it myself."

"Alright, but all it takes is one little touch…" He reached a finger toward one of her sweet pea vines.

"Don't you dare!" She grabbed his hand and pulled him away from her garden.

He laughed out loud, which made her laugh, too.

Alder wrapped an arm around her waist, holding her close. She leaned on him as they walked toward the house together.

"Mommy, Daddy! Papa says giants are real! But that's not true, is it?" The little girl rushed to join her parents.

Charlie and Alder exchanged a sly smile.

"Listen to your Papa…" Charlie mock-scolded her daughter.

They all laughed and crowded around the picture book.

On the cover, a girl gazed into the distance. Beside her hovered a glowing ball.

And between the mountains, among the trees, stood a very tall man.

The giant.

THE END

Read more of Charlie's story!
in the *Charlie and the Giants* series.

  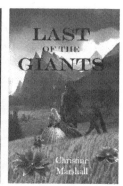

Available on Amazon and
CMarshallFantasy Etsy shop

Christine's ***Charlie and the Giants*** books are filled with magic, mythical creatures, and an *awesome* female protagonist that has to figure out who she wants to become.

If you love books that will help you forget the real world for a little while, are full of surprising characters, and will keep you guessing, then these are the perfect books for you!

Read Jessamine's, Juliette's, and Sariah's origin stories in
A Series of Retellings

Jessamine   *Juliette*   *Sariah*

The first three books in the *Charlie and the Giants* series. Learn why Jessamine became so wicked. Find out why Juliette loves the giants so much. Read Sariah's inspiring but heartbreaking story. These origin stories for three of the critical characters in the *Charlie and the Giants* series are framed as fairytale retellings full of twists and turns that you'll never see coming.

Available on Amazon and CMarshallFantasy Etsy shop

Thanks for Reading!

I hope you enjoyed this book!
If you feel up to it, please leave a review on Amazon and Goodreads. For indie authors like me, reviews are our lifeblood. Why not help a girl out, it'll only take a few minutes!

Check me out on social media!

Facebook: Christine K. Marshall-author
www.facebook.com/christinemarshallauthor

Instagram: @the_christine_marshall_24
www.instagram.com/the_christine_marshall_24

Tiktok: www.tiktok.com/@christinemarshallfantasy

Amazon: the_christine_marshall
https://www.amazon.com/author/the_christine_marshall

Goodreads: Christine_Marshall
   www.goodreads.com/author/show/22364476.Christine_Marshall

Email: christinemarshall24@gmail.com

Acknowledgements

No book is written alone! Though my fingers did all the typing, the **Charlie and the Giants** trilogy would not have been possible without a handful of amazing people.

Beta readers: Steve, Belle, Sophie, and Pepper. Thank you for your precious feedback, finding the inconsistencies, coming up with solutions, and laughing and gasping in all the right places.

Moral support: Sumedha and Shaylen, you guys are my BFFs! Thank you for your constant support and encouragement. And thanks, Shaylen, for snorting when you laugh.

Character inspiration: Hannah and Luke, you two are the best. Your antics made these books better.

Amazing art: My husband and other half, Steve: You are the Alder to my Charlie.

About the Author

When Christine isn't spinning tales on her laptop, she probably has a book and a chocolate chip cookie in hand. She loves all kinds of books: fantasy, sci-fi, historical fiction, non-fiction, and even textbooks.

She also loves to play her ukulele, stand in the rain, stay up late, and try new foods… but not all at the same time! Christine has moved over 20 times in the past 20 years, and firmly believes that people are more important than things.

Made in the USA
Columbia, SC
27 July 2023

20797376R00219